I0627610

RAVISHING CAMILLE

THOSE NOTORIOUS AMERICANS, BOOK 5, STEAMY FAMILY SAGA OF THE GILDED AGE

CERISE DELAND

Copyright © 2021 by Wilma Jo-Ann Power writing as Cerise DeLand

All rights reserved.

No part of this book may be reproduced in any form or by any electronic or mechanical means, including information storage and retrieval systems, without written permission from the author, except for the use of brief quotations in a book review.

ISBN for Digital: 978-1-953878-09-0

ISBN for Print: 978-1-953878-10-6

Photographic credit: The Killian Group Images

Cover Art: Wicked Smart Designs

❀ Created with Vellum

Money can buy anything, can't it? Those brash Americans--their dollars and charms work wonders. Until they learn that money can buy anything...but love.

She'd wanted him for years...and denied she cared.

As a step-brother, he'd loved her.

But she's older now and even more delectable. Should he walk away? Can he?

Pierce Hanniford returns to England after tripling his fortune in China. He's come for business. Not pleasure. And definitely not for love.

Camille Bereston decided years ago that Pierce was not for her. He's her step-brother, famous, restless, a savvy Shanghai *taipan* and a menace...to her heart.

She has ambitions to marry. Funny that none of her candidates seems good enough.

Yet Camille excites him as no woman ever has and he must have her, no matter the cost.

But should she take an older, experienced rogue as her lover...and should she claim him forever as her only love?

WILD LILY, BOOK 1
DARING WIDOW, BOOK 2
SWEET SIREN, BOOK 3

SCANDALOUS HEIRESS, Book 4
RAVISHING CAMILLE, Book 5

CERISE DELAND

SUBSCRIBE TO
Cerise's Bon Bons!

CHAPTER 1

Southhampton Docks, England
July 31, 1888

"This time will be different." Camille Bereston vowed as she watched Pierce Hanniford stride down the gangplank of the newest of the Hanniford family steamers, the *Manchu Empress*. Her rebellious heart hammered, silly thing. Her strapping step-brother was just a friend. Always had been. "We won't torment each other any longer."

Her step-father Killian Hanniford, who stood beside her, lifted a distinct black brow at her declaration. "The two of you have always understood each other far better than many people ever do. If you change, how will we know that you still care?"

Smiling, she tipped her head and viewed her dashing step-father. Pierce was the younger version of his sire, quick and decisive. Both men knew her too well. And she had always been eager to cover her attraction to Pierce. Today, she'd do it with a nod toward reason. "We're older, Papa. We should know better than to tease each other to hissy fits."

"Is that what you did?" He tossed away her observation, seemingly unconcerned as he examined his oldest child who returned from China this morning after two years.

How long Pierce would remain in England was the routine question. But this time, he'd written to his father that he intended to stay longer than he usually did. He had many problems to solve, he declared, with his partners in Europe. Running part of his father's shipping company operating in the Pacific plus his own world-wide empire was a huge challenge. Plus for the past six years, he also owned half of the import-export company originally begun by his brother-in-law, Lord Victor Cole. Killian had mentioned at dinner last night to Camille and to her mother, who was his second wife, that he was pleased Pierce questioned his perpetual journeys around the world. Perhaps he'd even find a woman he loved and begin a family of his own. "At thirty-seven, he's more than old enough."

"And wealthy enough," added her mother. "I doubt he need travel so often. He's built his staff carefully for years. You have taught him well, my darling."

Camille clasped her hands together and, much as she wished not to show it, she bristled with anticipation. As a young girl of fifteen, she had become infatuated with her older, debonair step-brother Pierce. She sighed, knowing she would admire him now anew.

Why not? Pierce Hanniford had always displayed ambition equal to his accomplished father's and today his wealth equalled it. His education had come, not at colleges, but in the rough and tumble of the world of business and finance.

And with his father's advice he had built his own empire. He owned copper and iron plants worldwide. His steel mills produced hundreds of tons, bought by governments and private companies. Ships, railroads and towering new buildings were made of Hanniford girders, pipes and electrical wiring. He was quoted in board rooms and newspapers. He was shrewd, accomplished, careful—and a millionaire. That he was also a bachelor meant he was a worthy catch for any ambitious woman.

Camille knew a few Englishwomen who'd read headlines of his arrival and planned to enchant him. Naive creatures. Pierce was not easily enamored. A man with such worldly experience did not tolerate simpering debutants or bold demimondes. He preferred a more refined approach. Usually his own toward a lady. Never the other way round. And Camille loved that about him. Erudite, sophisticated Pierce.

He waved to them, his smile broad, his silver gaze sweeping from his father to her...and holding.

She gulped...and waved back.

He was quite irresistible. As ever. Damn her soul to admit it. But she saw the ladies on the wharf who noticed him and whispered. His Black Irish good looks had always drawn more eyes to him than hers alone. He merited the regard, too. What woman would not swoon at his ink-black hair that blew in the breeze or his bronze complexion and ruddy cheeks that spoke of his robust health?

To say nothing of his wealth that shown like a beacon in the midday sun. In the precisely cut pearl grey suit, the aquamarine satin waistcoat, the straw bowler he carried in his hands, he was the epitome of a man of the world. Even if his walk were not one that said he bestrode the earth like Goliath, even if his shoulders were not broad as heaven, nor his height regal, or his hair a thick shock of glistening ebony, he could intimidate any man in his path. He was a quiet, deliberate man. Never prone to impulse. All those qualities caused most women to gape at his masculine *savoir faire* while his smile could lure them like lemmings to lust.

But not me.

No longer me.

He grinned at her, proving her point. Her knees did not go weak. Her blood did not rush. If her entire body swayed toward him, swooping her up like iron fragments to a magnet, she dared not admit it.

This time will be different.

Pierce took the last few yards of the gangway and rushed to embrace both his father and her at once. His arm crushed her close. Her broad-brimmed hat tipped and destroyed her carefully arranged chignon. Her breasts tingled at his embrace. Her fingers clutched his lapels. And her heart picked up a primitive tattoo. And in the next second, he kissed her cheek. His lips were firm, as ever before, warm as always. Yet his affection held a chill that two years away had created.

Surprise crept up her spine. She soothed it with logic that he was not for her, never had been. Plus she had suitors now. If she were so inclined to encourage them.

"Sir!" Pierce beamed at his father. "I am so happy to see you so well!"

"And you!" Killian clapped him on the back.

"And look at you!" Pierce tipped up her chin with two fingers. His examination with those silver eyes destroyed her firm resolve. "My God. You grow more stunning every year."

Then to her expectation and silly disappointment, he pecked her on both cheeks and pushed her to arms' length. Slowly he inspected her with the brotherly admiration that proved his usual approach to his little step-sister.

She set her jaw and flashed her eyes at him, determined to

show him her independence from his charms. "And you, dear sir, breathe every inch the accomplished man of the world."

After all, she had no intentions of shilly-shallying. She needed their relationship to develop differently from the past. At twenty-four, she was considered past her prime, on the shelf, too. But she didn't care for others' definition of her. No. She wanted things. Things she could not buy with her small but satisfying income. She wanted to make a difference in the world, for women especially. Women who had no wealthy family, no education, no hope of a life that was not drudgery from dawn to dusk. And for. herself? Yes, she had ambitions too. She wanted affection, a man of her own, a husband at the most, a faithful and inventive lover at the least.

That she had wanted that from this man from age fifteen was a fantasy, nourished by her irrepressible romantic illusions and her penchant for happy endings. Even her family experience with all of her relatives in marriages founded on love and devotion conspired against her hope that Pierce might one day be hers. Still, even today, as old and wise as she was, she stood here under his spell, absorbing his approval, his praise, as if she were that young girl. Yes, she still wanted him. Elusive as he was. Savagely masculine as no other. Fiercely independent as only a Hanniford male could be.

"Hmm," he said with a twinkle in those magnificent iridescent eyes of his. "And you, my dear, look like the successful author in your finery and your devil-may-care appeal."

"Ah. Do not flatter me too much, Hanniford." She pressed the flat of her hand to his chest where she was intrigued to feel his heart beat quickly. "We don't want the world to think you'd be taken in by ruffles and lace."

He put his arm around her waist and pulled her to his

side. But he glanced at his father. "I see while I've been gone you've taught her no diplomacy."

"Aye, we try!" Killian sighed, an Irish rogue's twinkle in his eyes, his brogue heavy in his words. "Our girl is too headstrong to be swayed by appeals to the ordinary."

Camille stepped away from Pierce's hold and shot open her parasol. "You two must learn to be more kind to a poor spinster who must make her way in the world."

The two men feigned horror.

Pierce curled her arm in his. "Give over, my sweet, you are too delicious to leave alone."

I dare not believe that. She'd rid herself of that delusion years ago. Ba! To him, she was a pest, worthy of teasing and easily left alone! "We'll see how long you have that view of me, sir."

He patted her hand. "I'll have a long time, this time."

She had to ask, had to know how long he'd remain in her sights, disrupting her life and fooling with her intentions. "How long do you stay?"

He scanned the horizon. "I haven't decided yet."

That made her wary. She had plans for her life that did not include focusing on him each day.

"I might just stay put this time."

"In London?" Hope warred with sanity that he might remain close. Little good his proximity would do her, god help her.

He inhaled and pursed his magnificent lips. "There. Paris. New York. I've not been seen in any of those offices for more than three years. I must. I should." Examining him, she found only mirth and good intentions.

Relief swept through her. She hated that it did. He had to leave. Would leave. He always did. Besides, she could count two probable suitors she could prefer and for good reasons, too. Both were stable, endearing. Neither liked to travel farther than Paris or Biarritz.

Killian scanned the dock. "Pierce, have you no valet?"

"No, sir. He became ill as we docked in Hong Kong and I left him there to recover. He'll return home to Shanghai. I got on well enough without him. We trained the ship's staff well in such services. I was fine."

"So then your luggage, Pierce? How many pieces have you?"

"Four," he told his father.

"Give me the tickets and I'll arrange it."

Pierce took them from his inside coat pocket and handed them over. "Two trunks in the hold. Two suitcases in my stateroom."

Killian hailed a porter and gave him the tickets. "We are the silver grey coach marked with an H in the far alley. Bring them all to us."

As Killian paid the porter, Pierce faced her with a dour expression. "I'm really very happy to see you, Camille. Glad you came. Very glad. I want so much to resume our friendship."

Ah, yes. Friends. That was only what they were. "Unique wasn't it?"

"Always." He lifted a hand as if he meant to touch her face. But he paused midway. When they'd first met, he'd made a habit of tapping the end of her nose.

She arched her brows and lured him. "Go on!"

He laughed. "You're older."

"As are you. But do it!" She egged him on. "You won't be happy until you do!"

"You're quite smashing and my dear friend!" he said and touched her.

Like old brandy, this sparring between them filled her

with happiness and a longing for more. She had to divert herself with some gay foolishness.

"Dear sir," she teased him, "I am the official welcoming party and I'm thrilled to be here." She tugged at her gloves, ignoring her urge to push up on her toes, kiss him and demonstrate how this more mature woman did not define friendship.

But Pierce leaned down, one of his hands on her shoulder. A foot taller than she, he'd always seemed enormous to her. Enormously protective. Excessively brotherly. Impossibly indifferent. "You look like a wise old owl to me."

She shivered in a dramatic rejection. "Wise and old. Hmmm. Yes. Next year, by society's rules, I shall officially become a spinster. But I am not decrepit yet!"

"God help us, a spinster? Aren't we done with that idea yet?"

"You have not been away that long, my brother. We're not even done with royal debuts and dowries, either."

"A disaster," he mourned.

"Tell me!"

"I hope you never lose your insights into society's foibles."

"Never. It's fodder for my novels." She wrote romances that scared and seared and delighted her female readership. "My readers exclaim over my heroines. How hard they must fight to keep their integrity." *And their lovers.*

"And your heroes?"

"Ah!" She lifted a finger in the air. "How devilish, how reclusive. How secretive."

He threw back his head to chuckle over that. "Dear God. Do you paint them all like that?"

She grinned at him. *You are my every brooding hero.* "Each and every one."

"Oh Camille!" He hugged her to his side again and her body burned wherever his touched. "I was right to come home. I needed to laugh with you. With all of you," Pierce added as Killian made his way toward them, his work ordering luggage done.

So there it was. Pierce's assessment of her. The inherent insult sparked her disappointment.

After all, she was worth more to anyone than simply someone to laugh with. Much more.

CHAPTER 2

"Shall we go to the carriage?" Killian asked them.

"Let's." Pierce offered Camille his arm. She took it and hooked her other arm through Killian's. The three of them wove through the throng along the cobbled street.

The bustle of the port filled his senses with the old comforts of the land he'd called home for most of the past decade. English shouted among the dock workers and murmured among the passengers brought a smile to his lips. Squared architecture, white Palladian Greco-Roman forms and red brick muscular Victorian dripping with too much decor had him nodding. The aromas of pasties full of potato and meat from the shops wafted, heavy on the briny sea breeze. The paved roads of Macadam and sturdy well-fed horses painted a picture of structure and order lacking in the treaty ports where chaos reigned among the coolies. Grooms and footmen in livery added to the illusion of order and precision. The lack of flimsy rickshaws led by emaciated barefoot runners spoke of the vast differences that still prevailed between the imperial western powers and the rigid and backward empire of China.

This homecoming was what he'd craved for many months. After receiving a letter from his step-mother late last spring, his desire to return to England and his family had grown each day.

He squeezed Camille's hand with the joy of being home.

Purposely, this time, he'd journeyed home more quickly than he usually did. Possessed of a need to bask in the affection of his family, he'd avoided his usual stops in ports around the world to meet with others for business. In Bombay, he'd disembarked only for one night while the *Empress* restocked her supplies and took on new cargo. He'd cabled ahead to an old school chum who lived in Jaffa in Palestine to meet him in port one evening for dinner in the souk there.

But his journey—a month and a half long as it was—had not prepared him, no matter his admonitions to himself, for first sight of his father and Miss Camille Bereston. His father, still a brawny Irish fellow, looked chipper as ever. But with more silver in his hair, more lines fanning from the the corners of his eyes, the man who had built an empire, a fortune and a family of nothing more than ambition, energy and devotion was growing older. At fifty-seven, shipping and industry mogul Killian Hanniford appeared to be more pensive, but still a hearty creature. Pierce made a note that at some point he would have a word with his father about his health and be very careful not to poke the man's hard scrabble pride.

As for Camille, she was as ever incomparable and he fought to keep his gaze off her. He'd learned about fabric, silks especially, because he exported them all over the world. By his own Chinese silk weavers, he'd been taught color, drape, weight, warp and weft. Camille might not know all of that, but she knew what looked good on her.

He appreciated her understanding of it, too—and he

smiled. In a day gown of jade cotton twill trimmed in deep golden ribbon at her bodice, she seemed to glow like a pearl. Her little spencer jacket hugged her long arms and framed the square décolleté of her gown to illustrate how her perfect breasts perched above a wasp-like waist. He'd watched her grow up, loving her choices of color and fabric, watching her turn men's heads, inspiring envy in women's, eschewing a coming-out, spending her days scribbling and then selling her first novel at age eighteen.

He'd known her for a decade. he had only one idea why her looks should make his heart skip a beat. She had changed. Of course, she had! And quite a bit since last he'd laid eyes on her two years ago. At twenty-two, she'd still had a few features of girlhood about her. Chubby cheeks. Small breasts. An inability to tame her thick locks of honey red hair.

The red in her hair that had been so blinding when she was fifteen that her mother declared she looked more like a poppy than a camellia, had since burned down to old gold. Her eyes, a fathomless brown color that varied with the light, searched and smoldered and seared beneath long earthy brown and gold lashes. Her looks had once amused him. Today...today they arrested him and suddenly, he was possessed of this yearning to put his mouth to her eyelids. To feel them flutter beneath his lips. To taste the lush cream of her cheek and put his hands over her large ripe...

He shot to attention. *Absurd, Hanniford.*

"How was crossing the Channel?" Killian asked. "*Lloyd's* published reports of a storm last night."

"From Bordeaux, yes, terrible. My entire trip was riddled with storms. Straightaway in the China Sea, we encountered a hurricane or as the Chinese call their violent storms, *tai-feng.* Big wind."

"A typhoon," she put in the bastardized English of the Mandarin.

"Exactly. How did you know?" he asked her.

She arched a long golden brow. "We do read here in Britain more than just the *Times*."

"Planning on using such color in one of your novels?" He had to tease her on her success.

She had to tease him. "I thought so. A wicked storm rages over a jagged cliff house. The mansion would be owned by a rich American *tai-pan*."

"Dark." He had read two of her novels and wondered at her characterization. Her men said little, kept their contemplations to themselves and struggled with finding the right woman to love.

"And brooding," she added with a nod.

"Do you write any light-hearted fellows?"

She shook her head. "It's extremely difficult."

"Don't you know any?"

"A few."

Who? He wanted to meet them, learn what they could tell him about...her.

That was silly. He knew her. Had known her for years.

"Any complaints about the accommodations on the *Empress*?" His father wanted to hear every detail of Pierce's experience on the maiden voyage of the newest luxury steamer of the Hanniford Oriental Steamship Company.

"None! The bed was comfortable. The dining room service exceptional. The saloon's bar well stocked."

"The electric lights worked?"

"Every time!"

"Exactly as you said they would." His father chuckled. "It will be profitable then."

"It will. Did you want a tour to see for yourself?"

"I do. But I'll return tomorrow for that."

"I'll notify the captain, if you like."

"No. I prefer to arrive unannounced."

Pierce nodded. "Of course."

From the corner of his eye, he caught a glimpse of the other passengers hastening down the gangplank. Among them was his best friend from Shanghai and he hailed the man to join them. "Here's a friend I want you to meet!"

Li Wa-Ren Macfarlane owned one of the biggest and most prosperous export-import companies in the British sector of Shanghai. One-quarter Han Chinese, Lee Warren—as he Anglicized his name when dealing with Westerners—was the son of a Scottish *tai-pan* and his half-Chinese wife. Lee had joined the *Manchu Empress* in Venice, and from there, the two men had spent the voyage by entertaining each other with stories of past adventures. They'd also devised a new business proposal to sell steel to a progressive Confucian viceroy who wanted to modernize the southern Kwangtung countryside near Hong Kong and Macao by building railroads.

"Lee! I'd like you to meet my father and my step-sister."

A tall reed-like fellow, Lee strode forward with delight written on his long face. He wore a superbly cut suit, this one of midnight black. Beneath, he wore a jade silk brocade waistcoat embroidered with yellow and red dragons, the symbols of the Wa-ren-Macfarlane House.

"Allow me to present my friend, Mister Lee Warren Macfarlane. My step-sister, Miss Camille Bereston. And my father, Mister Killian Hanniford."

"I am most honored to meet you both." He doffed his hat and shook hands with them. With serene blue eyes, he smiled at Killian and Camille.

"Are you abroad for a long time?" Pierce's father was always keen to meet other entrepreneurs.

"A few weeks here in London, yes." Lee spoke with a British accent.

Pierce could see the wheels turning in both his father's and Camille's heads. Pierce could bet that his father wanted to learn more about the man's business. Camille wanted to learn more about the man's background.

"Then I visit Paris and Berlin for a few weeks each before I return here, then sail to New York."

Killian grinned. "If you are here in Southhampton for a few days, we would like to have you to our house in Brighton for dinner."

"I am most appreciative." He glanced to one side as his young Chinese manservant presented himself for instructions for his luggage. "Perhaps I might come another time as I am on a train to London this afternoon."

"We will see you in the city then," Camille chimed in. "A few of the family go up to town soon and we would like to show you about!"

A flash of amusement lit Lee's deep blue eyes. He was used to the feisty western women in Shanghai International Quarters who took charge of social engagements—and often, business too.

Pierce grinned. "Lee and I spoke of this on board. He stays at the Langham Hotel in town."

"Thank you for the invitation. I accept and look forward to it."

Pierce was pleased. "I told Lee that we'd make reservations for the theatre."

"Superb!" Camille was her industrious self. "If you like, we'll go dancing, too."

Lee chuckled. "In Shanghai, we have Wednesday dance parties. Strauss is a favorite of mine. I like to waltz. Do you waltz, Miss Bereston?"

"I certainly do." Camille clasped her hands together,

aglow with admiration. "In London, we do it at home. But in Paris, they do it in the streets. We will see you enjoying yourself, Mister Macfarlane. In no time, I dare say, sir, you will be a sensation."

"I hope not too much! I have negotiations to engage in."

"Waltzing is like negotiating, is it not?" she asked, an impish twinkle in her devilish dark eyes. "One must navigate the floor with precision and grace in time with the movement of the spheres."

"So true, Miss Bereston!" Lee appreciated a woman who could steer a conversation with humor and complexity. Such a good time talking to a woman, Lee had not had in months. And Pierce knew it to be true. The two of them had lost a lady whom they both adored only ten months ago. Neither had yet gotten over her death.

"Thank you for the invitations. I look forward to seeing you again." Lee went off toward his own hired hack.

"Intriguing man," Killian said. "You've known him long?"

"Five years. One of the most successful men in Shanghai. He speaks His own dialect of Ningpo but also formal Mandarin. His English, as you heard, is superb. And he speaks better French than I could ever manage. And yes, he is Chinese. One quarter, to be precise."

They settled into the carriage, he backward, as his father and Camille took the seat facing him.

"Tell me about everyone," he urged his father. "All well, I do hope."

"Liv has had a summer cold and decided to stay home with the boys," his father said of his wife of eleven years. "Liam and Dylan fought the sniffles last week. Hence, they could not come, but are bursting at the seams to reacquaint themselves with their older brother."

"And Ada?" His youngest sister lived in Brighton, minutes from his father and step-mother Liv's home. Married to

Lord Victor Cole who was a member of Parliament, Ada was pregnant with twins.

"She is very selective about where she goes," Killian said. "These babies are slowing her down."

"As must her brood of three boys," he added.

"She longs for girls this time," Camille offered.

"A new challenge for her," Pierce said and crossed one leg over the other. "She's like a steam engine, never stops."

That brought a smile to Camille's lips. "She's as popular as Victor in his borough. They love her."

"No surprise there. She probably tells the ladies each chance she gets that she favors women's rights."

"As she should," said Camille. "We need the vote. And more ability to handle our own finances."

"You handle your own," Pierce said, but checked Killian's suddenly tight expression. "A great advancement."

She firmed her full lips, but stared at him.

He frowned. "The Marriage Law of a few years ago granted that to a woman of means."

She frowned and crossed one leg over the other.

Not pleased at all, eh? "Why do you look like you ate a prune?"

Killian turned to his step-daughter. "Better tell him."

"Tell him what?" Pierce asked when she clamped her lips together.

"I want to ensure that my earnings from my novels are only mine." She brushed a hand along the contours of one long leg and fastened her dark chocolate gaze to his. Since she'd turned eighteen, she had penned one novel each year. Maybe more, if he was not counting carefully. All were popular and profitable enough for her to have rented out a London flat last autumn, so Liv told him in her letters. All of her novels were mysteries starring young women who fell in love with secretive men who hid ugly secrets and lived in eery castles.

"Why wouldn't they be?" What had happened that she questioned this?

She scowled. "I want to ensure that all my money remains mine."

Pierce shook his head. "Why wouldn't it be? You wrote the books. You own them."

She huffed. "Not the first two."

"Why not?" Pierce checked his father's grim expression.

"They persuaded me to sell them all the rights for a pittance."

"All?" He sputtered. "How much of a pittance?"

"Thirty pounds for the first. And the right to republish until hell freezes over!"

"How can they have done that?" He could not believe she'd been so cheated.

"I got smarter after that and demanded a percentage of the net sales."

"I should hope so! And hired a lawyer too."

"Oh, indeed. The law suit continues." She folded her arms.

"Well, well then, so what's this that you fear your money is not yours to keep? I know you have your own bank account." Every Hanniford did. She too. Pierce remembered the day he and his father had gone with her to the City to open it. "Your money is only yours. Isn't it?"

When neither his father nor she uttered a word more, he sat back. "Just tell me."

"I'm going to get married."

Married. The word sank like a stone to his guts. Still he said, "Why that's—" *Impossible.* "That's marvelous!"

"Yes," she said in such a measured way that he could have thought she was agreeing to another scoop of vanilla ice or a peach cotton for a new gown. "It is."

Who is he? "Who is the lucky fellow?"

She shifted an iota among the squabs. "I haven't decided."

"What?" He laughed, relieved, confused. "How can you not know who you will marry?"

She met his gaze frankly. "I entertain two different gentlemen. Both are inclined to ask. But I've not decided which I will accept."

"Dear heavens!" He chuckled, cast at sea. "I don't know whether to congratulate you or dip you in the Channel for a nice cold swim."

"Do try," said his father. "I have. To no avail."

Pierce let his jaw drop. But looking at her brought forth no counter arguments from her. He was quite simply stunned. Camille was no social butterfly. Had refused a debut and all the fuss to accompany it. His father, step-mother and his sisters, too, had written often about her. She had sent fewer letters than they to him, but still he knew much about her life and her choices.

She navigated social rungs with her sass and flare. Her parents' social connections brought her the cream of society, and her own success as a novelist brought many in the literary world to her, clamoring for friendship. She had her own small apartment in London with a part-time maid. Enough money to live on. Enough friends to amuse her and gratify her need for gaiety. She was twenty-four, stunning and in need of no one to lighten her days. Which left, of course, what to do with the dark of her nights. "Why marry at all?"

"Ah," said his father with a nod. "The heart of the matter."

She waved a hand. "I grow older, you see. A woman must catch a man in her prime. Before her looks wither and she can no longer charm a stranger."

"What?" He scoffed. Camille had little tolerance for the

fripperies of female conventions. "True feminists do not need a man."

She shrugged a shoulder. "I do not need one. I'd simply find one useful."

"Poor fellow." He was horrified and trying—for the sake of comity—to be mightily amused.

"I want fun, too. With a man who'll adore me now and hopefully still will when I'm ninety-five."

"Do these men love you?"

"They might."

"Might?" He sputtered.

"I'm not certain yet."

Killian rolled his eyes at Pierce.

"How can you learn?" he persisted with her.

"Oh," she said with a hint of sarcasm, "a woman knows."

He frowned at her. "You cannot consider a marriage to any man who doesn't praise the ground you walk on."

"Thank you. I agree."

He focused out the window. Saw nothing. When would she marry? And go where? He'd come home, anticipating she'd be here. Lifting his spirits when he needed her. And he did now... He shook off the thought. "Who are they? These paragons of desirability?"

"You'll meet them," she said.

"When?"

"Soon. They come to dinner. The first comes tonight."

He folded his arms. "I can hardly wait."

She cast a jaundiced eye at his posture."Hunh! You certainly won't do them the justice they deserve, if you are set against them from the beginning."

Well. That from her was a stinging blow. "I am sorry, Camille. It's just a shock."

"I wouldn't pick simpletons. Besides, you knew someday I'd marry."

Did I?

"Everyone else has married. Even you wanted to last year."

He folded in on himself with that reminder. His loss of May was a wound, still tender. "Marriage is what we Hannifords do."

"Even this Bereston," she added with a smart little tip of her head. "I wish to join the ranks, that's all."

He nodded. Odd. Ironic. He'd come home to renew his ties with family. He considered remaining here, commanding his business empire and helping his father with his. He hadn't counted on Camille not being a part of that new life.

He had assumed she'd always be here. Why, he couldn't say. But that was silly, wasn't it? She'd go off as had his two sisters Lily and Ada. His cousin, Marianne, too, had married a Frenchman. Even his father had created a new existence after he'd fallen in love with Olivia. Like her mother, Camille would want her own life, more than an apartment in town and her own money. Like every other person, she'd want her own house, her own man and children.

But he'd been wrong to think of her as a fixture in his life. Wrong as he was about so much.

Frowning, he settled back to focus on the crisp sea air of Brighton. The rigid right angles of the architecture, the aromas of wheat bread and sugared treats from the hawkers on the wharves. The black hansoms and the stout Cleveland Bays pulling them. The ladies in painfully restricted corsets, their massive piles of hair wound up high beneath huge feathered hats, the men in severely tailored suits. No kaleidoscope of colored robes on the women. No bleeding bare feet. No aromas of onion and ginger. No offal trailing in the gutters from the ubiquitous fresh kill stalls. Not the singing tones of six Chinese dialects.

This was England. This was his country as much as

America. He'd been away so long that he'd forgotten the comfort of home and familiarity. He'd forgotten.

But a few things had changed. He should've predicted it. Prepared for it.

He inhaled and accepted the inevitable.

This time his visit with his family would be different.

CHAPTER 3

*H*anniford Manor stood in the eyebrow of a hill east of Brighton. A curving drive added grace to the Palladian mansion of creamy stone that overlooked the turbulent waters of the English Channel. What Pierce viewed as they rode toward it along the winding lane was a peaceful abode spread out like an elegant lady over the flowering landscape.

The architecture was more Grecian than ornate Victorian and the gardens sweeping up to the front portico reflected more the wild spirit of English love of flowers than any structured plots he'd glimpsed behind tall walls in Shanghai or Kamakura. His step-mother Liv and his father had built the house together just as they were falling in love a decade ago. It stood as testament to their success, his father—a tycoon of world-wide fame and his step-mother—an acclaimed interior designer.

The garden with its waist-high blossoms of every color of the rainbow set waves of remembrance upon him. Transfixed, he envisioned the tiny house in Baltimore near the docks where he had grown up with his sisters Lily and Ada, his cousin Marianne Roland and his widowed father. That garden outside the kitchen door had bloomed in riotous profusion from spring to autumn. Huge bushes of rhododendrons served as shelter for the rose bushes and tulips that Marianne had tended so diligently. His charming cousin, the daughter of his father's sister and her husband, was now the renowned artist, Madame la Duchesse de Remy. She was the only member of the family he did not expect to see here today as she made her home in France with her husband, a sculptor of international renown.

Fighting nostalgia, Pierce leaned toward the window to get a better look as the carriage rounded the drive. "I think Liv has been working more in the garden than on her business. The roses are spectacular."

"Gush over them, will you please?" Killian said with mischief twinkling in his bright gaze. "She complains that they do not fare well this year."

"But that is not for lack of Mama's attention!" Camille grimaced. "Dylan decided last week to feed them worms he'd dug up in the copse and the little buggers liked the rose leaves far too much!"

Dylan was Liv's and his father's youngest son. "And Liam, I assume, chastised him?" Their older son William, age eight and known as Liam, was a fellow who liked his life as regimented as their father. As Pierce remembered, the boy often chided his younger brother about his antics.

"He did." Killian offered, accepting his sons' differing humors. "They've been particularly devilish the past week, eager to meet you."

"Liam," said Camille with a pointed look, "has questions for you about China."

"Be prepared!" Killian lifted a finger in the air. "He has them written in a copy book."

"Ah. I'm ready for him," Pierce said, gratified.

Killian winced. "He wants you to teach him how to write calligraphy."

Pierce winced. "Well, now. That is a challenge. I can teach him a bit of Shanghai dialect. But calligraphy takes a master. A Chinese scholar who's been at it for a decade or more. Not me!"

"Dylan however," said Camille with a grin, "is a different kettle of fish."

"He wants to learn about Chinese worms?" Pierce made a silly guess.

She nodded. "And birds. He loves birds. Plants. Peach trees."

Pierce chuckled.

Camille laughed with him. "Peaches are his favorite fruit."

He glanced at his father. "I would say we have a budding biologist in the family."

"And a welcoming party," Camille added pointing to the crowd assembling under the portico. "Each intending to keep you talking all night long!"

My god. He counted four adults and eleven children waving and jockeying for position along the edges of the carriage-way. He hooted. "Who is *not* here? Only...Julian."

"He apologizes," said Killian about his son-in-law, the Duke of Seton who was married to Pierce's oldest sister, Lily. "He had an important meeting with the Prime Minister in London. He arrives tomorrow."

Pierce admired the array of his family aligned before him. "What a tribe!"

"Handsome, aren't they?" Camille said with sweet affection ringing in her words.

Pierce could not get enough of their strong good looks. His step-mother, Liv, with fiery red hair piled high. His youngest sister, Ada, the one who'd been a sprite, his irritant, ever jovial, round—huge, really—with her fourth pregnancy.

Her husband, Victor, a member of Parliament who'd won his seat with Ada's help. Lily, his oldest sister, her ebony hair glistening in an elaborate coif, taller than Ada, elegant in form but her exuberant self with arms wide, embracing two tall boys and a smaller wiggling one. Beside them, one little girl with a cherub's face jumped up and down yelling his name. She was the spitting image of her mother, Lily, and Pierce remembered her as a tiny gremlin who had stalked his every move. Elizabeth clapped her hands in joy. Next to her stood Ada's two step-daughters, Vivienne and Deirdre, sprouting up into adolescence, lithe strawberry blondes with abundant freckles to match. Next to them stood three very small boys, not so far apart in age, each with cinnamon hair and bright clear blue eyes. Resembling Ada, they were oldest to squirming youngest, Ethan, Oliver and Michael.

The most striking feature of the crowd had to be the number of boys. Liv's and his father's two. Ada's three. And Lily's three, her oldest Garrett, her youngest son Artie, and the boy she and her husband, the duke of Seton, had taken as their own six years ago, Nathaniel, after his father had died and his mother, Seton's sister, had abandoned him to them.

Nate looked none the worse for it, thank God. Pierce had a sudden memory of his beautiful mother, Elanna. Self-centered, self-indulgent Elanna who had been made to marry a man she abhorred. But she had done her duty to give him an heir, then had left him, trailing in her wake tales of liaisons so scandalous no one would receive her...except Lily and the duke.

He himself had thought her scintillating, tragic, pitiable and...yes, enthralling. Wickedly so. Luckily, he'd seen what destruction she'd caused so very many, including her son, this innocent boy. But Nathaniel had landed safely with this family.

With all of them.

The boys, stair-steps in age to each other, all with black or brown hair, a few with auburn glints, Ada's with the lighter hair, fidgeting, eager to run to him, intent as sin and handsome beyond description. Take them from their mothers' sides in a few minutes and he'd have trouble sorting who belonged to whom.

"How do you survive all that energy?" he asked, awash in admiration.

"We send them off to deal with each other!" Killian gazed upon his progeny with no small pride.

"They've learned the art of survival." Camille considered them with a wry smile.

"Useful in any endeavor," said his father.

The carriage rolled to a stop.

A groom jumped down from the rear and the carriage bounced as he pulled open the door.

"After you," Camille said and swept a hand toward the clamoring crowd.

"Go on, son." His father sat back. "We've been waiting for you forever."

He met the silver of his father's eyes and noted the tears of joy lining his black lashes. His own threatened. "Yes, sir. Thank you."

Camille was alert to the appearance of the family butler at the drawing room doors.

Jenkins, his round eyes deceptively quick, scanned the room chock full of family. The short roly-poly fellow should have retired years ago and her step-father Killian argued with him for it, often. But to no avail.

"I know my work, sir," said the man who'd become butler at Hanniford Manor when it was days old. "I'll tell you when

I should depart. Not yet, sir. I still know who's to get what here. When I don't, or I drool in my soup, I shall warn you, sir. Never doubt."

Tonight he knew that the first person who should welcome Camille's special guest should be she. She, alone. And she had instructed him so before they gathered in the salon. "I don't want the poor man washed overboard by family before he's had a chance to utter his name, Jenkins."

"Understood, Miss Camille." He'd bowed and promised compliance.

So now, as the Hannifords milled among each other and the adults drank their aperitifs and the children their lemonade, the butler hailed her from the far threshold.

"Excuse me, please," she said to Ada and got to her feet. "I think Lord Turnbowe has arrived."

The butler waited by the doors. "Your friend, Miss."

"Thank you, Jenkins. I'll go alone to welcome him. Mama has her hands full."

Her mother had caught a glimpse of the butler's intentions and would have risen. But Camille pointed toward the foyer and smiled at her mother. The woman resumed her chair to finish a story she told to Ada's three little boys and Lily's five-year-old, Beth. She was relating tales of her fox hounds and two Spaniels whom she was training to follow her in her daily outings. One liver and white Spaniel puppy had taken to Beth the past few days and would not leave her side. Even now the tiny creature sat near the little girl.

Pierce stood chatting with Victor. But as Camille turned to leave, Pierce met her gaze and arched a brow in question.

She threw him a grin but strode toward the door.

A quiver of concern trickled up her spine. Pierce could be a harsh judge. She'd watched him at it when he met others on the street. Once he had criticized a friend of hers, a young girl who'd come for a party at the London house. She'd not

been in the house more than two hours when Pierce repri-
manded her for demanding instant service from the staff.
He'd been right to ask her to cease her demands, but tonight
she worried that he could see things of people so clearly and
quickly.

She wondered what his instant analysis would be of her
beau.

"Hamilton!" She met him with a smile. He was giving over
his Homburg hat, cape and walking stick.

Good man, he beamed at her with those large mud-
colored eyes of his. "Kind of you to have me. And on a whim
too."

"I'm so glad you called to say you were here for a few
days. My mother and father are pleased to welcome you." She
hooked her arm through his. She'd not been so friendly
toward him before this, but well, tonight was the night for
that. "I must warn you that we are quite a horde of people.
My step-brother has arrived just this afternoon from
Shanghai and it's a reunion of huge proportions."

"I don't wish to intrude."

"Not at all." She patted his hand. "I shall introduce you to
each but don't feel as though you must remember everyone.
We have children dining with us. It's the custom. But the
younger ones will go on to the nursery before we are called
in to table."

"I shall do my best to remember each one."

She was sure he would. He could not be a successful
manager of his father's coal mining investments were he less
than devoted to details.

In fact, Hamilton was quite simply perfection. His wide
shoulders, his height, clipped red hair, trim beard, the line of
his stance, all about him spoke of precision and strength.
She'd known him for more than a year now. Met him at her
friend's house. Lady Brianna Price was the Earl of Bourke's

daughter, at twenty-five on the shelf, but appreciating every minute of her freedom. She and Brianna had a few things in common. One of them was an appreciation for Lord Hamilton Turnbowe. Another was a special enjoyment of his cousin, another jovial type, the Marquess of Dunvarnon.

The two women could not decide which man to favor more. And if Camille were honest, she could not say she would choose one before Brianna made her own choice. Cowardly of her, but she liked them both. Others too.

And if she had to marry, why not marry a man whom other women favored too? It meant one chose well, didn't it?

If one had to choose at all, that is.

And she should.

The sooner the better.

Pierce sat back as the footman placed the dessert before him.

"*Chocolat diplomat!*" He chuckled that his step-mother remembered his favorite French treat.

"Why not?" Liv winked at him from the far end of the table.

"Do you have chocolate in Shanghai?" Liam, his eight-year-old half-brother who sat to his left, piped up.

"Indeed we do. It's a favorite of the English ladies and the French."

"Not the Chinese?" Liam stopped, fork and spoon mid-air, and frowned, confused that such a thing could ever occur.

"They have other favorites. Almonds and peaches."

"Oh, well." Liam nodded in agreement, his curly black hair dropping over his forehead. "Good choices."

Pierce glanced down the dinner table and admired the comely multitude before him. He'd not been with such a crowd in a long time. His dining room in Albany Road in the Quarter could hold thirty and be cleared by his footmen to make room for a small orchestra and dancing. But he'd not invited many to his house in the past ten months. Only business associates. Certainly, he hadn't forgotten how to mingle with friends, but he had forgotten how to enjoy himself.

He grinned. The sight of those who looked so much like him warmed him as little had this past year.

"You like the looks of us, I think!" Lily, his sister, addressed him from directly across the table, her glass of port aloft in a toast to him. She wore a pearl blue gown an exact match for her crystal blue eyes—and a characteristically impudent smile.

"I do! Each of you appears splendidly healthy."

A flicker of laughter passed over her features. "Couldn't kill us with a pitchfork."

"We owe that to fine dining," said his father who commanded the head of the table and nodded to his wife at the other end.

"And from whom did we inherit that need to eat well?" Ada tossed her thick mahogany tresses.

"Grandpapa!" said Lily's oldest son, Garrett. "Papa says he made everyone clean their plates."

"He did indeed." Pierce glanced to his right at the boy beside him who was the imitation of Killian with midnight black hair and quicksilver eyes. "Has anyone told you why he thought that so important, Garrett?"

The boy met his gaze with a sincere concern, severe for a child of eight years. "Because he starved in Ireland."

"Indeed," Pierce said and glanced up at the man who had saved money earned on the Dublin and Waterford docks to buy passage for himself and his younger sister to the new world. "Hunger is a frightening feeling. As if you're a ghost of yourself. Transparent."

His father stared at him, but did not see him. Lily and Ada did the same, pausing to recall what their father had told them of the hours of his own mother dying from lack of a crust of bread. Pierce had never felt that hollow gnawing, but he'd seen it all too often on the wharves of Shanghai and in the cantons where the villagers with far too many children and far too little food to feed them, left babies in the streets to starve.

"I understand, sir," said Nathaniel who was Lily's nephew, "that many in China die of want."

"That they do," he replied, recognizing in the handsome boy his resemblance to his dark-haired mother.

"Why is that?" the boy wondered. "Has the Chinese emperor no interest to improve the lot of his people?"

Well, Pierce was certainly put to his tasks to provide these children with what they wished to learn of his far-off home. "The Emperor Kuang-shu is young but he is becoming devoted to that. He faces many difficulties, beginning with government officials who are opposed to change."

"Why not vote them out?" asked Vivienne. She was a young girl sprouting into a willowy young lady and one of Ada's two step-daughters.

Pierce thought that a viable question from a child whose father sat in the House of Commons. "Because those officials are not elected. They take examinations to qualify to serve in their territories. The exams don't test their understanding of how to raise rice or nurture chickens, but what they know of a set of rules put down by a philosopher who lived two thousand years ago."

"Who's he?" asked Vivienne as if the man were an upstart.

Pierce suppressed a smile. "His name was Confucius."

Camille's friend, Hamilton Turnbowe was spellbound. He wasn't the only one, either. Each child—and many of the adults—at the table was aghast or confused.

Turnbowe put down his fork and knife. "But how then, Mister Hanniford, do these officials govern?"

"Very badly, I'm afraid. And please, sir, call me Pierce."

The man was still curious and he leaned forward, the better to see Pierce from far down the long table. "Of course. Pierce. Why not change the examinations? Make them more useful?"

"That would be a bit like trying to make all Englishmen speak Latin. Difficult, troubling, and dare I say, irrelevant to the fact that the Chinese masses need a basic education first. Few of them read or write."

"That sounds fine!" joked Garrett.

"We could ride horses all day!" His cousin Nate joined in.

"Mama," said Vivienne with a devilish grin, "would not have to host so many receptions for Papa's constituents."

Ada swallowed her bite of dessert and took the high road with a grin. "I would find a way!"

Vivienne turned to Pierce. "She loves politics more than Papa does, I think. But many people make her cranky."

"Is that so?" Pierce knew Ada's point of view on the subject of those who refused to change anything in society. But he took stock of the expressions on the other women's faces. Not one of them—not his step-mother or Lily or Camille—objected. In fact, they winced.

"It is," said Lily with a frown at Ada.

"I am just very great with child," she admonished them all with wide eyes and playful indignity.

"Right you are." Camille nodded. "We've encouraged her to do more gardening lately than political work."

"In my condition?" She opened one hand before her very large pregnant form. "I cannot bend down to dig in the earth. But if you must know…" She bristled and took to her dessert for a moment, then gave it up with a clank of her fork and knife to her plate. "I have stopped my weekly receptions."

Pierce saw her statement as one meant as much to affirm Lily's point, but also to assure the rest of the family that she was easing up on her schedule. "Your mama knows how to take care of all of you and takes special care of herself, I am certain. She learned long ago, you see, how important that is."

Their father chuckled, a twinkle in his eye directed at Pierce. "You'll tell the story of her escapade?"

"No!" Ada objected with a snort. "Don't you dare!"

"Your mother is resourceful, Vivienne." Pierce took his attention to his dessert, but only briefly. "I shall tell you later of how she decided one day to go to the wharves in Baltimore, looking for the taffy lady."

Vivienne made a face. "Mama, you liked taffy? Ohhhh, no."

"I was young, Viv. What did I know?"

"So what did she do, Uncle Pierce?" This came from Liam, who sat across the table.

Pierce picked up his port, took a sip and began. "We lived on a street not far from the docks in the center of town. Papa had his factory between the dock and the railroad tracks. Many afternoons after school, Lily and I would take Ada and walk to the water to buy fresh crabs and oysters from the fishmongers for supper. But the treat Ada loved most of all was taffy. And we bought it from an elderly lady who hoisted her tent there on Fridays. One day, Lily was sick."

"I had a deep cough and Papa told me to stay in bed." Lily added.

"Where was your mother?"

Pierce recalled the long debilitating illness of their mother who died soon after this incident. "She was in bed, very ill herself. So Lily and I were in charge of Ada."

Vivienne looked appalled. "Didn't you have a nanny?"

"No nanny. No maids," he said. "We got on by ourselves."

"And you could walk to the docks by yourselves?" Nate was agog, but obviously liking that idea.

"We could and did."

Killian inhaled. "We were not wealthy. And I worked many hours a day."

"I learned to cook," Lily added with a smile full of pride. "So did Pierce."

A general round of ouuus and ahhhs went up from the children.

"What did you cook, Uncle Pierce?" Garrett, Lily's oldest, had to know.

"Fried fish. Potatoes."

"Crab soup," Ada said with a sparkle in her eyes. "Good too. Do you still cook, Pierce?"

"No. You're delaying the story, Ada." He chastised her as older brothers often did.

She tipped up her chin in defiance. "Hurry up then."

"Our Ada ran away from home one Friday," he said.

"It was Good Friday and we were to go to mass," Lily said. "We usually went to the docks after church. But this Friday morning, we had only enough money to buy fish for our supper. Not enough to buy taffy and when we told Ada, she was mad."

"I went to our bedroom in the attic and—"

"You didn't have your own bedroom, Mama?" Vivienne was incredulous.

"No, Viv," Ada replied. "We three slept together in the attic. Anyway, I was angry and sad. You see our mother was dying."

Silence filled the room.

"I was five years old and had no idea why my mother couldn't stay with us. I thought she had decided she didn't love us anymore."

Pierce glanced at his father who cast his gaze to his plate.

"So I ran down the back stairs and off to see Mrs. O'Dougherty. Across the streets filled with Union soldiers and across the railroad tracks to the hucksters' tents. But she wasn't there. She'd gone to mass and her husband tended the stall."

Pierce focused on Ada with a compassionate smile. "Lily and I had tracked Ada and came upon her just as Mr. O'Dougherty picked Ada up by the neck of her dress."

"He was tipsy." Lily said with horror in her words.

"Tipsy?" asked Vivienne. "What's that?"

"Drunk. He'd had too much whiskey," said Pierce. "And he was about to throw Ada into the water."

"No!" Nate said, full of indignation.

"He wanted my money," Ada said. "But I had none. I'd gone to see Mrs. O'Dougherty expecting she'd give me a piece of taffy for free. But that day I learned that nothing is free." She beamed at Pierce. "Except love. My brother who was a very tall, very skinny but a very scrappy thirteen-year-old launched himself at the very tall, very fat and very inebriated Mr. O'Dougherty and kicked him in the shins. The old man just crumbled."

"Well," said Pierce with humility, "that was because Lily joined in the fray and bit his arm."

"I had good teeth," Lily affirmed with a smug nod.

"And the tenacity of a barracuda!" Pierce snorted. "O'Dougherty bellowed."

"And he dropped me in a shot. I was grateful, of course. But angry at Lily and Pierce that they'd found me. Plus I still had no taffy."

"Did you send her to her room, Grandpapa?" Garrett had to know. "Or spank her?"

"No. That night when I got home and Pierce and Lily told me what had happened, I had a talk with your aunt Ada. I told her she must never go anywhere without company or without a coin or two."

"Most of all," Ada said with a kindly glance at her father, "he told me that those who love me must always know where I am and how I am."

"And we always did," Pierce said, ignoring the one time six years ago when she'd been abducted and her husband Victor, Julian and Pierce had saved her.

Ada smiled at him with gratitude that he didn't bring up that fateful night. "And after that, we each got five cents each week to spend as we wished. On taffy or lemon drops. I gave up lemon drops and I saved my money for a new porcelain doll. It took me nearly two years to have enough."

"And I," Pierce said with pride, "was permitted to join my father's stevedore gang on the docks on Saturdays."

"You were punished for Aunt Ada running away?" Garrett was outraged.

Pierce laughed. "Far from it. Before Ada ran away, I'd often begged Grandpapa to let me work loading and unloading cargo."

"When he attacked Mr. O'Dougherty," his father said, "I realized he had not only muscles, but skills at defending himself and others. I knew time on the docks with the long-shoremen would improve his chances of winning whatever he wanted."

"And did it?" Camille asked him.

"I learned from the best how to prepare for what I want and to earn what I get."

Down toward Liv's end of the table, tonight's guest and only non-family member Lord Hamilton Turnbowe acknowledged that with good humor along with the rest of them. Camille's beau was a hale and hearty fellow, as tall as Pierce, but more massive. If Pierce were to compare him to anyone, he'd say he looked the part of a rough-and-tumble wrestler. He fit into his precisely cut dinner clothes with the mark of a man of wealth and an eye for the earthen colors that best matched his dark complexion. Handsome? Pierce left that decision to women. He appealed to Camille so he was clearly acceptable. He had a wide brow and hair the color of Irish peat. He was the second son of a viscount and earned his income in trade. What the man knew of sound management Pierce had not had any time during drinks to discern.

But he did know one thing from those hours in the man's company with all others in the family. Turnbowe was taken with Camille.

That gave Pierce satisfaction.

Of course it did.

Of course.

CHAPTER 4

*P*ierce strode into the first floor breakfast room just as the hall clock struck eight-thirty. The room could hold ten easily but today no one else was dining. Not that he had expected anyone to still be lazing about. Most in the family were usually up with the chickens.

"Good morning, Jenkins." The butler held his post by the far door to the kitchen. "Am I destroying your impression of me as first up and out the door?"

"Never, sir. You've had a long journey and a full evening last night. Coffee or tea?" Jenkins had come to know each Hanniford's favored morning drink, but the man was always careful to ask anyone who had traveled abroad recently if his or her preference had changed.

"Coffee, Jenkins. We have a good assortment of beans in the Settlement," he told the man as he took the chair offered by the footman. "But I do prefer whatever it is Cook orders."

Jenkins took the compliment with a nod. "Shall I serve you?"

"No need." He'd noticed quite a few hot salvers on the

side-board. "I will do it. What morning papers do we receive, Jenkins?"

"Your father took the *Times* up to his office with him. He told me to tell you he apologizes but he had an issue that he wished to study. And he asks for you to see him after you've finished, if you would."

"I will." He caught sight of a stack of newspapers on the side buffet. "I'll be quite satisfied with what's in that pile."

"We do have the *London Daily News*. And the *Homeward Mail of India and China* of yesterday."

"Enough to amuse me, I'm certain."

"Does one get a constant source of honest news in Shanghai?" The butler indicated the *Homeward Mail* that reported the doings in the treaty ports and countryside to the British. But the man had another interest in that he was known to read anything in print, books in the house library included. "Regularly, I mean?"

"One gets…"—he flourished a hand—"summaries at first. More than a month old. I think the *Homeward Mail* gets the news here as quickly as any. But it focuses on India. China and Japan come second."

"A shame, sir. How do you decide on matters without the latest maritime reports or pricing of goods?"

Pierce shrugged. "It can be a guessing game. But the assurance one does the right thing comes from the fact that we all make the same assumptions together."

"Decision by consensus, sir?"

"Better than no decisions at all, eh?"

"Well! Hello! You're up!"

Pierce directed his attention to the vision in the doorway. Attired in a walking suit of starched white linen with a pink blouse, Camille was the picture of summer. She carried in her hand a huge deep rose straw hat with paper mache camellias in a spectrum of pink to red. Her hair, that abun-

dant wealth of auburn and gold, she'd caught up in an elaborate array of waves and curls. Little gold earrings twinkled at
her ears. And to top it off, she wore a broad smile.

"I am, yes. Good morning!" He indicated the chair next to
him. "Are you my company?"

"I've already eaten, thank you. I'm off to town."

"This early?"

She nodded and one of her golden curls came loose.
"Devil take it! Yes, this early." She put her little straw reticule
to the seat of one chair and began to work on her coiffure.
With both arms in the air, she spanned her silk blouse across
her generous breasts. He would have to be a dead man not to
notice their fullness.

He swallowed hard. She was, always had been, so graced
with good looks.

She jabbed a pin to her hair, but her efforts were for
naught. The thing kept escaping her. "Ohh!!! I'm...yes, I'm to
meet a friend for coffee and then she comes with me to my
autographing party."

Disappointment zipped through him that she wouldn't
dine with him. The outline of her breasts engendered a very
different emotion. Strong, it was, and a challenge to the linen
of his trousers. He cleared his throat. "An autographing?
Where?"

"In the Lanes. Winslow's Book Shop."

"Near the bakery?"

She removed the hair pin that would not stick right. "Yes."

"Sit down."

"No, I can't. I'm late and I must get my maid to fix my
hair."

"If you sit, I will fix your hair."

She pulled back to wrinkle a brow at him. "You?"

"Yes." He rose from his chair and pointed at the chair
beside him. "Sit."

She got this silly look of disbelief on her face. "You do hair?"

"I do."

"Since when?"

Since May showed me how to pin up hers. "A few years now. I'm good, too. Sit and you will see."

She cast about, glancing at the footman who widened his eyes and at Jenkins who lifted his brows. She plunked down in the chair. "All right. Show me what you can do."

He put his hands to her shoulders, the silk at the neckline of her blouse a sensuous enticement to slip his fingers up along her throat and her perfect little ears. Well, that would not do! He lifted the offending curl and pulled it straight out to view the structure beneath. "I see the problem."

"What?"

"Foundation insecurity..."

"What?" She snorted in laughter.

"The hair beneath is not secured in the manner it should be. This thing!" He pulled out a long roll stuffed with pale blonde netting. He set it before her eyes and she squealed.

"You wear this every day?" he demanded.

"Put that back! What are you doing? If you destroy my lovely curls...!"

"Not I, my sweet. Dear God. What the hell is this?" He took out a pin and another roll, similar to the first, fell free.

"Oh you are impossible," she groaned. "Do put that back!"

"I can't!"

She crossed her arms and huffed. "Or won't!"

"I have an idea." He parted this hank of hair from that and then back again. He really did not have any idea but he would try. "Scaffolding is what your maid built."

"Well, you are destroying my entire coif!"

He snorted. "It needs it. Without security, it will fall, dear girl!"

"As if you know!"

"I do." He put his hands to her shoulders and patted her with strumming fingers. "Now sit still."

"But hurry. I must be going!"

"Perfection takes time."

She huffed and puffed.

"Stop it," he ordered and found his way through the pins. Then he remembered how May had described the process of formal Chinese styling. That was an art that consisted of tiers of hair piled in irregular fashion to get height and stability.

"Pierce?" She egged him on.

"In a minute, pet."

"Really! How can you tell?"

He fished out the hairpins, picked that coil of hair from its moorings and re-wound the length to secure it to the other side of her head. "Your maid is good, but she should have taken more time to do...this!" He sank the pin in tight to her scalp. "And this." He put the other pin in.

She turned her head this way and that. "It feels more stable."

"It is."

"But it is pretty?" She flashed her dark chocolate eyes at his, searching for...*what?*

All humor gone, he stared at her squarely. *You'd be ravishing in absolutely nothing.* "Go look."

He folded his arms. Better that than to lift her from her chair by her shoulders and taste her...*No. That wouldn't do.* "Go on. The hall mirror will prove my worth."

She dragged her gaze from his, shot to her feet and grabbed her reticule and her floppy hat. "Thank you."

"You're welcome," he said as he watched her turn.

She walked away, waggling her fingers at him in good-bye, her backside swinging seductively in the white linen.

"What time is your autographing?" he called after her.

"Noon!" She kept walking.

~

He knocked lightly on the open door of his father's office.

Their eyes met, his father's probing as he waved Pierce inside. "Come in! Do! I'm glad you slept late. We think we're so healthy and travel doesn't diminish us, but we soon learn on land we are wrong."

Pierce walked about the office he knew so well. The floor-to-ceiling mahogany bookshelves on two walls, cabinets on the other. A table for his father's personal wireless cable and radio. The smell of beeswax, old paper and leather. The three globes in one corner by the far bay windows, the flat mahogany table in the center of the large room, an eight-foot expanse on which his father spread out intricate maps of the world dotted with Hanniford Enterprises offices. Maritime maps with shipping lanes mixed, one upon another filled with intricate detail, scaled in useful proportions. He fingered his father's newest acquisition, a drawing of the Bund waterfront of Shanghai, a gift from him to his father last Christmas.

He didn't wish to think too much of business for a few days. He'd come home to enjoy his family and friends first. The problems that plagued him could wait. He lived too much focused on them alone and had lost sleep over it. He was tired of that kind of life. Alone. Obsessed with work.

Wandering to the tall bay window that overlooked the front lawns, he paused to watch Camille accept the hand of a coachman who assisted her up into the family brougham. Her young maid jumped up into the carriage beside her, the two of them chatting gaily in the morning sunlight.

Pierce smiled to himself that he'd fixed her coiffure to no

avail. The caleche of the carriage was collapsed. By the time Camille and her servant arrived at her friend's, her hair would be a shambles. She'd simply have to fix it again.

He grinned and his fingers itched to fix it once more for her.

As the coachman flicked the reins and she disappeared, he turned to his father. "I didn't stop often this time to visit with many of our friends. I hope you don't mind that. Forty-three days was long enough for me. I just...wanted to come home."

"However, you came, we're delighted to have you at last."

Pierce considered his father's perspicacity. Warmed by it, he understood this shrewd man saw much in his children and their behavior because he took time to examine them and truly know them. If Pierce ever married and had children, he would attempt to be as good at securing such insight into his offspring as Killian Hanniford. "I thought I'd take a few days here with you before I go up to London. I told Victor last night I'd come visit him this afternoon, but aside from that, I'm eager to do nothing."

"Wise. I hope you'll enjoy a respite from your work. You look like you need it."

So do you. Pierce inhaled. Discussion of his father's health had to originate with him.

"Is there anything special you'd like to do while you're here with us?"

"Yes!" He laughed. "No gentlemen's clubs. No meetings or dinners."

"Do trust me, we've planned nothing formal."

"We've had such little time together these past six years, Papa. I'm pleased to take the opportunity to learn from the master."

His father chuckled. "Flattery gets you everywhere."

Pierce sighed dramatically. "You always could smell blarney at twenty yards." *Except this is none and you know it.*

His father extended a hand to the brown leather chairs near the fireplace. Today, no fire burned. The air was warm. The sea breeze misty with the flavor of salt flowed through the open windows.

"I will go up to London in a week or so." He sank to the comfort of the opposite chair and brushed a hand down his tan linen trousers. "I realize it's summer and no sane Englishman does business in August, but I must make the most of my time here."

His father's face fell. "You've set a date to return to Shanghai? I thought you were flexible."

"I am. Really. Call me undecided. But as for business matters, you know I cannot sit still while we wait for every lord and lady to return from the country! I do want to go to London soon and settle a few problems."

"I understand. I could never wait for their summer hiatus either. And it seems they've gotten worse in the past ten years since they've had a taste of jungles and deserts the world over. Personally, I've always gotten more done in a room with two men. But the Europeans have a different method."

"They're too used to negotiating everything from their marriages to their cattle sales in drawing rooms."

"Forgive me then, if I want to discuss a few matters of business with you here, even if you are on holiday." His father filled his pipe and took a damn long time doing it.

"What bothers you?" he asked at last.

His father arched a brow. "You know me well."

Pierce laughed. "You taught me to pay attention!"

"Ah." The man demurred. "Your success, Pierce, is your own. Look at the Shanghai company. You took over what Victor had built and tripled it."

"He admitted his heart was not in it." Pierce liked Ada's personable husband, whose ambition to sit in Parliament was more to his taste than haggling with Chinese merchants. "I wanted a new adventure."

His father examined his pipe, then put it down unlit. "You wanted more than that."

"I did." He was old enough to admit it. He was wiser now to not commit those errors again. "I made a few mistakes. I was not proud of them and I needed to grab a new challenge to find the contrast."

"They were not business mistakes, Pierce."

His father met his gaze. If he waited for Pierce to discuss Elanna, the Countess of Carbury, he would wait forever. Pierce knew what had happened to the woman who was so rebellious, so hateful of her husband that she had ruined her life with countless affairs and numerous public displays of anger toward her husband. True, the Earl of Carbury had been a bully, but she had learned how to best him at it. When he died six years ago, she could have seized the opportunity to take her young son Nate home and in time, marry one of the men she had favored. Instead, she packed up her son and left him with her brother Julian, the duke of Seton, and his wife, Lily. Nathaniel, who was born on the same day as Lily's and the duke's oldest son Garrett, lived with them and was as well cared for as one of their own.

Pierce's attraction to Elanna was an ill-founded obsession with her boldness. He knew it then. He understood it, even if he could not disentangle himself from her lure. He'd not gone near her and had not had an affair, though some in the family thought he might have gone that far. But no. He'd been sane enough to avoid that. He had watched on in horror as she ruined her life.

In the end, she had destroyed her husband, herself and nearly so, her only child. The knowledge of that was so stark that anyone with any sense understood it. As had he. Only on a logical level, however. On an emotional one, he had sympathized with her. And yes, he had lusted after her. Foolish of him. He knew better. He'd met a thousand women, appreciated them, desired a few, enjoyed their company, their intellect. He'd had mistresses, too. Each for very limited times and discreetly so. But Elanna had been a fascination, a fire in him, as if he could not believe someone could be so destructive. She was a geyser, irrepressible. Like fireworks, unpredictable. But she was also venomous. Mercurial, self-centered, irredeemable. Even as he wanted her, he'd been mystified by his desire for her. And too, he was ashamed of his infatuation with her.

When she'd disappeared, he wanted to as well. His brother-in-law Victor's offer to take on half share of his Shanghai Trading Company had been his saving grace. It had been the perfect solution to his need to escape, building his own steel and iron works by proxy here in Europe. But in China in six years, he'd expanded Victor's company, now half his, transforming it into the largest foreign-owned textile export company in the east coast region of Kiang-su province. In that time, he also added more exports of tea and fine porcelains, increasing his own wealth to the point that he finally felt whole, accomplished and satisfied.

His father smiled at him, all empathy. "But you're here now and well."

"I am, Da."

"We worried about you after you wrote that you'd lost the woman you planned to marry."

He considered the empty black grate. "I wanted to call in her Methodist minister even as she lay dying, but she wouldn't have it. She said she had gone to her temple and consulted her Buddhist fate teller about our friendship. The man had read her stones and declared our 'friendship' would remain intact, eternal. He said that after May was gone, I would soon become whole. May said she would not taint that wholeness to take any part of me away from my future."

"She is not yet gone from you a year, Pierce."

"In many ways, she will never be. She was a creature of her environment. Part Scots. Part Chinese. One-quarter really because her mother was the daughter of an English clerk and his Chinese wife. Her father is full Scots, descended from Highlander rebels who love taking a bite out of Englishmen's ambitions.

"She was educated, quick-witted, spoke Cantonese and Mandarin, Spanish as well as English. She saw the values of Confucian devotion to harmony and Buddhist principles of peace. But she also valued the virtues of aggressive western men. Few can. We can be beasts abroad."

"Anywhere, Pierce. I saw it in the shipment of black men from Benin. I saw it as Rebels fought Yankees to bitter death. You don't have to live outside your own culture to be a menace to others and your own integrity."

"So true." Pierce sighed. May had gumption, like Elanna. Yet was unlike her, in so many ways. "She had patience and a humility that allowed her to view the other as one to value. May was her name. May Warren Macfarlane, a child of both East and West. I miss her."

"Your friend, Mister Macfarlane, is, I assume, her relative?"

"Her brother. A fine man. As was she a fine woman. He'll have trouble here in Europe, you know."

"Prejudice." His father nodded and drummed his fingers on his desk. "We can help him."

Pierce found solace in his father's acceptance of everyone as his equal. That was part of what Killian stood for and what Pierce had learned made his father great. "I plan on it."

"A few will ignore him."

Pierce nodded. "Because he is different. Looks different.

Understands a culture so far from our own. Many will try to cheat him."

His father winced. "And? Will he survive here?"

"Has he the stamina? The nerve? Oh, indeed. They will not know how to cope with one who beats them with his wits. When he outmaneuvers them, they will blame him. There will be trouble."

"Does he realize this?"

"He does. He's had the best education in Shanghai with those who cannot fathom that a Chinese can best them at their own game." Pierce was done with this subject and he wanted to know what concerned his father. "But you wanted to talk about our business. What is it that worries you?"

"I am having a problem with laborers in Liverpool. Strikes. Nasty business. It weighs on me."

"Yes. Workers demanding more. They're doing it everywhere. New York, Paris. People want compensation for their hard work."

"I've no objection to higher wages. You know I never have. But banding together to beat my office workers with clubs is not the way to win my heart or the point. There is an element. Bullies. Reminds me of the gangs on the docks in Waterford and Dublin in the years before I left. I won't stand for it."

"Tell me what their demands are. We'll find a way."

"I hoped you'd help me with the negotiations. You have the temperament for it. Not that I don't, but you have more patience than I. What's more, I dare say, you take the longer view."

Pierce widened his eyes. "Kind of you, Da. But I doubt you've read the newspapers' analysis of my tactics in Shanghai."

"With the Russians who wanted to buy out your porcelain suppliers?" His father laughed.

"Ha! Or the Germans who wanted to undercut my prices for steel."

His father scoffed. "And failed because they had no idea you paid your people very well. The Germans value strength not resilience. They had no idea what they were up against. I value you for your ability to see others' reasoning. So. What do you say about this Liverpool problem? Will you handle this for me?"

Pierce nodded. "I welcome the chance to help you. Have you called for meetings with the workers?"

"I promised them to begin mid-September."

"Four weeks from now?"

"Approximately yes. Might that fit your schedule?"

"I guess I won't return to Shanghai for a while," he said with a smile.

"Or ever?"

Pierce lifted a hand. "To be determined."

CHAPTER 5

"Come along, Ivy." Camille motioned for her maid to catch up to her and her friend Brianna Price.

The girl loved to dawdle before the shop windows. Especially the baker's. Not that Camille could blame her. She herself would buy everything she desired. And she did desire a lot. Not simply from the bakery. But shirtwaists from the dressmaker's, cotton caps from the linen drapers, crocheted canezous from the lacemakers. All goods, any goods to make a woman's life easier, brighter. Yes, she would buy it and pass it on to Wattledge House where young women who had nothing, discovered they were about to have that most precious and—for them, each one single and destitute—the most damning thing of all—a baby. "I promise we'll take tea and luncheon after my reading."

"Ha!" Brianna tossed her head, today enfolded into in a peach straw affair with white egret plumage sticking out at obtuse angles. "You love to eat more than she does."

Camille rolled her eyes. "You know me too well."

"And if you could skip this event to go dine, you would."

"And you," Camille said and arched both brows at her

tall, regal friend, "would join me. But one must keep up appearances and earn one's daily bread. And today—" she said as she swung wide the front door to Winslow's Book Shop, "—I also promise to read a shorter passage of my newest."

"Thank heavens." Brianna swept in behind her and kept the little bell over the door ding-aling-ing. Ivy scurried in behind her. "I'm tired of this new man."

Camille tugged off her gloves, eager to talk with the proprietor and get her event underway. "'The Recluse of Harrowgate Aerie' is quite a fellow. I loved him. So did my publisher and he says, to date, so do more than six thousand British women."

"Ah, yes. The Earl of Harrowgate may be a silent, brooding beast who marries the heroine for her fortune, but better yet, he is profitable."

"He is quite delicious." Camille craned her neck to see if Mister Winslow or his wife were perhaps in the back storage room. "Once he reforms."

"I'd marry him before that." Brianna fluttered her long red lashes at Camille. "Tall, swarthy, a world traveler who understands how a woman must be made to feel...shall we say... welcome in his home as well as his bed?"

"Indeed. After she is half scared to death by his majordomo."

"Who looks rather like a ghost. I say, my dear, you frightened me with him. I'd give him his notice."

"Ah! The butler and his master! The stuff of exciting literature." Camille meandered back through two bookshelves. "Let's go over here and see if they've set up...yes, they have my desk."

"Only two rows of chairs," Brianna worried.

"If more arrive, they'll stand but many simply buy the book and hurry on home."

"Of course, they do. To devour your words," said Brianna with knowing eyes.

Camille grinned, then put down her reticule to the chair and fished inside for her favorite ink pen while Brianna perused the far shelves. She set to work to remove the pins from her hat and shake the contraption loose from the hair that Pierce had nailed to her head.

"There you are! Miss Bereston!" Mister Winslow was a short roly-poly fellow with huge blue eyes, a few wisps of white hair and a sing-song voice. He was, in spirit, as soothing and pleasant as the mellifluous sound of his family name. Someday soon, Camille would have to create a character as dulcet and euphonious as he was. A striking contrast to her usual characterizations of her mysterious heroes, he would be a secondary actor, sorry to say.

"Good afternoon, Mister Winslow." She stepped forward to greet him and shake his hand. "How well you look."

"I am, Miss. As is my wife." He turned aside to allow his shorter, even rounder spouse to approach and welcome her. "We are so pleased to have you."

The trilling of the tiny bell above his front door announced the arrival of others and his pudgy gremlin's face lit up with joy. "You hear that! We will have a large gathering today. So happy, we are, to welcome one of our own from our own town."

Camille thanked him as Brianna made her way toward them. "And I'm sure you remember Lady Brianna Price?"

"Indeed I do, my lady. Welcome."

"Thank you, sir." She indicated the four books in her arms. "As you can see, I simply cannot leave without a bit of light reading for the evening."

Camille leaned over to read one spine. "'*A Vindication of the Rights of Woman*'?" The diatribe by Mary Wollstonecraft was a favorite of her friend's. "Another copy?"

Brianna looked pained. "My cat shredded mine."

Camille choked on laughter. "Is your cat still alive?"

She narrowed her dark eyes in menace. "In hiding."

"Smart feline."

Winslow grinned, ever happy to see customers who loved his wares. "And I hope you will avail yourself of a copy of your friend's book today, too."

"I will but I can speak certainly to its worth to any and all potential customers."

"Lady Brianna, "Camille put in, "reads my drafts before I send them to my typist. I'm hideous at missing words and she is my first and most necessary editor."

"Never fear, though, Mister Winslow!" Brianna had a finger in the air, all drama at the ready. "I shall buy not just one but four copies today."

"Three!" He clasped his stubby little fingers together in utmost glee. "I know your friend is honored."

Brianna cast a jaundiced eye at Camille. "Honored that my mother, my maiden aunt and my older sister cannot live without their autographed copy of the next Camille Bereston gothic romance. And that I need the last copy for myself. My cat, you see, will be quarantined."

Camille had crossed her arms at her friend's soliloquy and stood back against the edge of the signing table. "Hmmm. We here simply hope that Wilkie Collins is proud of how we have amplified his suspense tales."

"So say nothing of Charlotte Bronte and her *Jane*, eh?" Brianna gave them both a wince.

Ladies of all ages, heights and demeanors approached Camille and circled round them.

"Oh, Miss Bereston! I am so honored to meet you."

"My, my, Miss Bereston. Your novels are my most wonderful enthusiasm."

"Comforting," said another lady.

"You must write more. I simply cannot live without you in my day."

As the women formed a cadre near Camille, she began to make her way to the back of the table. Taking her chair, she brushed out her white linen skirt and tucked in—once more —her errant curls.

She caught Mister Winslow's eye and nodded. He was very good about letting her know when to begin. She'd told him her preference for a one-hour event, and he had always kindly agreed. The group before her continued to buzz in expectation and the bell at the front door kept ringing nonstop.

When at last all seats before her were full, Winslow rose up on his toes and lifted his bushy brows. He nodded and made his way to the front to one side of the desk where she sat. A stack of her new novel was piled at her right hand. Four copies of each of her previous nine were arrayed to her left hand, so that any readers who had missed one might buy a copy and have a complete library of her works.

He began with an introduction, citing once more that she lived with her family to the east in Hove. He always began that way, as if to note for his modest, middle class clientele that she was acceptable, moderate, a woman of substance and some virtue. His introductions always evoked a sense of pride in what she was, what she appeared to be and yet, pricked at her conscious of what she was not. Not yet, in any case. Not totally independent.

She shook off her reflections. She was working toward her goal. She was.

"Good afternoon, ladies!" She began with her hands and heart open to those like her who loved to get lost in the written word and especially those who put their hard-earned pin money into a few hours of pleasure reading her novels. Among those here, she recognized a few who'd attended these readings before. Many now brought their friends with them to meet her and listen to her read from her own pages. "I'm delighted so many of you are here. I thought I'd begin by reading a passage of the newest."

Murmurs of approval rose up from her crowd.

"Marvelous!" She opened a copy of the book and leafed through it. The fragrance of ink on paper, the crisp sound of pages pried apart for the first time sent shivers of excitement through her. The satin texture of the cover beneath her fingertips aroused frissons of delight she'd experienced as a child when she first took a new book, a new treasure, a new adventure in her hands.

"Shall we take a peek at Harrowgate Aerie?"

"Indeed!"

"Yes, please!"

"I hope it is as chilling as Mannerton Court," one woman confided to her friend beside her.

Camille loved it when her readers remembered her previous works. "I hope so too! Ahem. Oh, let me see. Here we are! The aerie."

She cleared her throat.

"'Above the treetops, upon a black jagged cliff, something drew my eye. Tall, pointed, reaching for the swirling thunderous clouds. I sat forward in the coach and trained my eyes on the needle. Oh! No needle, but a spire. And not just one but two...three. As the coachman drew us forward along the serpentine drive, I marveled that anyone found his or her way in or out amid the neglected overgrowth that scraped and poked at the sides of the carriage. Sleet and wind buffeted the coach. I shivered in the chill.

But sat straighter, taller. I would not be cowed!

At one turn, the brush cleared, the house appeared. And oh, it was no mere house, but a mansion of Minoan proportions.

How could I live here with a man I did not know?'"

~

Pierce stepped down from the Hanniford curricle. He hadn't been to the shops in the Lanes in years. The sight of the bustle along the winding passages through shops and hawkers of every kind reminded him of the chaos of the merchants and beggars in the Chinese quarter of Shanghai. Here the sounds were understandable, English. The attire, western. The manners of the women more sedate. The manners of the men, what few there were out shopping, milder still. Folks buying and haggling with each other, others stopping to admire goods in the windows or to handle fruits and vegetables for sale from seated gypsies.

"Do return home, Sam," he told his father's groom. "Fetch me at Lord Victor's office at three."

Before he'd left the house, Pierce had inquired of the man if Miss Bereston had requested a carriage return for her. She had but it was to arrive at the corner of North Street at two. His appointment with Victor was set for one-thirty on the Steine at his office, so Pierce would have to offer to take Camille to luncheon another day.

"Aye, sir. Three it'll be!" The groom nodded and flicked the reins.

Pierce secured his straw hat and took the lane to his right. He passed a knife peddler, a perfumery and a china shop. In the next circle, he came to a stop and questioned his memory of where the book store was.

He spun around when a commotion on the other side of the fountain had everyone pausing to stare. A lady in a violet walking dress glared at the gentleman before her.

"I won't!" she told him.

He reached out to her, but she swayed away from him.

"You cannot set this right unless you end it, I tell you."

Whatever his response was—and Pierce could wager a goodly sum it was a refusal of her demand—she set her teeth and then, slapped him.

He recoiled.

His face, above his trimmed light brown beard, went red. His eyes, dark blue, gleamed with bitterness. Aware of those who witnessed the confrontation, he surveyed the crowd, swallowed hard and turned his back on the lady.

The lady—and Pierce saw now on closer examination— was not quite deserving of ascription to that class. Her gown was fashionable. Fitting her voluptuous form to perfection, but the fabric was faded. Her bodice lower than a woman of style or of social standing would wear to shop at midday. Her hair, as abundant and wild Scottish red as his step-mother Liv's, was piled haphazardly upon her head. And her hat was a pitiful thing that had seen a better year and a fuller feather. She was, quite simply, of the demi-monde. And the gentleman? Better attired, a dandy in his summer tan linen trousers and navy frock coat, he wore his cravat at an angle that bespoke either of lack of a valet or hasty dressing.

All in all, a quarrel between a man and his paramour presented the onlookers with a spectacle that had them shaking their heads, whispering and walking on.

So did he.

But after he came to another fork in the lanes, frustration beset him. He surrendered to go inside the tea salon and ask for directions to Winslow's Book Shop.

Within two short minutes, he was there, opening the spruce green door and setting the bell a-jingle. He removed his hat and threaded his fingers through his hair. The bookshop had long been a favorite haunt of his when he'd lived here in England. The smell of beeswax polish mingled with the fragrances of hundreds of books, paper and ink, soothed him. It was good to be home.

He stopped, absorbing the sound of a voice that filled him with more contentment.

She was easy to find. Always had been. Her husky contralto, a symphony like dark notes of cognac, drew him past one shelf and the next. Talking of an old manor house on a craggy hill on some gloomy, godforsaken shore, she was reading her own words with an ease and certain relish that brought a grin to his lips.

He rounded a corner and the sight of her stopped him cold.

If her voice charmed him, the lovely rest of her arrested him. He had been so blithe yesterday. Complimentary as any man was to a beautiful woman in his family. Jovial in his praise as a man is toward a young lady he's not seen in years. But this, the looks of her, in her element took his breath.

She came to the end of a passage and something induced her to look up and peruse her audience. She spied him, standing as he was, arms crossed, his back to the wall of shelves, chock full of books, floor to ceiling. She fluttered her dark golden lashes in nervous surprise.

He gave her a wink and she flushed, overjoyed.

He lifted his finger and made a little circle in the air for her to proceed. She tipped her head to and fro, her mellow eyes wide to chasten him. Losing, she gave a laugh, then went back to her recitation.

"'I caught my breath and pulled my frayed wool collar up against my throat.

The coach stopped.

The door opened. The groom reached in to offer his hand. I took it. I did, demanding my body to calm.

With quick steps, I took the stoned path to the forbidding black front door.

It swung wide to admit me.

There stood the liveried butler. Tall, pallid and proud, he had the pinched look of one who remains too much indoors. Without a word of welcome, he indicated I should surrender my cloak, my gloves, even my hat.

I did not argue.

"This way, Miss Parton." He was too officious. Too formal.

The chill had followed me inside.

He led me up the curving ivory marble stairs, past pastorals so gay I marveled at how sweetly they belied the grim aura of the rest of the gloomy manse. Down a long corridor we walked until he led me into a library of stunning proportions. Thirty-feet-high, shelves of books and portfolios of every size and shape and age sat upon the rich mahogany. And from the shadows emerged a man of dark, appealing proportions. He stared straight at me.

My bones dissolved at the scorching silver fires of his gaze. I stood, enraptured, speechless. He approached, took my hand and raised it to his warm lips—and kissed my flesh.

He lifted his dark head and drew himself up to his full and impressive height. "Welcome to your new home," he said. "We shall be married tomorrow."

"No, sir," I replied. For I had fresh resolve to leave the ugly place tomorrow morning.'"

Pierce agreed with her.

The hero was rather a dolt. He had decided to marry a young woman but had no intentions of first ingratiating himself with the obvious charms of the chit. The man was an idiot, but what did Pierce know of trends in fiction for ladies or even indeed what some wanted in a man. He himself had indefinite ideas of how a woman could add to the quality of his life.

He stilled at that train of thought. For what he wanted in

a woman had been May Macfarlane. She'd been a surprise, a female full of action and opinion. And she was gone.

She had been out of reach of him from the very start of their relationship. Short as it was, business at the root, friendship in the bud, admiration in the flowering...

And then it died when she had.

He blinked, stood taller and heard the little bell ting-a-ling over the door. He paid no attention to the newcomer's footsteps, until he turned out of curiosity to view the patron who had such a hard footfall.

The fellow who stood there was the one from his altercation in the Lanes with the prostitute. He'd tidied himself up, his cravat properly tied, his navy linen afternoon coat buttoned, his pale wheat-colored hair combed. But he was that particular distasteful man.

And to Pierce's disgust, he grinned at Camille with an exuberance that implied they were much more than friends.

CHAPTER 6

*P*ierce pulled open the door to the bookshop, cursing beneath his breath. Nostrils flaring, he strode east toward the Steine and Victor's office.

The man was a bounder.

"I'm so pleased you came!" Camille had strolled up to the creature who'd argued with the prostitute in the Lanes. "Allow me to introduce you, Pierce. This is Mister Aldridge Connor. My step-brother, Mister Pierce Hanniford."

The man had done the acceptable and nodded obligingly. He gave no indication of shame so evidently, he'd been unaware Pierce witnessed the altercation minutes ago. "Mister Hanniford. Very fine to meet you, indeed. One hears so much about your successes. Newly arrived from Hong Kong."

"Shanghai, actually. I hope all you hear is kind."

"Rippingly so! I understand you're to meet with the British Engineering Society."

"Among others."

A faint twitch of his pale brow told Pierce the man caught

63

a whiff of his disapproval. "I understand you have a holding in the ironworks that fits out the Paris Eiffel Tower."

"I wanted to negotiate that. But it was not possible." No one provided the wrought iron for the tower except Monsieur Eiffel.

"Wish I had heard of it. I would have bought in."

Connor was grandstanding here because no one but Eiffel could have bought in. Eiffel demanded it. "Are you an investor in public projects like the Tower?"

"Occasionally, yes." Connor spun toward Camille. "Forgive me, my dear, I must leave you. I was in the neighborhood and had to come say hello. I will see you next Thursday evening."

"You will. Eight o'clock."

"What," he asked Camille when the man exited their company, "are you doing with that fellow next Thursday?"

"He's coming to dinner," she'd said on a cheery note and turned to meet a few more readers.

She'd left him with his mouth hanging open.

The very idea that that man was one of the two she considered marrying turned him to dust. If she ever uttered the word, Pierce would first strangle ignoble Mister Conner.

He stuffed his fury long enough to pay the shopkeeper for two copies of Camille's novels he did not own. Out in the lane, he strode toward Victor's muttering to himself. "Absurd! The man could not polish her shoes!"

His brother-in-law Lord Victor Cole had his local office in the Steine, which was the main thoroughfare north to south through the city of Brighton. Rounding the park fronted by the Royal Pavilion, he shook his head at that disastrous interpretation of fine Muslim construction which had been built in the early decades of the century by the old Prince Regent, later George the Fourth. Purchased by the town in eighteen-fifty from Queen Victoria who hated it, the building had been preserved as a museum.

As a commemorative to the former king, the palace was a hodge-podge of the west's interpretation of an Indian Muslim ruler's glory. The interior with its striking mustard yellows and sapphire blues, its silk Chinese carpets and Soochow pottery and laughing Buddhas was more a declaration of western colonialism than a true example of fine Eastern sculpture, furnishings or decor. The enormous iron dragon that hung from the dining room ceiling attested to the showiness of old George's appreciations. One day, Pierce would like to erect another palace to show the British what simple aesthetics true Chinese architecture could bring to one's sense of peace and order.

Focus on his interests and the heat of the summer sun seeped into his foul mood. He applauded his decision to walk here. After so many days on the steamer, he'd needed a good walk in open air. His head was clear. So too his purpose. Camille could not marry that man. He would forbid it.

Dodging a hack and an omnibus, he crossed from the park to the opposite side of the street. Homes here were especially grand. Most of them were refurbished mansions from the era of that same Prince Regent. The houses toward the south, the shore and the Marine Parade tended to be offices more than domiciles.

Victor had purchased one five years ago and made it into his local establishment for constituents to visit him. A second son of the seventh Duke of Brentwood, he had begun his professional life in trade. But when he suffered from the scandals created by his first wife, he took his family to Shanghai. The escape proved to be a shelter from the storm, but also a very profitable venture for him. He'd specialized in exporting silk and decorative art to Europeans and Americans. Others more avaricious than he had focused on the illegal opium trade, but he had never ventured to that dark commerce. When Victor married Pierce's younger sister Ada six years ago, he hoped he might remain in Britain and build his business. He and Pierce had come to an agreement whereby Pierce bought rights to Victor's company and he would go to Shanghai to build the enterprise. Victor also received a portion of Hanniford Enterprises. Bound together in such a way, they mutually benefitted from the other's success.

What had been profitable as a trading company focused on those goods Victor had favored. Pierce had added more teas and porcelains. Pierce also supervised the Shanghai construction of a few Hanniford steamers. Steel production had increased the company's profits by forty percent. While that started slowly because of the lack of industrially-minded or scientifically educated Chinese nationals, Pierce sought to remedy that by offering students scholarships to American colleges and stipends to study at American factories. A year abroad for five young Chinese men was beginning to pay dividends in social ways too. The fact that they were from the families of Confucian provincial governors who had an eye to developing commerce in China aided his efforts.

The *Manchu Empress*, the very ship that Pierce had sailed home in, was the second such steamer built and launched from their Shanghai docks. A beauty five decks high, steel clad, sported running water and electric lighting, marble halls and brass fittings. She had four first class suites accommodating four to eight passengers each. The *Empress* had gained the admiration of the passengers, a few port officials in Jaffa, as well as the longshoremen who worked the docks where she put in. In Hong Kong, Aden and Southhampton, the *Empress* had made a great splash.

Pierce had not only expanded his father's shipping business in the Far East but he had also improved Victor's company. Hundreds of thousands of dollars for both. Soon to be double that for the shipping company, as Pierce had recently secured orders from a major Japanese *samurai* house in Tokyo to sell them blueprints so that they could construct their own steamship liners.

He strode up the stone steps of Victor's office and opened the door. Inside, two of his brother-in-law's assistants sat behind their broad desks. Both shot to their feet.

"Sir!" The young woman, dressed in plain white shirtwaist blouse and long black serge skirt, greeted him. "I am happy to greet you. Lord Victor is in. May I say who is calling?"

"Miss Herndon," the bald middle-aged man who occupied the next desk looked apologetic. "This is Mister Pierce Hanniford. Lord Victor's managing partner in Shanghai. Forgive her, sir, Miss Herndon is new with us."

She was nigh unto apoplectic as she took his gloves and hat. "I am sorry, Mister Hanniford."

"No harm done, Miss Herndon. I'm pleased to meet you. How have you been, Mister Banfield? You do look well."

Victor's assistant always added more to his waistline each time Pierce returned. This was no exception. "Thank you, sir. Chipper, I am."

"Your wife, too, I do hope?"

"Indeed, sir."

"Lord Victor wrote me that you are soon to have a new addition to the family."

Banfield's very fair skin blushed bright pink. "Oh, yes, sir. Thank you, sir. We expect our new blessing next month."

"Superb." Pierce thought a moment. "How many is that then? Five?"

"Six, sir."

"Remarkable." If every couple kept on as he saw so many did with a new baby each year, the world would soon be ocean-to-ocean people. If they were all to live well, many would have to build towering apartments and yet leave acres of green spaces to offset the concrete and glass. He himself had long ago known that everyone would need unblemished roads and sturdy sanitation pipes. He'd built them in Shanghai and if he could, he'd build in every city around the world. For that, he'd need trained staff, organization and a great deal of study. It was a different sort of enterprise than what he was used to. The ambition lured him, daunting as it was.

"Come this way, sir." Banfield led him up the wide marble stairs.

Victor removed his rimless spectacles and stood to greet him, his hand out. "Had some sun, did you?"

"I was in the Lanes and thought I'd walk over. I dropped in to hear Camille entertain her minions with a reading from her latest." He hoisted his two books. "I bought more."

"Always a good idea. Please...." He indicated two of four large chairs near the broad bay window overlooking the back walled garden. A cheerful office—the yellow walls lined with shelves and heavy oak cabinets—showed Victor's devotion to order. Even his desk was clean, save for one large appointment book spread across the four-foot-wide expanse. "Camille does enjoy all that autographing business. Smart thing too. It gets her out of her little hideaway. Brandy? Tea?"

"Tea would be welcome, yes." He sank into the chair, irritation with that horrid Connor shadowing the sunshine's restoration of his humor. "Hideaway? What do you mean?"

"She gets an idea and closets herself up for hours at a stretch. Not good for her health although she loves every minute of her seclusion. Now then." Victor faced his assistant. "Mister Banfield, that full tea we debated, we really do need it."

"On my way, sir." The man clapped his hands and spun to it.

"I do not wish to trouble you, Victor."

"None at all. We have a standing order from the tea shop around the corner. And I'm hungry, too."

"Excellent. I wanted to take Camille to luncheon before I came but she was occupied with a friend."

"Lady Brianna Price?"

"The very one." Pierce nodded. An earnest and peppy woman. Victor and Pierce wrote lengthy letters to each other, detailing everything from the intricate business items to the family goings-on as well. Friends were not omitted from the descriptions. Nor were, in Victor's case, details about constituents or public policy debates. "Is she that woman who makes your hair stand on end?"

Victor snorted as he sank into the chair opposite. "In the flesh. I like her, never doubt. But if she could have my seat, she'd do me in with a grin and a bash on the head."

"I've read a bit about her. Wants voting rights for women. Assistance for women in the family way."

"Scholarships to colleges for those women who qualify for admission to medical studies."

"All fine ideas," Pierce noted with a chuckle.

"Say you and I and she and Camille. Plus your father and mother."

Pierce winced. "Makes six of us. And the rest of the family."

Victor sighed. "Not quite enough to pass a bill up to the Lords."

"Exciting concepts though."

"Truly," Victor agreed. "What else can you regale me with?"

"Ah, well! I bring you news. First, as you might expect, just before I left, I signed the deal with the Mitsubishi family in Tokyo for them to buy the blueprints for construction of five passenger steamers."

"Like the *Manchu Empress*?" Victor was grinning.

And Pierce followed. "Replicas. They need do nothing but follow the blueprints. Add more amenities, if they wish. With this and their government contracts for the mail service, they become the leading steamship company in Japan."

"Killian knows?"

"I told him yesterday. He's thrilled."

"You and I should be celebrating. I'll get that brandy." Victor got up. "And the other news we should celebrate?"

"Increased sales of silks to Germany and the United States. Porcelains too." Pierce liked giving Victor news of increasing profits in the silk and porcelain trade. That had formed core of Victor's business and was what Pierce managed for him. Victor's profits in Pierce's businesses were fewer because his investments were smaller. "But the other news is that on the voyage, Lee Macfarlane and I devised a plan to encourage Li Hung-chang to buy more steel from us to complete the Shanghai railway north to Peking and south to Wuhan."

Victor paused, his frown showing his surprise and worry. "The Chinese have started and stopped efforts like this so often. You will pardon me if I don't get excited over this until you tell me the details."

"I understand. Macfarlane and we split the investment, work and proceeds. We use only Shanghai laborers speaking the local dialect. We use our own Chinese engineers who have been American-trained. Lee will conduct all the meetings. Only he and his staff, only men who are true Ningpo natives."

"That will make the viceroy happy."

The imperial viceroy in charge of the province near Shanghai was Li Hung-chang, an aged Confucian bureaucrat who'd been appointed by the emperor to solve many problems. While Li was at heart a staunch conservative Confucian, he also saw the value of improving his country's railroads and infrastructure. But he faced enormous opposition from most of his colleagues who thought of foreigners as arrogant purveyors of tools that would destroy the peace of the empire.

They were right, of course. The Opium Wars of the forties and fifties had disturbed it. That narcotic trade, still illegally conducted and mostly by Americans merchants, destroyed the health of millions of Chinese, as well as the internal economy of the empire. The Tai-Ping Rebellion, initially a peasants' revolt led by a man who declared himself as the brother of Jesus Christ, had swept the countryside, killing more than thirty million. Now those who prospered in China were the thousands of British, American, French and Germans who lived along the coast. Those who had arrived later—the Russians and the newly revitalized Japanese—added to the contrast which the impoverished Chinese peasants witnessed.

"The viceroy will remain happy too, because," Pierce said, "Lee Macfarlane will ensure that all on the project speak only the Ningpo dialect."

"Ah. And the Court won't have any criticisms that we do not permit Mandarin into the mix?"

"A delicate balance. Lee says he'll hire two men from Peking who speak both dialects. Their job will be to negotiate any conflicts."

"No rebellions this time. No riots." Victor frowned.

"That's what killed Jardine and Matheson's attempt to construct the Shanghai railway ten years ago. But after a man died on the tracks during construction, the emperor demanded it be stopped. We cannot afford to have that happen here."

"I know. We are not as well-funded as Jardine. Another reason why working with Lee Macfarlane is an excellent proposition is because he has capital to match our own."

Victor shifted in his chair. "You trust him?"

"I do." Pierce cocked his head. "Don't you?"

Victor smacked his lips. "I never had many dealings with Lee. I liked him personally. But I will say that his father was a wily bugger."

"Lee is not his father."

"You're certain?"

"I grew to know him well these past few years. He was helpful to me five years ago when I first arrived and wanted to start the gas works in the Settlement. And he is very forthright with me about his predictions of rebellions against the emperor."

Victor flinched. "I fear it too. Not just against the emperor. We could see more rebellions like the Tai-ping and they could be focused on getting rid of us."

"All the more reason to help them modernize as quickly as they can. I'm excited about the prospect of a railroad. I plan to work on a good price for it and cable Li Hung-chang soon. I want to make it very attractive."

"Do it." Victor nodded.

Pierce inhaled, pleased that Victor liked his idea. "You and I have done well. Macfarlane too. But the French and Germans resent that the British and Americans have prospered more. Did you know that the Germans persuaded the governor of Chi-li province to hire German officers of the High Command to teach in his new military academy?"

Victor frowned. "Not good. The French must have something to say against that, too."

"They're very unhappy. They go at the Germans often in City Council meetings," Pierce said with disdain.

"Here too, they argue over anything." Victor ran his hands through his curly auburn hair. "The Germans have the haughty attitude of victors and the French carry a resentment of the Germans."

"War, again, do you think?"

"They both build for it. And one aspect I want you to be careful of when you go to Paris is to trim our involvement with French weapons manufacturers. I won't sell anyone steel and contribute to a war."

"I agree." Pierce was adamant. "Just as we don't deal in opium, we won't deal in rifles or cannon."

Victor examined him for a long minute. "What is your assessment of our new comprador?"

"Wang Su-yi?" Pierce had appointed the company's new Chinese manager last winter. He was thirty-four and had worked as assistant to their former go-between for more than four years. "He is very competent. Forthright."

"And honest?"

A perennial problem with Chinese representatives of western countries in the treaty ports was the tendency of the comprador to take 'squeeze' from his own countrymen for goods traded or favors rendered. "I've seen no evidence he is receiving fees. I told him when I appointed him, I would not stand for it. He knew we did not approve of it and knew his predecessors had not done it. In any case, Jonathan Stewart is vigilant."

Victor had not known the American Stewart when he worked in Shanghai. "But he's been your assistant only a few months."

"I trust him, Victor."

"He began work with Lee Macfarlane's father," Victor sat back. "So we know he must be well trained."

"Indeed. And shrewd." Pierce laughed. "Really, Stewart is excellent. He comes with very good recommendations."

"From Lee and from his sister." Victor nodded.

"Yes. From both. I trust Lee and I'd like you to visit with him and become reacquainted. Unfortunately, though he's in London now, he's soon off to Paris and Berlin. I think he returns here before he sails off to New York. So if you think you might come to London soon, I can arrange a luncheon. If that is not possible, I could arrange for you both to meet here before he goes on to catch his boat in Southampton."

"That is a possibility because I doubt I'll go to London. Ada is so very pregnant and due soon. I will leave the particulars of working with Macfarlane to you. I trust your judgment, Pierce. Always have. You do set my mind at ease."

"Thank you." Pierce sat forward, his elbows on his knees. "Will you set mine at ease, please?"

"Of course. About what?"

"Do you know Mister Aldridge Connor?"

Victor barked in laughter. "I may take a long while to ease your thoughts about that fellow."

Pierce met Victor's gaze with sad trepidation. "So it's worse than I thought."

"What do you know?"

Pierce recounted the scene he'd witnessed in the Lanes.

Victor brushed a hand down his trousers. "Why am I not surprised?"

Pierce recoiled at that answer. "He does this often?"

Victor brightened. "Fight in the Lanes? Or get slapped by a lady of the night?"

"Both."

"He has been known to have liaisons with women who are not of his sterling class."

"As I feared. Is that his only fault?"

"Wishing for more, are you?" Victor knit his brows in feigned horror.

"Is there more?"

Victor inhaled. "Word has it that his father's estate is nearing bankruptcy. The good baron has had a few mistresses who have cost him dearly."

"Well, hell. Courting ladies of the night is an inherited trait." Pierce had a fierce disdain for a man who could not control his body or his finances. "So his father has a title. And land."

"The title is old. Twelfth century, I do believe. The land is a major tract in Kent. But Baron Beckford has not attended to its upkeep. He has some property that abuts Julian's and they've had words about repairing bridges and roads. Our brother-in-law, as you well know, is very attentive to his tenants and his land. Anyone who fails to do their part anywhere near his own holdings, gets a piece of Julian's mind."

Pierce winced. "I'd not live long."

A knock came at the far door.

"Come!" Victor bid and his assistants trotted in, each carrying trays piled high with sandwiches and cakes, tarts of strawberry and creme, and a tea service, cups and saucers clattering.

Both men waited until the side board had been laid, then they rose to avail themselves of the offerings. They sat to partake of the fare before Pierce went on.

"Camille says she wants to marry."

"She has been saying that since she was sixteen."

"What?" He laughed but Victor did not. "How do you know that?"

"Liv often repeats it whenever Camille has a bout of the 'Lonelies.'"

Pierce made a face. "Which are what?"

"She says she is the only one who is not matched and she'll marry before the year is out."

"I see. Why?"

"Because we are all married. Paired off. She feels…out of place."

"I'm not married."

"But you, old man, are often not here."

"Right. Well, in her 'Lonelies' she cannot think of marrying this man!"

"Agreed!"

"But he comes to dinner next Thursday."

"Oh, god." Victor laughed in resigned horror.

"You'll be there? You'd better. He can be cowed. I've seen him. He knows he's not good enough for her."

"I do believe we are invited, yes. And yes, he can be *informed*—shall we say—that he'd not fit."

"Superb. If he dares to ask for her hand, I don't want to be the only one shooting him where he stands."

CHAPTER 7

*D*inner that evening was the four of them. He was grateful, knowing it would be just his father and Liv, Camille and him in private conversation. He'd planned all afternoon to have a word with her. When she had not appeared until after five, he decided he'd catch her after dinner.

But right after dessert, Camille had announced her decision to retire. "I must go up."

Neither his father nor Liv made any objections. So how could he, eh? But he was too concerned to let her go without making plain to her his opinion of the man she thought of fondly.

He wandered onto the patio facing the sea, seeking a calmness he required if he were to make a successful point.

And so, after a few minutes in which he pined for a meditative moment, he resigned himself to what peace he'd garnered and took the stairs. Instead of going left to his own suite, he went right to knock on the door to hers.

"Yes?" She flung open the door and blinked at the sight of him. "Oh! I thought you were Ivy. Is...something wrong?"

"No. Yes, actually." He noted her confusion and the fact that her hair flowed over her shoulders in a cape of gold. And she was dressed—or rather not, in a pale pink charmeuse silk robe that clung to her plush figure like a second skin. She'd even removed her corset because he detected the large round outline of her nipples beneath the supple caress of the silk. He swallowed back his unbrotherly observations. "May I come in?"

Unusual as it was for a man who was not a woman's husband to ask for admission to her boudoir, he and she had always had a casual approach to their status as step-siblings. Since their very introduction, they'd been freer with each other and free of many dictums proscribed for interactions of single men with unmarried women. She'd come to his rooms to talk about novels or the theatre and he'd often gone to talk in her sitting room about sights and experiences abroad. She was, he had to say, the most gracious listener, rapt in her attentions to his descriptions of the impressions of sights and sounds of any place in the world. She had no preferences but wanted his impressions of anywhere he'd been. Lisbon, Aden or Yokohama, she cared to learn about them all. She was also curious, eloquent in her questions, insightful in her comments.

"I want to go," she'd often told him in that rapturous whisper of one who makes promises to oneself. The Ming dragons of Peking. The church in Jerusalem where Christ's tomb lay. The Doge's Palace in Venice. "I must see all the wonders of the world."

He'd long since given up telling her she must wait and take care. "So much of the world is unsafe."

"You go!" she'd object. "I must too."

Now for him to warn her off this man seemed a similar attempt, doomed to fail. She was headstrong. Once decided, difficult to dissuade.

Tonight might be the same. He had to try.

"Come in." She pulled wide the door and stepped aside. She tipped her head, curious, as he paused. Her gaze went down his black dinner attire. "Well? Do you sit? Or are you just here for a moment?"

"A few minutes," he said, her easy acceptance unsettling and putting him adrift in his own intentions.

"Well, then. I will sit." She did, taking the huge pink and yellow flowered chintz beside the darkened fireplace. She had turned the gas lamps in the room low and the pink aura from the sconces fell over her in shades of summer sun. And in the clinging silk with her long waves of dark red-gold curls about her shoulders and curving around her pointed breasts, she seemed to glow like a Renaissance painting of Venus on the half shell.

He cleared his throat.

"Pierce?"

He could not continue to look at her...and allow her to see how inappropriately he appreciated her figure. Flustered like a boy, he strode to the fireplace and braced himself, two hands to the mantel.

"What is it?"

"I enjoyed your reading today."

She gave a laugh. "Oh, do not patronize me, dear sir."

He spun. He'd train his eyes on her face. He would. He had a devil of a time of it, though. "I don't. You're very good."

"Thank you." But she gave him a challenging arch of her brows. "But I write for my readers. Not for Dickens's or Thackery's or Hugo's. Just mine. I don't wish to be other. So if you are humoring me with your faint praise..."

He stood taller. "But I'm not. You write dramatic prose, good prose, substantial characters."

She narrowed her eyes. "I take the compliment. Many

men look down upon what I write. For women. About women."

"Who dares to criticize you?" If he asked the question to lead her toward an answer he hoped he'd get, he had to acknowledge that such was no less than what he often did with business associates. But she was not that, at all.

Not...at all.

She was...always would be...his talented...young...step-sister.

She bristled. "Many men proclaim their superior abilities to review literature."

"Ah. Yes, I understand." What else did he understand? That she had been his to protect and on occasion when she was younger, his to escort informally at family functions. His to accompany and converse with. Yes. His to laugh with. Always.

"I don't care what they think." She crossed her arms.

And in the doing, she pushed up the contours of her breasts in such a manner that out of respect, he sought to cover his mighty response by seeking the opposite chair.

Now she tipped her head the other way. "Pierce? What bothers you?"

If you knew, you'd shove me out the door. "I wonder how long you've known Aldridge Connor."

She shrugged. "Two years. Three. Why?"

"Is he one you consider for the honor of becoming your husband?"

She sputtered in laughter. "My, my! Do you need all those words to ask me if I love him?"

"I do."

That took her aback.

"Do you?" He had to know.

"Love him?"

He nodded.

She knit her brows. "I haven't decided."

"Ha!" he crowed and slapped a hand on one knee, whether in delight or disbelief, he couldn't say. "You don't know?"

"If I love him?"

"Yes!"

She glanced about the room. Then came back to focus on him. "No."

"But you should!"

"That's what I'm discovering!" She smiled but when he didn't respond, the corner of her mouth turned down.

Was she angry or confused? He couldn't tell. Damn! He had to continue with this! "Don't you see?"

"What?" She looked truly perplexed.

"If you have to *decide* or *discover*, then it isn't love."

"How do you know?"

"Because..."

She waved him off. "Because you've been in love. Well, good. Wonderful. How did it happen for you?"

"What?"

"Over time? One night at dinner? A walk in the park?" She leaned forward and her breasts swayed toward him, the nipples hard and peaked and his trousers absurdly tight.

He crossed one leg over the other, hoping he effected a bit of camouflage. "Over time. Months."

"Well, there you have it! Your own proof."

"But you say you've known him for years!"

She curled a shoulder. "Here. There. A waltz. A ride in Hyde Park. Not so well really."

"Exactly!" Triumphant, he felt his anger flare. "Does he like your novels?"

"I haven't asked."

He snorted. "Don't you think you should?"

"I don't care if he likes them or not."

"Don't you think he should approve?"

"He should. Every man should. Again, whether he approves or not will not mean hide nor hair to me."

"Ba! Really? Then why are you worried you won't have control over your income after marriage?"

"Is one the same as the other?"

"Related! It's about respect! And you know it!" He was angry. But loving the repartee and that he had control of the conflict. He'd keep it. "Has he sent you flowers?"

She drew back in her chair. "Last week."

"Have you met his family?"

"Yes. Years ago."

Dear God. "Has he kissed you?"

"Yes."

Arrogant man! "Did you like it?"

"Why?" She glared at him.

Wonderful. He'd made her angry. She'd answer him now.

But she clasped her hands together and regarded him much as his first tutor of Mandarin had. With tolerance. "What are you getting at, Pierce?"

"What did you feel when he kissed you?"

The corners of her mouth turned down and she seemed to melt into the chair. "Why?" she asked on a breath.

He read her lips more than heard the sound.

"Why?" She asked once more when he seemed transfixed.

But he stirred and frowned at her. "Because you would know...feel so many things if you love him."

"Would I?" *If I kissed you, what would I know?*

"Of course you would. What sort of kiss was it?"

She should laugh. But she had cotton in her mouth. "What sort of kisses are there?"

"Oh, come now, Camille. You know."

She did give him her skepticism then. "Do I? Tell me."

"Did he peck you on the cheek?"

Yes.

"Or draw you against him?"

That too.

"Did he take his time or rush you into it?"

Wouldn't I want both? One upon the other?

She shot to her feet, unable to sit, her blood hot, a squirming liquid flame deep in her belly.

He stared at her. "Is that what he does to you? Makes you need to move?"

No! You do!

She swung toward the mantel. It was her turn now to face away from him. Why had he before? Because he wished to conceal his anger and his power. Be the protective brother. The one who would ward her off a man whom he…

Oh, she saw now. "You didn't like him, did you?"

"No, by God, I did not."

"Why?" She whirled around to see him standing directly behind her. This close, his cologne was a lure of sandalwood and some eastern fragrance she'd noted on him before but could not name. More devastating to her independence was his bright gaze that flowed into hers like molten quicksilver. "Why?" she repeated in a whisper.

One hand of his came up. And in the next moment, he brushed a fingertip across her bottom lip. His move was a brand.

Her hope was a flame.

"How would you kiss a woman you loved?" *Oh, yes.* She was a fool to ask.

But in her curiosity, she knew power. Because he blinked and yet he did not pull away, she had the control. Instead, he stood immobile as she stepped against him. She lifted on her toes, for he was so tall. And she slanted her head to one side, her gaze fastened on his, her mouth a heartbeat away from his. "How would you?"

"Camille." Her name was not a sound.

She heard it as a warning, but took it as an appeal. One she'd waited for nearly half her life. One she would take advantage of now. For if anything, she was a woman of action. And in regard to him, she'd always been a woman of desire.

She sought purchase with her fingers going round his upper arms. "Shall I kiss you on the cheek?"

He gave a small shake of his head.

Accepting his feeble answer, she put her lips to his nose. A peck. An acknowledgment of affection. "Like one gives a child." *Or a brother.*

He seemed to vibrate beneath her hands.

Beneath her fingertips, he went still as death. Her time grew short and so she pulled away ever so slightly and said, "But I would want more from a man I cared for. Much more."

Her education in the art of kissing was poor. She'd had weak precedents. A wet thing from a twelve-yer-old boy who'd come to visit with his parents. A grasping thing from an Eton lad who petted her with clammy hands before he tried to stick his tongue down her throat. A ravenous thing from a sullen lord who should have known better than to seize her as if he were a pirate and she his booty. Only once had she been swept away by the artfulness of a man who knew his way around a bedroom and a woman. She'd enjoyed the kiss…or rather kisses, but later, refused the man his suit.

So it was her imagination and her eternal curiosity about Pierce as a lover that led her on. A frantic seizure of the minute, the night, the topic, led her to brush her lips on his and stifle the moan that rose in her throat.

She took his broad firm mouth with her own in a grand claim that had him drawing her near and allowing her the range of his lips. He was hers, faintly groaning in objection or passion, she did not know. But he pulled her flush to his torso and she surged with triumph at the rigid expression of his lack of control.

Surrendering to what she wanted, she slid her hands up his shoulders and cupped his nape. Her fingers wound through his satin hair. He hauled her closer, his cock harder, slipping against the hollow between her thighs as he kissed her.

His lips were warm, reverent. At once, he pulled back and stared at her, shock his first emotion. But need was his next as he cupped her cheek, sighed her name and took her mouth once more. This time, he savored her mouth in lazy caresses. She clutched him closer and he darted the tip of his tongue between her lips. But with one touch, he gasped and was gone.

She hung in his arms, triumph rushing through her veins.

He stared down into her eyes.

She swallowed.

He searched her expression. Of course, he did.

He searched for himself. For his motivation. For definition of his own desire.

She let him do as he wished, but regarded him with languor, for she had no such query.

She knew what she wanted.

Him. Always him. Ever him.

And she had him in this moment. As she had always wanted the fullness of his passion. The madness of his attentions.

"Forgive me." He stepped back even as he braced her arms to ensure she stood upright.

Well. Just barely. But gentleman that he was, and lady that

she had been born to be, she would stand and she would forgive.

He cleared his throat. "That was…"

Exquisite.

"I apologize, Camille. That should not have happened."

I wanted it to. "I'm the one who started it." *And I won't apologize.*

He gave her a watery smile. "We will forget this."

Not if I can make you remember.

"Good night."

With a few quick steps, he strode away.

For long afterward, she walked the floor of her bedroom and relived every word, every move, every ecstasy. Her body hummed with the tenor of his words. Pulsed with the imprint of his lips. Glowed with the impression that he wished to protect her from a man he did not like.

Good.

She paused to study her reflection in her cheval glass. Her hair mussed. Her dark eyes vivid. Her nipples, rigid. Her body, swollen in liquid yearning.

Protection was not precisely what she would have prescribed.

But on that she might build.

She had plotted fiction wherein the couples learned to care for each other. She knew each one's past, their motives, their aspirations, their faults. Here she knew well her own.

But Pierce's?

His life was not a mystery. Nor his character. But aside from his desire to remain her friend, she could not fathom what he thought of her.

Or if he might change his mind.

CHAPTER 8

*H*e stayed well away from her the next few days. It was rather easy. She chose to write in her rooms, coming down to dine or walk along the beach, then return to her work.

They did not speak or even give the other any indication that they remembered the kiss in her bedroom. He thought he did well at that. She seemed superb at it, so they marched onward. But the truth was that only a few times in his life Pierce Hanniford had been ashamed of himself. This was the worst. What had he been thinking to permit himself to do such a thing as kiss her?

He damned well had no idea.

Two evenings later, Connor came to dinner. Polite, socially adroit, he seemed presentable. But his veneer was thin. Pierce saw beneath to the shrewdness of the man.

Connor was nothing but suave, natty and on his game. His quarry, of course, was Camille, who knew her worth and did her duty to act as his hostess, his introduction to her wider family. Her mother, Liv, greeted him as if she had no qualms about his character. His father—the man who'd met thousands and conquered others for millions—took Connor's measure and left him to others to pick apart. Ada and her husband Victor had showed no hint of disapproving of him. Pierce noted his father's affable manner toward the man, ever an indication that Killian was waiting to be impressed. Liv was her usual self, a magnificent and accommodating hostess. Camille appeared sprightly, irritatingly friendly toward the man.

Connor, it appeared, had not won much favor.

To Pierce, the man simply was not suitable.

He hated the fellow.

"Good morning!" His step-mother Liv greeted him the next morning. It was unusual for the lady of the house in England to come down for her breakfast. But Liv, formerly Lady Savage the widow of a minor English nobleman, now his father's wife, had eaten her breakfast from a tray in her room only twice. Both times had been after she'd given birth to Liam and Dylan. And then, each time, for fewer than seven days.

An interior designer and decorator of mansions and townhomes all over Britain, she was a successful business woman who claimed she had little time to fritter away. Like his father, she was devoted to her work and loved each moment. This morning, though it was fifteen past seven, she took her place at the table and spread her napkin. "You're up early."

"I have new monthly reports I need to review so I thought I'd get started." He finished the last of his coffee. "In fact, I am off to Victor's office."

"Your father was up at dawn. No good company there, I must say. But are you running off, too, now just as I get here?" She appealed to him with a false look of dismay. "I wanted to talk to you and I haven't had any time alone with you."

"Oh?" He couldn't help fearing the topic. He doubted Camille would share with anyone what had happened between them a few nights ago. He certainly had not, nor would he ever. But he took it as a measure of his remorse that he went lifeless at the possibility. Instead, he forced himself to sit back. "What's on your mind?"

"You."

He took a breath. "Why?"

"You've not been yourself since you arrived. I thought perhaps there might be something I've failed to provide or that you feel..." She lifted her shoulders. "Homesick?"

He barked in laughter. "You've gone out of your way, Liv. The footman, James, is an excellent valet. My shoes are buffed so high, I can shave in the reflection. The cuisine is superb. I think you have ordered up balmy weather. So not a thing is missing. You've made me very comfortable. And no, I am not homesick, Liv. I am home."

She met his gaze with a long examination for truth. "Good. I wanted to affirm that before I went on and made a fool of myself."

"You'll never do that." He acknowledged the footman's silent offer to refill his coffee cup. "Talk to me."

"I have a favor to ask."

"Anything."

"I open a show in London a week Wednesday. New fabrics and cabinetmakers, architects I'm working with. Two days later we are all slated to go to Paris for Remy's new joint exhibition with Claude Monet. I have yours and Victor's silks, thank you very much. But I'm having a few problems with shipments of the silks from Lyon. Camille has always helped me with such problems in the past. She says she'd gladly help me now that I'm rather in a crunch."

"What can I do to help?"

"Camille had planned to go up to London with me in three days. She must meet with her publisher there, and so she said she'd happily help me with my suppliers. But now I'd like her to go early for me because I am having problems receiving my supplies."

"And what precisely do you need me to do?"

"I cannot go up to London earlier because all my correspondence for the shipments come here. It won't do for me to use cables. One doesn't cable pages of orders. I'm hoping that you'd go up to London with her."

"To give her a hand with the suppliers?"

"Oh, no, she'd hate that. The implication would be that she couldn't do the transactions properly. And she can."

"And?" He gave her a crooked smile.

"You do plan to go to London yourself."

"I do. I have a few urgent matters to take care of. I'm to meet with Victor's and my man in the City and then my own manager, too." His correspondence with his father's men in Liverpool about laborers' wages was ongoing. That meeting in mid-September did not affect his trip to London or Paris.

She tipped her head and smiled. "So then, it sounds convenient. I hoped I might ask you to go with Camille as a chaperone of sorts, but also as an escort."

He struggled with that. But how could he refuse her? "Oh, well, Liv…"

She licked her lips. "You see, it's more than that. I know you and she have a special relationship."

Special? I'm not certain I know what to term it.

"You're her friend. And she looks up to you."

As a friend? An advisor? How could that prick both his pride and his conscience?

"And I hoped you might take her dancing…"

"Dancing?"

"She loves to dance. And she hates to rattle around in that big house alone."

Alone. With Camille. He liked that idea. So did his body.

She inhaled. "Oh, hell. She needs diversion. She's got it in her head that she's interested in marrying."

"Not Aldridge Connor?"

"Yes. Maybe. I'm not sure. He's certainly interested in her!"

Pierce snorted. "He's not suitable material for any woman."

"You didn't like him?"

"Not last night nor when I first met him last week at her autographing party."

"Rascal." She huffed. Took a sip of her coffee and glared out the window over his shoulder. "He's relentless."

"Is he?"

"Very much so," she said. "Victor knows him better than any of us and he thinks Connor wants our connections and her money."

"Her dowry." His father had put fifteen thousand dollars a year in each Hanniford girl's bank account from the day they were ten years old. His father had not known Camille at age ten, but he had opened an account for her after his and Liv's marriage. What her savings might total now with interest could be five, ten, or fifteen times that. Not as much as a Vanderbilt heiress, but still useful to any husband who sought to use his wife's wealth to pay debt.

"Exactly." Liv winced. "She's not scatterbrained. Not foolish. And I doubt she'd accept him. I know she wants a loving relationship."

"She won't get it with him."

"I agree. But I worry. In the last few months, she's seemed more determined to find someone. And soon."

Pierce grabbed hold of his self-control. If he went with Camille to London, he'd go as her chaperone. An older man with his beautiful young charge. A mature man—hell, a roué —who could not control the surge of excitement that stiffened his cock and his desire to...

To what? Save her from another man? A n'er-do-well who wanted her as an ornament on his arm. Or as a nubile wife with a dowry that could prop up his estate.

Pierce shifted in his chair, arguing with his rebelliously aroused body. He leaned forward and toyed with his coffee dup. "And you want me to show her a good time...and offer a foil to old Aldridge?"

"That's the crux of it, yes. Would you?"

What could he say? 'No?' Never! Or 'Yes.' *I'll show her such a good time that she'll forget the cad. And then what?*

He'd spend his days keeping his distance and showing her what a good time her step-brother could offer.

Bugger it all. *How helpful was that?* A guest at a banquet where he could not dine!

"What do you say, Pierce? Will you? I'd owe you my gratitude."

To get rid of Connor, he'd do anything. "Of course, Liv. I'd be delighted to go."

Pierce had cultivated the habit when at the Brighton house to stroll the beach. Morning was his best hour to clear his mind. Soon after he'd arrived in Shanghai six years ago, he'd taken the advice of his Number One houseboy to learn Buddhist meditation. He'd studied with a withered old monk at the nearby Amida temple how to sit and let the world leave him.

He preferred to seek the serenity near the water on his veranda facing the East China Sea. When in Brighton, he sat crosslegged on the terrace. Afterward he'd go down to the shore to enjoy the air and sea. When the weather was fine, he'd go down at night too. Late.

He'd take the cliff walk down from the veranda at the leeward side of the house facing the sea, remove his shoes and socks and leave them on the rocks. The rough sand and smooth rocks of the Brighton beach had never bothered his sensibilities. He'd gone on in any case. His solitude and desire for the peace of salt and sand and sea more compelling than any hardship he'd encounter walking the rugged surface.

Camille knew this. She'd noted how he'd taken up this habit once more now that he was home.

So it was easy to find him.

Easy to surprise him.

She walked toward him, her hair loose and flying away in the cool wind from the water, her own shoes and stockings stacked on the same rocks as his. She wore no corset, no chemise. Purposely, of course. What she'd felt nights ago, her body fluid and giving in his arms, is what she'd hoped to have again. She had wrapped a cherry cashmere shawl over her shoulders and shivered at the soft ripple of French silk that slipped over her skin as she walked toward him in her green and purple ottoman print pyjamas. Since their kiss days ago, she and he had not talked privately. She'd not sought him out. Nor he, her. She hadn't expected it. Hadn't wanted it.

Instead, she'd wanted this. Her approach to him. Days afterward. With time for both of them to think. She had no idea what his perspective was on their intimacy. Fearing what he might think, she didn't want to learn his conclusions. She'd rather—as Americans said—let sleeping dogs lie.

But there came a time to rise and deal. Since her mother had told her this afternoon that she'd asked Pierce to go with her to London day after tomorrow, that time was now. Tonight. And she chose it to be here on the beach.

"What are you doing here?" He faced her, yards away, his bold lean frame a silhouette in the shadows of the bright round yellow moon. He wore dark trousers, a white shirt open at the throat, a heavy half-cut dressing gown, whose collar he'd turned up along his throat. His thick dark hair blew wild in the wind. And if he was surprised or dismayed by her joining him, he seemed in his tone only curious.

"I hoped to catch you." She liked that phrase.

He opened his arms wide and flapped them to his side. "You've found me. But what you'll catch is your death, you know?"

She shook her head and smiled. *Keep this friendly.* "I won't get ill. I've got too much to do."

He turned aside, a hand out to invite her to go with him. "Want to walk or did you have a bone to pick with me?"

She grinned at that. "I'd like to walk, yes. And no arguments from me."

"No?" He paused to check her expression. What he saw there reassured him because he gave a huff of laughter and walked on. "I expected you to object."

He thought they spoke of him going away with her. But she'd address the bigger issue. "I've always had fun with you. Why would I object?"

He stopped again. This time the moonlight was upon his face and she saw the magnificent lines of his handsome bone structure and deep inside her, every bit of her stirred. She swayed, her thighs crushed together to deny the hot gush of need that darted through her. She wanted him again as she'd felt him nights ago, flush against her, his body rigid, his penis full and urgent, wanting her despite himself. He did not move to take her in his arms, though his nostrils flared and his eyes burned silver fire. He stared at her as if she were a woman he had to have. A woman who was a stranger. "You don't mind that I'm to be your keeper?"

That he termed it that way made her very happy, though of course, no man would ever really be such for her. "Is that what you'll be? Ho-ho! Try that and you'll be sorry."

He caught her wrist and pulled her to a stop. "I want to show you a good time."

Ah. She approved of that idea, too. "I'd like nothing better."

Anger flashed across his sharp features. A muscle in his jaw ticked. "Your mother doesn't care for Connor."

"I know. Papa doesn't find him charming either."

"And you? You never really told me the other night."

Yes. Let's talk about the other night. "I'm…discovering."

Pierce widened his eyes. "It would be best if you discovered him gone."

She chuckled. "I know you must have reasons. Aside from his father's profligacy, I do mean. But please allow me to discover what the reasons are all by myself."

"Camille." He shook his head. "There are so many good men, darling."

Darling. She licked her lips, in love with the sound of that on his tongue.

He caught a sharp breath, dropped her wrist and took up his stroll again, hands jammed in his dressing gown pockets. "I thought we'd go to the theatre."

"Yes. Let's call on your Mister Macfarlane at the Langham and take him to the theater and dinner. Sarah Bernhardt is playing. I forget where. No matter. I could arrange a dinner party at the house, too. My publisher, his wife. You'll like them. Mama's man of business for the City exhibition. His wife. Do you think your Mister Macfarlane would like to be paired with Lady Brianna? Just for dinner, of course. I'll see if she goes to London soon."

He stopped, the look on his face a cross between hilarity and pride. "You've got us all planned out."

Paired off, too. As if we were a couple. "I do. Do you mind?" She tried to look puzzled, but she knew he adored people who thought ahead, planned completely. That's who she was. Always had been.

"No!" He shook his head and scanned the heavens with a grin on his face.

Ah, so, he had worried, had he? "Good."

"We'll have a wonderful time," he said, then scowled. "Connor is not expected to be in London, is he?"

"No."

"You do realize that if he appears I will have to shoot him."

She tisked. "Just a nick, please."

"To see if he bleeds?" He scolded her with wicked narrowed eyes.

She laughed and cuffed him. But in the move, she put a foot wrong on a stone and slipped.

He caught her. And up against his warm hard chest, her breasts flowered and her nipples heated. Her lips parted. She sought his gaze.

There again was his desire for her flat against her thigh. She clamped her legs together.

He plunged his fingers so deeply into her hair, she could feel his nails against her scalp. And when she thought he would have kissed her, she put the flat of her hand to his heart.

Then she forced herself to smile, a tremulous offering of uncertainty, and she stepped back.

"Let's go home," he said in a voice she'd never heard. He

wound one arm of hers through his and patted her hand. *Like a brother. Again.* "It's late."

But what she knew in the marrow of her bones was that it was too late. Too late to ignore what she felt for him. Now. As a man. Too late to pretend what she felt did not exist. Or that it was affection for a sibling who was not even one. But a man who'd been her friend. Still was.

And now was so much more.

CHAPTER 9

Two days later, Pierce took Camille's hand to help her up the step into the train car. He'd purchased first class for four. James, his newly appointed valet, and Ivy, Camille's maid, had been thrilled with the news not only that they were to go to London, but also that they were to attend them in the first class cabins.

"Thank you." Camille had praised him for it when he'd told her about the tickets before dinner last night. An egalitarian if there ever was one, she approved of his largesse. "I usually sit with her in the second class cars."

"A young woman should not have to be concerned for her safety when traveling. Or at any time." His purchase of the servants' tickets had been out of concern for their welfare. Just as he had protected his sisters when they were little girls, he would protect any woman in any circumstances. Camille, as well.

But he had to be honest with himself about the purchase of the tickets. He had other reasons for wanting the two servants' presence. Their company meant he would be focused on Camille as his friend. Only his friend. In train compartments. In the Hanniford house in Piccadilly. In any room where she walked and drew his eyes and his anxiety.

She took the upholstered banquette facing forward, Ivy beside her. He faced her, James next to him.

She had donned a deep rose summer walking suit of cotton with fine hand embroidery of wild field lilies in the bodice. She'd always turned herself out in appropriate finery and this morning, she once more had him smiling at her elegance. Even her trim little lavender chip hat topped in more tiny lilies seemed gay. She made him the envy of a few men who passed them by. No wonder. The color illuminated the glow of her complexion. The fit illustrated the curve of her figure which no corset need elaborate.

He tore his gaze to the window and those passengers in the Brighton station who ran along the quay to catch their places in the second and third class coaches behind. He grew desperate to be on the road, away from the crush of their family. He had told himself he needed to see Camille alone without them. In her own environment. With her publisher and friends. With her mother's manager and business associates. That would soothe his ruffled feathers, his troubled mind. Help him see her as a person who was a business woman herself, organized, talented and artless.

Artless. An intriguing word that had come to him two nights ago during dinner when he had the occasion to watch her with her guest, the artful Mister Aldridge Connor.

"I had a note from Mister Connor this morning. Flowers too." She folded her hands and stared at him, one long golden brow arching.

He huffed. What a woman. Even with Ivy and James present, she would ask. "That's bad news."

"Why?" She waited and he held his tongue. "Come now. Ivy and James have seen him. Ivy, twice before. Be frank, Pierce."

Well now that was a challenge, wasn't it? *Do be frank, old man.* "Connor. Connor. Ah, yes. Connor. He speaks well. He dresses well. He does not smoke. He drinks, it seems, moderately." *He is determined to make you his wife.* "He is arrogant."

She crossed her arms and in that delicious rose attire, her breasts pushed up to ample heights, making him tingle.

Christ. He looked away.

"So you don't—?"

"Like him? You tell me! Why would I? Would he make you a faithful, caring spouse? Would he be good for you? Nurture you? Encourage your writing and your desire for political career? You must ask yourself that, not me, Camille."

Never me.

He'd sworn to himself to be honest with himself about this attraction he had to her, too. Over the years he'd been on his own in business, he'd made millions being brutally rational with himself about projects he favored. Ruthless in his analysis, he'd learned to separate desire from wisdom. He'd wanted to invest in a Japanese *zaibatsu* focused on building steel mills. But the conglomerate was very family-oriented and at heart resented westerners. He'd taken his money elsewhere.

At one time, he'd also advised the imperial viceroy of Foochow to finish the completion of public sewers. But the man had delayed. Then the city had suffered a flood and as a result, a bout of cholera. More than four hundred died. Pierce had pleaded with him to allow him to create better sewers in a two *li* area, a small but illustrative display. The viceroy refused.

He'd also proposed to open a school to teach Chinese students the fine points of electricity and plumbing. He'd told the viceroy he would fund the school. But the elders of the region learned of the proposal and favored the didactics of *feng shui*—wind and water—as rulers of the universe.

Pierce could not fight tradition, as much as he did not wish to fight family allegiance or prejudice against westerners.

Now he had to be wise about his disturbing new attraction to Camille. It was sexual awareness. No wonder. He'd not indulged in any intimacy for more than a year. He'd been grieving. Now looking at Camille, young and alive, gay and laughing and oh, so ripe for a man to love her, he was more than interested. Sadly.

He ran a hand through his hair.

She tipped her head in question.

He had to smile, didn't he? And he had to be smart about this. He was older than she. Much older. He could even scold himself and declare he was too old for her. But not quite doddering, was he? Not when he could be drawn to her lips and her breasts and...

He swallowed.

"Are you unwell?"

"He is not for you. And I will not say more. I am eager to be off."

"Ah." She pulled her leather portfolio closer to her and her elegant fingers riffled through it. She took out a folder and pencil and opened her paperwork. When he didn't move but continued to watch her, she put down her papers. "Did you bring work?"

Work? "I did. But I'm ready for my meetings."

"Lucky you." She went back to her columns.

He went back to his scrutiny of his attraction to her. She'd not said a word of reproach since the night of their kiss. Not looked guilty or sad. Just friendly.

He snorted.

That's what he had come to. Old and more than randy and not quite wise enough to contain his desire to become more than just her friend.

Dear God.

He opened his leather briefcase.

That's what he was and would only be. Her friend. Her *old* friend.

~

The house on Piccadilly was a grand old thing that Camille's step-father Killian had purchased from the original owner over five years ago. Her mother had redesigned much of the living spaces upstairs and improved the downstairs accommodations for the staff. Since Killian preferred to live in Brighton and use the London house for business during Parliament and the holidays, they kept a skeleton staff there at all times.

The new head of the London household staff was Reginald Brisbane.

That man had sent the family town coach to Victoria Station to fetch the four of them and the ride home was quick if hot in the August weather.

"I'd forgotten London in the heat," Pierce said, his finger to his collar as the coach came to a stop.

"I prefer the summer breezes, too," she said. "But upstairs you'll catch the cooler winds up from Dover."

The flurry of Brisbane and two footmen meeting them took over the activity. Soon they were up and out, inside and going up to their accommodations. Ivy, upstairs to the fourth floor maids' rooms. James, to the small valet's bedroom connected to Pierce's. Pierce to his suite and Camille to hers, opposite.

"I'll see you downstairs, will I?" she asked, chipper as she stood in her bedroom doorway. Staff had laid out a small luncheon for them in the apple green drawing room.

"In a few minutes, yes."

She closed the door and sank against it. He was worried.

She couldn't tell if that meant he was angry with her or himself. Or if he anticipated all sorts of antics from her now that they were alone.

She had no magic up her sleeve. She would never trick him. If he ever came to her as a lover, she wanted him fully committed. To her. She'd seen other girls lay traps for men they desired. Seen their mamas do it too. The result initially might have been what they thought they wanted, but in the end, many paid for their subterfuge. Two of her friends were now quite miserable. One endured a lonely life upon the moors of Yorkshire, badgered by a meddling mother-in-law and two brothers-in-law with salacious intentions upon her. Another lived apart from her husband. Having given him his heir and spare, she was now shunted aside as he took his interests to a mistress of very expensive tastes. Camille could never live like that.

She wanted a man who wanted her.

And no other.

CHAPTER 10

No. 110 Piccadilly
London, England

*I*f he anticipated that the two of them living together would bring him problems, Pierce was very wrong about the nature of temptation. Camille was easy to enjoy.

She arose early. A wonder, that. Few in the family had ever beat him to the table, even before he'd gone to China and learned the value of morning awareness. Keeping to his practice of meditation here, he was up early even though he had not slept well. He needed to continue with his own routine. His serenity depended on it. Pondering how close she was to him at night, feet away across the hall… dressed in next to nothing. Ah, serenity was elusive.

They breakfasted together the first and second mornings, or at the least, had coffee or tea while the other finished. She'd appear, as ever well turned out in one gauzy summery gown or another—and decidedly cheery. He, having tossed and turned with worry over his work and his attraction to her, was not as delightful a companion as she.

The third morning, she'd teased him about that.

"You look tired. Do you need more exercise?" she'd inquired after he grumbled behind his morning newspaper. "You didn't get much on that steamer, I'd say."

He'd peered over the edge, aware of the exact type of exertion he'd prefer and in which he could not indulge. "I didn't and I don't."

"We could go riding in Hyde Park."

He'd barked in reply. "You know I hate to ride."

"Me, too," she said, teasing him with a wiggle of her elegant brows.

That fourth morning, they'd asked the grooms to bring round the town coach. Pierce was off once again to an appointment with his manager in the City, while she would return a second time to visit with her publisher, not far away. Her meeting with Liv's supplier their first day had gone as well as could be expected, given delivery problems she could not solve.

"Do you mind if we go early and stop at my flat first?" she asked him. "I'd like to take the first draft of my recent manuscript. I forgot it when I went to see him the other day, and I need it now to refresh my thinking."

They'd had their coachman circle around to Eardley Crescent and he, curious about where and how she lived when she was submerged in her work, he asked if he might go up with her.

"It's not grand," she'd quickly warned as they stood before the door. "But it's mine, you see. Just mine."

"And that's why it's grand in its own way," he said. "Come on. Turn the key. Show me!"

When he followed her in, he was surprised. Contrary to

the current Victorian style to drip lace and cram bulky gewgaws into every inch, her two-room apartment was orderly, nearly simplistic in its appointments. One grand emerald velvet settee facing a small brick fireplace and two matching red tweed wool upholstered chairs dominated her compact living area. Against one wall stood her desk, an old unwieldy scuffed oak. Scrap notebooks, well thumbed, piled up in a teetering tower atop the otherwise clean expanse. A typewriter faced the wall, in exile, it appeared. A small circular wooden table and two chairs neared a window that overlooked the winding street. She had a tiny stove, wood fed. Beyond was, he assumed, her bedroom.

"I do hope you are not disappointed in me," she declared. "I'm cozy here. Just up the street is Earl's Court where Mama and I lived before she met your father. This feels like...home. And it is what I can afford from my sales. At three shillings per copy for a first edition, I sell enough to pay the rent. But after the first three months, most publishers make a 'railway' edition for travelers. And that gets me one shilling per copy."

"Camille, I am damned proud of you. Never doubt it. And I see why you want better royalty terms. I agree with your fight for them."

"Thank you." A lock of golden hair fell over her cheek.

He did not think, but acted. Stepping toward her, he pushed the fine silk threads behind her ear. "I can see you here. Working. Spartan, I'd say you are. No crocheted doilies. No wild potted ferns."

She pointed at him. "Right you are. One of my friends has a stuffed bear standing, claws out, in her drawing room. Her husband shot the beast on a trip to Montana." She shuddered theatrically. "He insists they display it."

"I'd hate it too." He chuckled as he followed her out and down the stairs two floors and into their carriage. "Last winter a tiger invaded a village along the Woosung River near the City and killed two elders and five children."

"No! How is that possible?"

He shrugged. "Many villages have no walls, natural or other, to shield them from predators or floods or landslides."

Her shock stilled her. "But you've brought engineers to the city! Even trained others!"

"I can only do so much. Progress is slow because the majority of officials do not see dams or plumbing as a necessity."

"That must be frustrating for you."

"For us all," he said as he handed her up into the town coach. He was damned tired of attending to the details of so many projects world-wide.

"Do you have plumbing in your house in Shanghai?" she asked after they were settled across from each other.

"Plumbing and electricity. Advances, but the rest of the house is built much as the Chinese do." He missed the serenity of his abode, but not how lonely he'd begun to feel inside it. "I have three stories. No cellar. The house is made of brick and wood. With five large rooms on the ground floor, four above and three above that. I have running water, hot and cold, three proper baths upstairs and a kitchen off the first floor back wing. *Feng-shui* rules, wind and water laws of the universe, demand the kitchen and the front door be appropriately situated for prosperity. My cook insisted. She is superstitious. So many from the villages are. But I don't care. I like her cooking and her. I like my houseman and valet, too."

"And your decor? Is it Chinese?"

"A mix. But I have very few pieces of furniture. I like the aesthetics of space and air. I've studied Buddhism with a friend who is a wise man. He taught me how to sit *tso-ch'an* which is to say, I meditate to understand the flow of the universe." He smiled at the interest in her eyes. Since he had seen who she was in her private abode, he thought it only fair he show her himself. "Shall I demonstrate?"

"Yes, please. When?"

"Tomorrow morning before breakfast."

She made a face.

"I know, but it's best that way. Your mind is open. Your body is clear. But you've got to be able to move easily for this. So you've got to wear those pyjamas you wore to the beach the night we walked together."

His mention of that night they nearly kissed a second time made her blink, but she did not blush or mention it.

He crossed one leg over the other and placed a firm focus on his coming business meeting. Or at least he tried.

The third morning, she rapped on his door just as the sun rose. She was barefoot, hair haphazardly pinned up, but she had donned her elegant silk top and trousers. The pattern was one he'd not been able to appreciate fully the other night in the dark. The violet with tiny peacocks of orange and red drew his eyes and his appreciation.

"You like my pyjamas?"

"I do." He recognized the print as one from the Bombay area.

She strode into his sitting room and yawned. "You'd better, because I am tired. And you look...plain."

He was dressed himself in white raw linen top and trousers. "I can have a set of these made for you. But only if you like this practice. Otherwise, your outfit will do well."

"Agreed. So. I'm ready. Teach me."

She was young and flexible. But she was not used to bending to touch her toes or to stand, warrior pose. Nor did she wear anything underneath that silk and when he touched her ribs to straighten her stance for warrior, he felt the fullness of her breast beneath his fingertips. And damn. She did not move. She made no remark, but waited for him to react.

It took the willpower of a saint not to snatch away his hand or to cup her breast—and to position her arms in right angles. Worse was the way the silk blouse fell around her neck and exposed the arch of her back, the points of her spine and in profile, the full curve of her breast and the points of her large pale pink nipples.

He burned. He fought. He argued with his cock.

"Sit now," he told her in some other man's voice. "Like this."

He readily sank to the Turkish rug and pulled his own shirt fully over his raging erection. His mind could not reach serenity. His body could not cool. He did not breathe.

She sat, all nubile temptation, peeking at him from one eye. "You seem to be a statue."

And hard as one, too.

"I don't know if I can sit for long." she told him.

"If you give it a few minutes, you can get into the flow. Try now. Five minutes."

She had been good and sat for more than the five. When she arose, he offered his hand and she grinned at him. "I will try again. Tomorrow."

"Ah. My attempt is not in vain."

"Never. Teach me anything. I am ready."

What he wanted to teach her would shock her to her core. "I'll remember that. Coffee now."

She raised a finger in the air. "Bath first. See you in half an hour."

~

If she could have run to her room, she would have soared like an eagle, screaming in frustration. She thrust open her sitting room door and fell back against it, gasping for sanity.

As if they were on fire, she tore off her blouse and stepped out of the trousers.

She lifted her breasts and thumbed her nipples, yearning for his fingers or better, his mouth. She clamped her thighs together, her flesh wet and empty. She let one hand drift down to separate her folds and she tapped the rigid pearl that pulsed in time with her heartbeat.

How could he touch her like that? So accidentally? So carefully. So quickly. As if…as if she were porcelain. Cold to his touch. Indifferent.

She walked to the wall pull and yanked the cord to summon Ivy. She needed a bath. Water. Soothing and hot. Inside her. As he should be. How could bending her this way and that and thrusting in odd poses and having his hands all over her bring her peace?

He must be a monk.

While she'd become a lunatic.

She paced her bedroom like one. Eager, full of raw desire for what she could not have. And why?

Why?

She was not his blood.

Not his sister.

Never had wanted to be thought of in that way, not by proclamation or proximity.

She straightened. The only reason she could not take him, have him as a lover, was because of possibilities. If she invited him to bed, what were the odds he'd accept? She must weigh them.

Then too if she took him to bed and he did not enjoy her, what were the possibilities that he'd no longer be her friend? That would crush her.

Ah. And if she took him to bed, what could the probability be that she'd find him boring? Commonplace? That she'd not want him wrapped around her, inside her, again and again?

She knew that answer. He was older, surely acquainted with the arts of love. If she asked him, if he accepted and she enjoyed herself, she could count good odds that she would be entranced. She'd never want to give him up. Never want another man. Her hopes to find a lover who would want her until the end of time would be dashed.

Then too she faced another problem. Her married friends had often exclaimed that a girl could not help but fall in love with a man who'd taken her and shown her passion. But she'd had one man on purpose to prove to herself that the popular belief was a misconception. She hadn't loved that man. Not before. Not after. But wanting Pierce, craving Pierce was a different desire. It was not a hope for education. Ha! No. Instead, it was a hope for culmination.

She loved him now. Loved him as he was. Devilishly handsome Pierce. Accomplished. Hard-working. Daring to take chances in business that Carnegie and J.P. Morgan and his father, Killian took daily. Winning.

And he'd had lovers. She'd overheard him, years ago, speak to Killian about them. About one whom he'd taken as a mistress and pensioned off, years ago. About his fascination with Elanna, Julian's sister, the Countess of Carbury. If he'd had an intimate relationship with Lee Macfarlane's sister, May, she was not certain. One did not have to go to bed with a person to be in love.

But she must tally up her probabilities for success with him. She could not continue in this limbo, yearning for him and gaining nothing but frustration.

She could lead him to her bed, and he could decide. She'd have to state well her reasons. And her promise that if he refused her, she would never mention it nor approach him again.

And if he came to her? If he agreed?

Oh, my.

She ran a hand along her belly to her hip bones and into the curls at the apex of her thighs. She bit her lip.

If he made love to her and he found her...lacking? Oh, that would be impossible to bear. But she might be nothing he'd want as a lover. The truth was, she had no way to know unless she invited him to it. She'd have to promise beforehand that she'd never reproach him. That she'd forget the moment, the impulse and how she adored him. That might be the most difficult of all results. But she would have to bear it.

She must.

She could not go on this way.

Instead, for her own sanity and peace, she would risk alienating him forever.

CHAPTER 11

She hurried downstairs to the first floor and found him sitting at the desk in the library, working over a sheaf of papers, pencil in hand.

"I'm off," she told him, yanking on her gloves.

Something in her nature made him snap his head to one side. His calculations suddenly mattered not as much as the sight of her, fresh and enticing. "Refresh my memory. Where are you going this morning?"

"Mama's man of business again. The other day he promised to notify me the instant he heard of the delivery of her French upholstery fabric. I haven't heard from him, and I'm worried. That ship was due in Dover yesterday afternoon. She must have that for the show."

"Yes. I recall now you said." His eyes, sharp and probing, ran over her, head to toe and back again. He must have liked her lime green day gown and gold-trimmed walking jacket because he smiled in that slow way that spread his magnificent lips in approval.

She quivered, alive in every nerve.

"As ever, your hat cannot remain on your head."

She patted her hair. A lock fell to her cheek and she tried to weave it up.

"Don't." He rose, pushing back his chair, and strode to her. "We must have a few words with Ivy about your hair."

She pulled back when he would have taken her curl and pushed it under her brim.

"Let me," he seemed to croon.

She shut her eyes as he did whatever it was with her hair. She could smell him, sandalwood—and perhaps, what? Jasmine? She could feel him, his heat, his deft fingers on her scalp. She could kiss him now, so easily on his lips and forget about her mother's business and her friends for luncheon. She could have him, as on the beach in Brighton before he knew to object. She could feed her own craving and fill her emptiness. She swayed toward him, and he caught her by the shoulders.

"Do you still wish me to meet your friends at luncheon?" His voice was hoarse.

Could he have trouble speaking being so very near to her? She opened her eyes.

He stared back, his silver gaze probing hers and falling to her mouth.

He licked his lower lip.

She caught her breath.

"Do you?" he asked on a breath.

What were they talking about?

His fingers dug into her upper arms. "Do you want me to come?"

Oh, you cannot imagine how much.

"Camille?"

She blinked. "Of course. Lunch." She'd not reneg on that. But she would do it in a moment if he wanted her now in bed. In that chair. Here, standing. Ohhh, she'd lie to herself if

114

she didn't admit that she'd do anything to be near him. But how wise was that?

Not at all. And if she was too quick, too rash or too wrong to try, she could ruin him and the entire family. Irrevocably.

And she mustn't. Mustn't destroy the family unity and camaraderie. The immense pleasure each took in the others' company. Her mother who'd worked so hard to give her a good life after the death of her father. Her step-father, Killian, who loved her and treated her as if she were his own. Her young half-brothers, William and Dylan, sweet boys. Her step-sisters, Lily and Ada and their families. Marianne and Remy and their children in Paris. Each one, accomplished and intelligent, who valued the family trust and bonds of respect. All wonderful giving people who were, above all, honorable. If she took Pierce to bed, if he would be so bold as to come, and love were not the cause nor the enduring bond, then she would have to leave the family circle because she'd broken it in the name of lust.

She tried to smile at him. But her heart was not in it.

She must be stalwart and logical. Find a way to discover if she loved this man so that she could honor him as his lover and as his wife. Because it was one thing for him to desire her, but if he could want her only as his lover, then there was no benefit in making love to him. Only disaster would come of it.

Had she known that? Instinctively?

Yes, she'd probably known that for a decade. If indeed he could never want her in the fullness of matrimony, then she must abandon all feelings for him, save friendship.

So she pulled back. Patted her hair above her ear and threw him a breezy toss of her head. "Two o'clock at Cafe Royal."

"I look forward to it."

~

Cafe Royal was an established restaurant in Regent Street off Piccadilly that served the best French cuisine and the finest British clientele. While many dined here or at Kettner's after theatre performances, for luncheon the literary set was the crowd that congregated.

Oscar Wilde was known to put in an appearance. His friend—Bram Stoker who managed the Lyceum Theater—brought in his associates most of whom were playwrites. While tales of writers' odd midnight hours swirled about, one could prove them true by looking into the weary complexions of the males. Like French *flaneurs* who kept *garçons* busy in Parisienne cafes, the men of the literary bunch in London appeared in their high starched collars and tweedy suits swilling down their wine, resembling high class pimps.

As Pierce was shown to the table where Camille and her friends sat, he welcomed the diversion from his struggles desiring her. This morning touching her wrist, her thigh, her breast had set him to grinding his teeth—and cursing his rebellious body. Christ, how he wanted to put his hands all over her. Claim her. Consume her.

He threw himself into the art of the business luncheon, expecting to meet somber young ladies of meager means who scribbled for a living.

From what Camille had told him about her pitiful royalties, he did not expect feathers and boas or stylish attire from her colleagues. Instead he faced Camille in her splendid green and gold and her two young friends who were so dressed to the teeth that they appeared to be princesses rather than novelists.

"Allow me to present Mister Pierce Hanniford, Rosalie. Pierce, this is my friend, Lady Rosalie Marchand."

He had understood that he was to be the showpiece of their luncheon. A lady does not invite a man to dine with her friends unless she wishes to display him like a male peacock. He didn't mind. He was Camille's male peacock, becoming more so by the second.

He greeted one lady and turned to the next. They were practically cooing at him in appreciation.

Camille did not seem to notice. "And this, Pierce, is my other talented friend, Miss Sheila Buford."

To neither woman did Camille introduce him as her step-brother. God in His Heaven knew, he did not feel brotherly toward her. When was the last time he had?

"My pleasure to meet you both. Lady Rosalie. Miss Buford."

"Let's dispense with all that, shall we?" Rosalie, a thin blue-eyed red head who looked like she belonged in the Highlands, flicked a dismissive hand.

"We are to be friends, and so I am Sheila and this is Rosalie," declared the other one who was blonde, buxom and as languid as someone on laudanum.

"We all went to finishing school together," Camille put in.

"But our instructors could not seem to polish us up!" Rosalie looked about for the waiter. "We need another bottle of champagne, don't you think?"

"He'll appear," Sheila said, but her attention was on Pierce. "We are here to learn about Shanghai, Mister Hanniford."

He was certain that they were here to inspect him, but he was here to discover the facets of Camille. Thus he played along with the social game. "I am at your service. But we may need more than two hours at lunch."

"I agree," said Rosalie with the shrug of her shoulders. "My grandfather had an interest in the East India Company long ago. Went out once. Took my father's youngest brother and the poor boy died of cholera. Grandpapa returned home and declared the Orient hell. Obviously," she said, her gaze drifting from his face to his shoulders, his navy blue afternoon frock coat and back to his lips, "you find it otherwise."

"I do."

"Well!" exclaimed Sheila with big brown eyes, "now that Rosalie has thoroughly alienated you, we must not discuss *'the Orient'* at all. Rosalie will trip over her tongue in an attempt to be—"

"Rational. Accepting. Not judgmental?" The woman in question offered.

"Exactly," said Sheila. "May we start again, Mister Hanniford?"

He glanced at Camille who sat calmly, a smile wreathing her perfect oval face. Unperturbed by his ability to fare this storm, she pursed those ripe lips of hers together and drove him mad with want.

How damn soon could he leave here and have her all to himself again?

His body wanted her now. In his lap. His mouth on hers.

He sat forward and sought the waiter himself. As they shared champagne and oysters *a la Greque*, he gave himself over to telling Rosalie and Sheila about the mechanics of rickshaws, the terrors of Triad coolie gangs, the subtle art of calligraphy and the beauty and squalor of Shanghai. In so doing, for his forbearance, he gained the approval of Camille who in recognition of his efforts, ran the toe of her shoe up his ankle. Once. Twice. She'd started that soon after they met years ago and gave it as homage for whatever he'd said or done. Then, he'd taken her approval with laughter—and marked it to their friendship. This afternoon, the friendship was there, beneath another emotion he mustn't dare to name. Oh yes, he continued his revelations about life in Shanghai. Plus he liked Rosalie and Sheila, because they were straight-forward in their likes and dislikes. They were looking for an education and so he did what he could, by Jove. But he did it because he craved that slide of Camille's toe along his ankle.

He answered it with his own toe to her foot.

Her gaze delved into his, a frank invitation to continue their play.

He choked back a laugh. He might as well be sixteen again! But damn his soul, he kept feeding information to Rosalie and Sheila. And playing footsie with the irresistible woman next to him.

He would have it that he admitted over the *flambé de tournadoes*—and the wicked torment of Camille's foot skimming up his shin—that he would do anything to please Camille Bereston and to revel in the torment of his hard full cock pressing against the constraints of his ridiculously tight trousers.

CHAPTER 12

"*I* thought we'd walk home from here," he told her as her friends climbed into a hansom cab. "I hope you don't mind."

"Not at all." She welcomed the chance to be out with him, on his arm for the world to see. She looped her arm through his, daring for just a second to press her breast to him and shielding her face from the sun by pulling down the brim of her straw hat. "The day is glorious and I've had four glasses of champagne that I must walk off."

As they strolled down the crowded by-ways of Piccadilly, he asked her what she thought of her friends' work. "Do they write as well as you?"

She could puff herself up with pride, but on this subject, not ever. "Better."

"Are you being humble?"

She chuckled. "No! I am being honest."

"Do they write gothic romances too?"

"Yes. Rosalie's are very dark. Think of *Dr. Jekyll and Mr. Hyde*." She feigned a shiver. "And Sheila writes a mystery in her plots. Mine are simple romances."

"Why writing?"

"Why not? If I could, I'd run for Parliament, but since I am of the weaker sex—" She paused to put the back of one hand dramatically to her brow. "—I must be more prudent. Writing stories, earning an income that way is respectable. If now and then, a few think it a bit risqué."

"But you don't write anything scandalous."

"That is all in the eye of the beholder, isn't it?"

As if she'd said something ridiculous, he frowned.

"What's the matter?"

"So much of what we do rests on what society thinks." A gust of wind had him clutching his navy bowler to his head. He turned away for a moment, killed whatever thought had made him wince, then came back to smile at her. "We think we are immune, but we never are."

That truth stabbed her. She was not immune to social mores or the knowledge that she must not damage her family—*their* family—in her quest to discern if he could love her. "I have heard you regard criticisms of how you run your companies as reason to reform them. You welcome suggestions."

"I do. One must be thoughtful of others."

"I agree. I understand you pay your employees well as opposed to others, like that American steel manufacturer, Carnegie."

"He'll come round," Pierce said, patting her hand. "He knows that Papa and I pay our workers a living wage. Most of the public approve of that. Carnegie will follow."

He led her toward the window of Skinner and Company. The window display drew her with a thousand lights arcing in the sunlight. She grinned at the beauty of the diamonds and rubies, but pointed toward one multi-strand necklace of pearls. "Those are gorgeous."

"They are. They're taken from the sea by divers. In the

south of Japan, they are exquisite finds. But otherwise, I can't say I admire most of what we see here. I know how such jewels are mined and believe me, it's the miners who pay dastardly prices for their excavation. Their lives are miserable. Ten or twelve hours a day in the pits of the earth, breathing bad air, working in the dark."

"I'd read some of that."

"For you, pearls," he said, contemplating her complexion. "Pearls to match your skin."

The sun was brilliant. The crowds around them, buzzing like bees to flowers. But he had eyes only for her, and she could not move. Not breathe, either. "You shall have them. The longest strand I can have them string."

She could not kiss him here. But oh, my, the temptation to do so flashed through her like a flood.

He reached out to brush an errant curl from her cheek and gave her a forced smile. "Let's go home. I've purchased four tickets for us for the theater tonight. Earlier, I called over to the Langham and the concierge delivered my invitation to Lee Macfarlane. He'll join us for *The Mikado* and dinner afterward."

Wonderful. She needed as much company as possible. "We need a fourth?"

"I hoped your friend Lady Brianna might be in town?"

"She is! They'd make a good pair."

"Exactly my thought."

Like us? Do you think we are a good pair?

Lee Macfarlane stepped inside the gilded vestibule of the Savoy Theater. With one wide-eyed assessment of the packed lobby, he found Pierce and wove through the throng toward him, Brianna and Camille.

That afternoon, Camille had sent a written invitation over to Brianna's home in Berkley Square. Brianna had written back in her bold script, "Of course! A new man!"

Camille's friend counted as many former suitors as she. In the six years since Brianna's formal debut at court, she had turned down three proposals of marriage. Her father, the persnickety Anglo-Irish Earl of Bourke, had resigned himself to her "foibles". Her mother had been furious. Her brother— the heir who wished to have his only sister off his hands before he inherited the earldom—had been sullen. Arguing against her only given reason each time, her brother claimed one need not wed a person who "intrigued" one. Brianna had asserted she'd not marry without a swell of daily curiosity... as well as sexual attraction. Her brother had married a little mouse for her money, so there was his rub.

Camille took one glance at Lee Macfarlane and from the corner of her eye saw Brianna tuck her chin into her throat as she examined the man from head to toe.

He did look regal in his black swallow-tailed evening suit, ivory satin waistcoat and elaborately tied silk cravat. Pierce wore similarly striking attire and Camille found herself smiling at the thought that many a lady here would want him or his friend...but have neither. Not while Brianna was near this man. Not while she was Pierce's partner...at least for tonight.

The thought of another in Pierce's attention stabbed her with sorrow. She forced herself to the matter of welcoming Mister Macfarlane.

"On a Wednesday evening," Lee greeted them all, "one would think the theatre would be poorly attended. Good evening, Pierce and Miss Bereston. I'm delighted we are a foursome." His sky-blue gaze landed on Brianna with a sensual intensity that had the lady parting her lips.

Pierce carried on with the introductions.

Camille extended her hand to him. "We thought you'd enjoy sterling company, and so we invited my former school friend to join us."

Lee bowed low over Brianna's hand with a slow appraisal of her upswept auburn hair and rosy lips. Then he lifted her hand and kissed it, a chivalrous charm that in the bright light of the foyer illuminated his instant desire. "I am delighted to meet you."

Brianna acknowledged him with a wide arch of her brows and no small bit of astonishment. At once, she seemed to shake herself and recovered her usual *elan*. "I'm quite honored to meet you, sir. I'm afraid, however, you won't be happy to have met me."

Given in good jest, her comments had him gazing at her in confusion. "And just how is that, Lady Brianna?"

"I promise to draw every detail from you about your home which means you'll miss the play entirely."

"I know Japan so well, my lady, that I shall not miss this performance, but prefer the honor of your full attention."

"You sway me with your compliment, sir."

"Wait until you feel the full force of my own questions," he said, so good at this banter that Camille grinned.

"You'll allow me to learn everything?"

Lee lifted her hand to his lips once more. "I ensure it."

Brianna blushed, her lashes fluttering. The man was newly arrived from another country only weeks ago and yet clearly knew how to charm an English woman.

Brianna tipped her fan at his chest, a more familiar gesture than their brief introduction might allow. Yet Lee took no umbrage. Just the opposite. He reached for her wrist, turned up her hand and plucked her fan from her fingers.

"A woman who enjoys the language of the sticks should possess her own incomparable ones." He deposited her fan on a waiter's stand. "I will send one to your home tomorrow before your breakfast."

Brianna—an heiress and aristocrat who was never smitten by any man easily—stared at him in what Camille would say was awe. "I'd like it in yellow," she told him in a voice that sounded very much as if she were in a trance.

"The color for an empress," he said and lifted her wrist—this time—for the blessing of his lips. "None other."

Camille arched both brows. Brianna did indeed shiver at this man's attentions.

"Shall we go up?" Pierce turned to Camille with laughter in his eyes.

Camille gave him her arm and they found the circular stairs off to the right and up to the entrance to the balcony boxes. She debated if sitting with Pierce in such proximity was a good idea. But in the regular floor seats, they might have been closer, their knees and thighs touching. When he opened the door to their box and he took her cloak to hang in the ante-room, his fingers lingered on her bare shoulders. She stilled. The four chairs in red velvet and cream brocade were no farther apart than the seats below. But each pairing of two sumptuous upholstered fauteuils gave an intimacy to the private space that implied more than simple affection between partners.

He took her hand and led her to the fore of the box. She peered over the railing. Below, a hundred or more mingled as they found their own seats. Some were in parties, others alone. Camille caught the eye of one former school friend of hers and Brianna's. She turned to tell her, but her friend was much too involved with Lee Macfarlane to tear herself away. In truth, he focused so intently on Brianna that he enjoyed himself as well.

Camille cast another look at those on the floor—and halted. Her gaze met those of Aldridge Connor. She smiled and inclined her head in acknowledgement. But he did not. He held a glass of wine or whiskey and downed it, then set his mouth in a firm line. In the next moment, he caught sight of Pierce and their two companions, but returned to scowl at Pierce.

She recoiled at Connor's animosity. His behavior, silent though it was and far removed, was nonetheless rude and oddly unsettling. She turned away.

And sat down. She opened her program but the print swam before her. That Connor should be so disconcerted by Pierce's presence confused her. She'd not felt any hostility between the men. Why should there be?

She sought a distraction, anything not to look down again to the house seats.

From the corner of her eye, she observed how Brianna and Lee whom she had just met seemed to live in a world of their own. They talked as if they were old friends. They laughed as if they cared not for any others in the world. They touched as if they had before.

Was this fascination? Of course it was.

Camille held her breath and caught a glimpse of dashing, darling Pierce. Desire burned her from the heart out. She had seen it this morning when Pierce touched her. Felt it this afternoon when they'd toyed with each other, their toes under the table, teasing each other as they had for years. Rejoiced in it on the walk home, the press of her aching breast to his arm.

Camille understood desire when she saw it because she had lived it for much of her life. All for Pierce. Since she'd been terribly young and knew no other men. Since she'd come under the spell of one man whose lure she could not escape, though God knew, she had tried. She bristled with the remembrance of how she'd admired Pierce when he was young, a man in his twenties, alive with the intentions to grow his own empire. To be his own man, a replica of his father and yet, unique unto himself in his style and interests.

She'd first met him in Brighton and waltzed with him on the Promenade, letting her fancy take her away with girlish ambitions to have him to herself. The years, her own schooling and friends, had taught her that adoration was not love. Fascination was often a fragile construct, meant to shatter in the face of reality. Desire, a fool's opiate, was heady but dangerous. Passion, a physical drive, was sated by quick attention to the cause. But love? The care for another that required respect for their reputation and their hopes. That demanded more than any blithe surrender to heady euphoria.

Did she love him?

She had always wanted Pierce for more than the blush of passion. Always. No other man had compared to his humor, his zeal, his family devotion. She wanted him for now, for tomorrow and all their tomorrows. But for the first time, she asked herself, could she match him in those sterling qualities? And could she honor and keep him as he so well deserved?

It was one thing to ask herself these things. She had a few answers.

She glanced over at Pierce. In profile to her, he was her ideal. The wealth of stark black hair. The clean brow, the perfect straight nose. His lips. Full. His jaw. Firm. His throat. The sum of him, healthy, strong and more handsome than any man she'd ever encountered.

Sensing her, he met her regard and his brilliant eyes caressed her. Her mouth, her nose, her hair, her heaving breasts in the low-cut shantung. He smiled and a melting sensation swept down to her loins. He took her hand and squeezed it, directing his gaze to her fingers as he toyed with

127

them. Through her gloves, she burned to touch him skin to skin.

She took her hand away. Her lips parted in apology, but no words came forth. Her nipples ached. She arched her back and shifted.

"Camille," he whispered as he lifted her hand and kissed the back. "Try to enjoy this."

She had to laugh. The play or his kisses? "It's very difficult."

"I agree." He inhaled and tore his attention to the stage. "We must."

She nodded and attempted it, didn't she? For the sake of propriety and their family.

She could not endure this kind of temptation for long. If she did not find words to ask him of his feelings for her, she would burst with need and do something rash, unforgivable.

Tonight, she would begin the discussion with him. She must. Did he see her as a woman, full grown, with a regard for him that bespoke of more than their shared past? Could he love her as a woman? As a wife?

She must learn. Then stay or leave.

She rubbed her arms.

"Are you comfortable?" Pierce leaned toward her, his gaze ablaze with concern. "If you're chilled…?"

"No. Not at all." She lifted her fan on the crocheted draw at her wrist. It was something to fiddle with instead of squirming at the enticing fragrance of Pierce, so near and provoking. But distraction came hard and she said, "I wondered that you chose *The Mikado*. I fear Mister Macfarlane may be offended."

"When I telephoned, I told him I'd purchased tickets for this. But I also said if he preferred to see Sarah Bernhardt, I'd change them. He's heard of the 'Divine Sarah'. And of Gilbert and Sullivan, too. But he told me he wanted to see the parody of Japanese society. He knows what he faces here, Camille. We have prejudice in Shanghai, too, you see. And it's worse there against those who straddle two cultures."

Money cures few ills, her mother always said. "Yet he seems to rise above it and does well in business."

Pierce's face was a study in pride in his friend. "Very well. He knows many discount his abilities. He's learned to show them he is their equal. His father has taught him the western way. His mother, the Chinese. In truth, I have watched him to learn finer methods."

She let her admiration show.

He must have understood because he said, "A man can always learn new things."

She nodded as the bright gold tapestry curtain rose. "A woman too."

CHAPTER 13

*H*er comment set him aback. How did she have to change?

He liked her as she was.

But the light in her eyes told him the ideas she considered were about him. And he feared she might consider leaving him and London. Despite the fact that she was twenty-four, she was so young. She had considered many to marry but wisely had chosen no one. Yet. She had no idea what the future might bring with a man she barely knew.

She knew him. Good, reliable *him*. He had the right of it to control his urges and touch her only as her friend. Her good friend.

He crossed his arms and focused on the musicale. How he hated it. The bastardization of the art of *kabuki* was one insult to the ancient culture of Japan. But the other was to the Japanese efforts at modernization. Those earnest people had aggressively begun to change their feudal country economically and politically and it had cost them a great price of upheaval. The emperor, a boy of intellect certainly, was now the head of a parliamentary state. The shogun—

once the premier executive for centuries—had been removed from power, sent to obscurity to the countryside for his failures to hold back the Western powers and the influences to his country. His samurai who had kept the peace and the order for centuries had lost their purpose and professions, feudal warlords though they had been. And while many might think that good, the men and their families had to find new ways to support themselves. Fine minds among them who reached out to Westerners, eager to help them form a parliament and revitalize, grasped the new concepts of funding businesses that would modernize the country. The Mitsubishi family started a mail order business and steamship operations. The Mitsui clan who had collected taxes, organized one of the major banks. The Suzuki produced steel and supplied the navy. Others opened grocery stores and construction families made cement and paved roads.

Over the past twenty odd years in that country, palanquins had given way to horse-drawn omnibuses. Candles to electricity. Fire to gas for cooking and heating.

Because the Japanese wished to change and enjoy the benefits of science and industry.

He frowned at the stage when one of the geisha appeared and made fun of the old samurai who bemoaned the loss of his honorable warrior-past.

One didn't have to abandon the past to make a bright future. Pierce knew it to be true, because he'd seen his father do it. Watched Lee Macfarlane do it, too.

He himself had done that in business in America, England, France and lately in the totally new and different culture of Shanghai. But now he questioned if he might also embrace the knowledge that he wanted Camille in a new way that did not abandon the friendship they'd had before, but built on it.

~

He shot to his feet when the curtain went down. In the cloak room, the two men donned their evening capes and helped the ladies with their wraps. Camille avoided his gaze and when he asked her if she enjoyed the opera, she forced a smile and nodded once. It was not like her to be out of sorts.

As they left their box and emerged into the grand circle, he offered his arm to her and strode alongside Lee and Brianna.

Lee's expressions during the performance had gone from insult to disgust. Like Pierce, Lee headed numerous projects with Japanese businessmen, most former samurai who were fearless but measured in their attempts to build railroads, ships and improve their ports. Fearing Lee might be furious at the play's portrayals of Japanese, Pierce had to hear his friend's reaction. "What did you think?"

"The Japanese are far more intelligent than those in the play." Lee scoffed. "I would hope the world might learn more from us in Asia than that we are foolish in our efforts to modernize."

Brianna touched his arm, her gesture a sign of empathy and concern. "I've read that the Japanese make great strides to build their country."

"They do. It takes courage to change that much. Leaders must be respectful of the past, but fearless."

"And well-financed?" she asked.

The look on Lee's face told Pierce that his friend found this lady extraordinary, not just in her looks or her charm but in her uncanny abilities to understand his challenges as a *tai-pan* in a mixed community.

"Indeed, my lady. To take a society from the tenth century to the nineteenth is no easy feat. Courage is necessary.

Compassion even more so. At the moment, the Japanese have a larger measure of both than we do in China."

Camille regarded Pierce as they headed toward the staircase. "There is so much more you could tell me about what you do abroad."

He appreciated her interest. "The story is complex. I can rattle on. You must warn me when I begin to bore you."

"But there should be no limits on a good education, don't you think?"

Gratified, he grinned as they rounded the landing. "I can begin any time."

"Tonight. Why not? Others should want to learn what you do and how you navigate the—"

She halted.

"What's the matter?" Her gaze led his downward.

At the foot of the circular stairs stood Aldridge Connor. His hand upon the bannister, he glared at them.

Pierce did not like the looks of him. Earnest, glassy-eyed. "No matter. Come."

They took the remaining steps, Lee and Brianna in front.

But as he and Camille reached the last step, Connor neared.

Pierce led her around him.

But Connor jumped in front. He bared his teeth, his eyes red.

Foxed, was he? Pierce stared at him and tightened his hold of Camille's arm. "Pardon us, sir."

"No," he seethed. "I know what you two are doing."

Pierce grumbled and stepped around Camille to shield her.

Connor danced backward, keeping pace. "You must not have her, Hanniford!"

"You are being rude, Connor."

He headed toward the door.

The brute yanked on his evening cape.

Pierce halted. And called to Lee.

Lee whirled, and took Camille in his embrace.

Pierce swung around and peeled Connor's fingers from the wool, crushing them into the man's fist. He smelled of alcohol. "Go home, sir. You are making a scene."

The man cupped his abused hand. Jeering, he followed them out the huge glass doors to the paved walk. "No. No! You're the one—you're the one making a scandal, Hanniford."

Lee and Pierce checked each other's expression and Lee nodded. His arm in the air, Lee hailed a hansom from those circling the broad Strand.

Other theatergoers, not hearing or seeing the urgency, scrambled to gain their own cabs. The crush was not the most polite and one of them pushed Pierce toward Connor.

The man—fuming—grabbed Pierce's lapels.

"You would be wise, Connor, to let go my coat." Pierce had met many a drunk man. Even if this one were sober however, he would not be a match for the arts Pierce had studied at the feet of an elderly Buddhist warrior monk.

"You mustn't have her." Connor leveraged stability from clutching Pierce's coat and rose on his toes.

Pierce winced at the man's rancid breath. "You talk foolishness, Connor. Do go home." And with that he grasped the man firmly by his shoulders and pushed him to the walk.

He'd just grasped Camille's forearm to help her up into the large black brougham that had pulled to the curb, when Connor grabbed her around the waist and dragged her backward.

She cried Pierce's name. Her eyes black with fright, she clawed at Connor's hands. He dragged her backward, one arm wrapped around her waist and the other crushing her breasts.

Pierce was on him in two steps.

But the beast gripped Camille with greater strength than Pierce anticipated a drunk could summon. Pierce circled round and hauled him backward to the red brick wall. The man clung to Camille, but when Pierce pried his hands away, her necklace of malachite and the teal **chiffon** of her bodice came away too.

She gasped and grabbed for her gown.

Pierce seized both of Connor's arms. But the man wriggled away, then swung round to punch Camille in the face.

She shrieked and Lee grabbed her up.

Pierce growled. With Connor's offending arm high up against his chest, he slowly, relentlessly bent it backward at such an angle that it snapped.

Connor screamed and sank to his knees. His face white, he braced himself on the pavement with one hand while his other hung limp from his elbow. "You bastard! You broke my arm."

Pierce took Camille from Lee's embrace, pressed her bosom to his chest and pulled her evening cloak over her torn gown.

The crowd around them muttered. Someone called out for a Bobby. A few men stepped to surround Connor as if to waylay him should he try to flee.

Pierce stared down at the man. "Now you'll go home, Connor. Never again come near Camille or me."

"She's a fancy piece. You can have her!" His jaw quivered as he whimpered. "But I see you already have."

A few in the crowd exclaimed. Others were horrified.

"Eh? What's the problem 'ere?" A tall, burly policeman in spotless black wool and stove-pipe hat stepped through the throng.

A few bystanders recounted Connor's assault.

Pierce was relieved to see him but eager to leave. "This

man accosted my lady. See to him. I'll give you a statement. Gladly. But in the morning. I'm Pierce Hanniford of Number One-ten Piccadilly. But I will take her home now. Call on me as you need."

~

Camille stood against him, her hands clutching the edges of his cape, her face pressed to his throat.

"Sweetheart, Lee has a carriage. Can you walk?"

She stared into his eyes, her own shrouded in shock. "Yes, yes."

Her cheek was red where Connor had hit her and her gown was a ruin. Her beads were gone, a red line around her throat where Connor had pulled off her jewelry. Pierce would kill the man if he came near her again.

"Shall we come with you?" Lee stood at the open cab door and helped Pierce hand Camille inside.

"No, we'll be home in a few minutes. Please, the two of you, claim our dinner reservations."

"I couldn't possibly dine," Brianna murmured.

Lee held her around the waist, close to his side. "Neither of us can. We'll go to my hotel and I'll order something simple. Call the concierge in the morning, will you? I need to know how you are."

Pierce agreed, swirled off his cape and climbed inside the dark confines of the carriage.

At this time of night when the theaters let out, coaches of all sizes circled the roads around Covent Garden and the Strand. Lee fortunately had managed to hail a large and well-appointed one.

Camille sat amid the thick black leather squabs, hunched over, her hands clasped tightly together as if she were praying—or mourning. Her bodice hung forward, the lines of her frilly corset visible, and her breasts swelling over the top.

He sat down beside her, pulled off his evening scarf and threw it to the opposite seat. Then he removed his own cape and tucked it up around her shoulders and throat. He lifted his legs to slide along the seat, sank backward and spread her body along his, head to toe. Like a wounded animal, she came to him. Her head, he firmly placed against his shoulder. Her face, she nestled into the hollow of his throat. Her arms went round him, squeezing him close. Her hair against his chin, her nose against his neck, her fingers digging into his sides, her legs tangled in his, she sank against him. He ran his hand down the crown of her hair. It fell in waves over her shoulder, her pins and evening toque long since gone in the melee.

"Pierce," she whispered. "Oh, Pierce." She shuddered and sobs wracked her long lithe body.

"Don't think of it. Just be at peace, here with me. No one will hurt you now, sweetheart. No one."

"He was hateful." She gulped, tears on her cheeks.

Pierce dug a handkerchief from his waistcoat inner pocket and dabbed them away. "More than."

"How could he do that?"

He winced and stroked her hair. "Don't think of it. He is a cad."

She took the handkerchief. "He made me a laughing stock."

For that alone, I could kill him. Were we in Shanghai, my houseman would suggest a gang whose only job was to avenge such insults to women and children.

She clutched him closer. "Oh, Pierce. He thinks that you and I are lovers."

He exhaled. "He was drunk, Camille. That was obvious. Others saw it all. They won't take what he said as truth."

But he saw the truth. Tonight he saw it.

"They'll talk anyway. They'll say horrible things." She wiped her cheeks and pulled back to gaze into his eyes. "I've lived a different life. But I'm not...not what he said."

Not my lover.

"I'm not."

He lifted her chin and turned her head this way and that. She'd have a bruise, the mark of that man's insult. Please god, might it be mild and temporary. "No, my darling. You're not."

But you should be.

~

When they arrived at home and the footman pulled open the coach door, Pierce gave him a quick look of dismissal and got out. As Camille emerged, he swept her up into his arms and marched to the front door.

Brisbane was there. "Sir! How can I help?"

"I want a bucket of ice. Hot soup, crackers, jams and brandy. And tell James he is to go to bed."

Brisbane frowned. "As you wish, sir."

He took the stairs at a clip as Camille murmured her displeasure. "You needn't do this. I can walk."

"I'm not letting you go."

"Pierce, please."

"No."

She curled her arms around his shoulders more tightly. "Thank you."

"Open the door," he told her when they stood before his.

She checked his gaze, but she swung it wide.

He strode inside and went straight through his sitting room to his bedroom.There he sat her down on his mattress and lifted his cape from her shoulders. First came her shoes and her gloves, then the remaining pins in her hair. He met her gaze. "Shall I call for Ivy or can I undo your gown and corset for you?"

She lifted her chin, her look with a dawn of thanks and wonder in it, too. "No. You."

He shifted, sitting behind her to unlace the elaborate ruined French silk. He'd buy her dozens of gowns, hundreds to take the place and erase the menace of that man.

"Stand a moment," he told her when he could not do her service without the full of her back available to him to remove the cloth. When she stood and he sent the supple fabric to the floor with a brush of his fingers, more of her bare skin was exposed to him. He hurried to unlace the ridiculous contraption that encased her. At the sight of her flawless skin and the dip of her waist against the subtle flair of her hip, he swallowed hard on desire and worked rapidly.

She swayed with his virulence and clamped a hand to her bosom to retain the corset to her chest and save her modesty. He slowed. God knew, he had no desire to hurt her more. And the sight of her curling her shoulders away from him told him she needed to maintain her reserve.

So as the thing gaped wider, he shot to his feet.

"Don't move." Off he went, eyes straight ahead, to his dressing room and pulled from a padded hangar the onyx and silver Chinese *han-fu* that served as his robe. Gazing to her right, he handed it to her. "Step out of that ugly thing and put this on."

He could hear her swallow, but she took it and let the frilly cream and pink undergarment drop to the carpet.

"Now lie down. Yes," he said, catching her question as she tipped her head. "There. Up on the pillows. I'll return." Spinning, he disappeared back into his dressing room to tug off his evening coat and waistcoat, cufflinks, shoes, stockings, black trousers and white shirt. In a rush to get back to her, he pulled out of his top drawer one set of the white linen shirt and pants he wore for daily meditation. Donned them. Belted them at his waist. Then padded barefoot back into the room.

At the corner, he stopped. She had watched the entryway for his return. Mute, she met his gaze as he returned to her. He settled beside her against the headboard, legs along her own and gathered her into his arms. With a sigh, he drew her near. The hard points of her full breasts pressed warmly against his chest and he ignored the implication of what they told him. She put her palm to the v of his bare skin beneath his throat—and though he told himself he shouldn't, he welcomed her caress. When she burrowed nearer to him and she put one leg over his own, he caught sight of her long white lacy garters and the clocked white hose she wore. He knew she moved to better balance herself against him and he warned himself that this was her way to accept his shelter and his protection. That it was also the way his raging erection fought with his logic and his good intentions had him putting his lips to her forehead and praying for strength.

"When Brisbane returns," she said, "tell him to send Ivy to bed as well."

The implications were manifold. One would be that the household might get the same impression that those outside the theater had. She had been mortified by that and frankly, so had he. He would guard against that for her sake. "The servants will know you are here with me."

"I want to be."

"Camille," he said and lifted her chin, "I mean to make you feel better. Not seduce you."

"You do make me feel better. Best, if you don't force me away until I want to go. And seduce me?"

Oh, the way she delved into the depths of his eyes and sought his good intentions helped him affirm in his own mind what this night's affection would become.

"No, you won't do that," she said with confidence, then sank again to his chest and snuggled there.

Firmly fixed by his own better angels, he offered up a small chuckle.

"Good. I like to hear you laugh."

"Sweetheart," he said and stroked her long tresses down the elegant line of her spine, "you are the one who needs to laugh."

"I'm not ready yet."

"Fine. You tell me when."

"I will. After you hold me awhile longer." At that, she curled herself more dearly against his side, one of her long legs inside his two, rubbing against the swell of his temptation and arousing his ethics against acting on it.

"You will have to stop doing that," he managed on a cracked voice as he spread his legs wider and pushed hers away from his cock.

She took that well and did not speak for a few minutes. He continued his stroking of her hair and back, learning the points of her vertebrae and wishing they were his to touch and count and treasure sans the Shanghai silk beneath his fingertips.

She traced little circles in the hair on his chest, content it seemed, to be still with him. "I'm not a virgin."

That took his breath. To reclaim it and his right mind, he examined the crown molding where the ceiling met the far wall. He must not make assumptions about her reasons to tell him that. "I hope you chose the man and moment."

"I did. But I wasn't happy with the results."

He feared to ask what they were.

"Except for one thing."

"Which was?"

"I realized that I didn't want to spend the rest of my nights in that man's bed."

"Ah." His head whirled with visions of her in some insensitive clod's embrace.

"You can continue to stroke my back now."

He resumed. "Right. Good. Why did you allow him?" Fool that he was, he had to know.

"I thought I should have an education and he seemed nice enough. And I liked him. Until afterward, when I was disappointed and confused."

He swallowed back the mad desire to strip the *han-fu* from her luscious curves and show her what a man should always do with her sweetness. "What did he do?"

She sank backward in his arms, her head in the crook of his elbow and considered him. In the mellow gaslight that his valet had left burning in the sconces, she looked at him with dreamy eyes and moist lips. He wanted to taste them all. But she broke his reverie when she answered. "I'm not quite certain what he did except to be fast and clumsy. Afterward he declared he was grateful! So grateful, he said he would go to Killian and ask for me. I had a difficult time convincing him he shouldn't. Only when I told him I would never marry, did he realize that to justify it all, I was fibbing."

"To cover your true feelings."

"That I didn't like his lovemaking. Yes."

"Poor bugger." The idiot should have known better.

"He was thirty years old. I thought he'd be...skilled and make it...wonderful."

"Age has nothing to do with the art of making love." *Do I hear myself saying this?*

"He was so mechanical."

Pierce cringed, his cock telling him the mechanics of making love to Camille would be long and rapturous and burn him from the inside out. "A magnificent experience begins with passion, not education."

She squirmed beneath his hands. Her body of its own accord tried to press her thighs together.

He pushed himself up and away before he fulfilled her needs and devoured her with kisses.

"Don't go," she pleaded with him.

He glanced over his shoulder. She lay on the bed like a cat, her hand to the midnight blue coverlet and her mellow eyes inviting his return.

"I think Brisbane should be back with the ice and—" He strode toward his sitting room, anywhere to get away from the manic temptation to consume her.

"Pierce?"

He stopped and should not have. One hand to the door frame, he stared at the floor and saw only the urge to turn back and take everything she offered.

"Don't you think I should have a proper education in the arts of making love?"

"A woman should be taught them by a man who adores her."

"I agree."

And three raps came at the far door.

She consoled herself that he wouldn't make love to her. He first would minister to her swollen cheek. Brisbane's tray full of broth and tea and brandy had included the chipped ice and wool cloths to wrap them in.

As Pierce approached with it, she turned to her back and closed her eyes.

His application was gentle.

Her appreciation great. She put her own hand to the compress and sighed. "I can do this."

"Do you feel like eating?"

"I'd like the brandy. Then the broth."

"I'll set a table for us here."

She lifted the corner of the cloth and peeked at him at his duties over one small table in the corner. "Will you tell me about the woman you wished to marry?"

He stilled and turned his gaze to hers. After the moment's pause, he strode to her and reached out his hand to help her up. She went, clutching his robe close about her.

They sat at the small round Chippendale table and were well into the brandy and then hot broth before he spoke. "May Macfarlane was twenty-two when I first met her five years ago. She was Lee's young sister, his only sibling. At her father's insistence, she was educated in Western history and algebra from age five. But she also had a traditional education in the Chinese arts of the fan, calligraphy and ancient Chinese literature. Her father was the oldest son of the Scotsman Ian Macfarlane, who'd gone to Hong Kong in eighteen-twelve to run gunpowder and opium. May had lived in the Shanghai British Quarter all her life, but she spoke Mandarin and Ningpo, the local dialect. She was also fluent in English and French. She could add a column of thirty figures in a minute and predict your profit or loss just by asking you when the source products were due to arrive.

"The first day I met her, she was pruning chrysanthemums from her private garden, singing an old Chinese opera ditty. She would have managed the Macfarlane factories equally with Lee. Their father decreed it. Lee had never quarreled with his decision. She was a strong woman with a determination to be her brother's equal. Any man's. I respected that. Valued it." He caught her gaze. "I had asked to marry her before she became ill. It's ironic that she died of cholera. For years, she had worked to modernize the water supply and sewerage system of the city."

Camille could understand Pierce's admiration. "I hope she loved you."

He nodded but his attention was on his tea cup. "She did. Not as many women would think of love. But then she was not like others. She was part this, part that, everything female, yet nothing like any other. She was of the Chinese past, of the British present and of a future for China that she wanted, but few others can envision. She wanted equality for women. A parliament. And education for the peasants. None of that is remotely a possibility for China now or, if you ask me, for decades to come. I loved her, but not…"

Camille searched his features and waited.

"Not as you might expect. I saw her as my equal. One who would be my partner. But I worried that she might never accept me as I completely was. A man of the West. Of America and England and France. She told me she was born in the sign of the snake. I was a horse. We could not work well. We would argue."

Camille idly stirred her broth. "And did you agree with her assessment?"

He sat back and inhaled. "I did. She was aggressive. Whereas I love the journey, to conquer the road. In any communication, I value the discussion, the debate, the arbitration more than I do the triumph. Lately I wish for fewer decisions about a multitude of projects. I wish for fewer details and more simplicity."

That gave her pause. For that was precisely what the two of them were doing here. Discussing the way forward. Toward simplicity. One good solution. She surrendered to it, aware it was best.

"And when she died, I let her go with a grief that marked my own death to the knowledge that I was best working with Westerners and only tangentially with Chinese. I didn't know it then, but I do now. I was preparing to come home."

"And will you return?"

His silver eyes locked on hers. "I've come to realize while I'm here that I want to stay here. I've talked with Victor briefly about it. We need to discuss it more. But I think that I left the company in good hands, and I'll return occasionally. They will prosper without me."

"I'd like to go."

He smiled, warming to her sentiment. "We'll have to see that you do. You will enjoy it."

With you, I would go anywhere. Still, she realized he had not committed to take her himself. She swallowed her disappointment in favor of learning more. "Do you still miss her?"

"I do. Time does help. She taught me much. And I will always remember her for her courage and her ingenuity. She taught me to think of women in a fuller way. As those who can and should be aggressive and claim what they want. Votes. Power. Money."

She grinned at him, but sobered at an old nagging question about his view of one woman in particular. "And your thoughts on Elanna?"

"Ah, well." He wiped his mouth with his napkin and poured more draughts of brandy into each glass. "I thought her assertive, argumentative, surely. But wrong-headed. Her husband was no better, demanding she be the idealized wife, loving, sympathetic, passionate. Yet he showed her none of that. What one gives, one gets. I sympathized with her. But she was a creature of a prison made by her husband, by society and by her own willful capacity for destruction. She paid for it. Dearly."

He sat for a moment, contemplating his brandy. "What you saw in me was my obsession with her. She was a firestorm, a catastrophe that destroyed all in her path. She was a tragic figure, lovely beyond imagining but erratic and foolish. Locked in a prison others had made and she made worse. I'd never met a woman who had so much life and so much desperation."

"Nathaniel is the one who truly suffered for it all." Elanna's and her husband's son had lived a horrid life with the two of them and only after his father's sudden and outrageous death had the little boy gone to live with his uncle Julian and his wife, Lily, Pierce's oldest sister.

"Thank heavens for Lily and Julian to take the boy in and give him the home and family he should have had."

"One thing this family does is support all its own." She reached across the small expanse to cover his fingers. "You and I won't tear it apart."

"Never." He got to his feet, her hand firmly in his, and lifted it to open her palm and kiss her there. "We will be careful."

The words robbed her of breath.

"I'll take you to your room now. You'll need that ice again."

She stood and went into his arms. Aching to lie against him in his bed, she pressed her forehead to his chest and wound her arms around his waist. "I'd rather stay with you."

"And I'd rather have you here." He lifted her chin. " But we mustn't. We'll talk again tomorrow."

CHAPTER 14

That morning, Pierce took the stairs down to the breakfast room at a run. He'd slept late, exhausted from last night's events and his preparations for his speech to her. Eager to get on with his discussion with her, he quickly donned informal trousers, a shirt, braces and a morning jacket. Having asked his valet if he knew if Miss Bereston was awake yet, he'd been surprised to learn that she'd dressed and dined more than an hour ago.

Where had she gone? He wanted this business of their future out in the open.

He reached for the pull in the empty breakfast room.

Brisbane appeared quickly. "She said she's going cycling, sir."

"Cycling?" She was that recovered from last night that she'd take out a bicycle?

"I believe, sir, you might still catch her in the mews."

He turned on his heel for the more convenient servants' stairs and took the exit to the family stables in the mews.

She was emerging from the door. She was dressed in a white cambric shirt, light tweed waistcoat of green and purple, and black balloon knickerbockers down her little half boots. Her legs straddled the black steel frame of a tall two-wheeled bicycle and her delicate ankles in fine purple stockings reminded him of last night when she had lain nearly naked against him.

"Good morning." He smiled.

She didn't. Nor did she meet his gaze. "Morning," she said with a brisk tip of her tam-o-shanter Irish hat.

Very well. Pretend last night did not happen? That won't be possible. "Brisbane said you were going out."

"I am."

"Where?" He would know. She shouldn't go anywhere alone, not with the likes of Aldridge Connor in town.

She sniffed and focused down the alleyway where a few of their neighbors led out their horses for their own morning rides. "Hyde Park."

"I want to go along. If you'll wait I'll—"

"You needn't." She faced him fully now and he could see that the bruise to her right cheek was turning a nasty purple. But she'd applied a heavy cover of powder. The jaunty cap helped to conceal the severity of Connor's blow.

"But I want to."

"Why?" She had her hand on her hip. "I'm capable—"

"To go alone is not wise, Camille. Come to think of it, where's your maid?"

"Ivy doesn't cycle."

"I see. So you thought you'd brave the world alone."

"I wanted time to myself." She set her jaw, her eyes narrowed in earnest endeavor.

"And if Connor decides to ride, too?"

"He won't."

"You can't be sure."

She mashed her lovely lips together and scowled at him. "I can. He never rides. He takes his curricle to the park."

"Even worse. He could run you down."

She pursed her lips and lifted her face to the sky. The long line of her creamy throat was exposed to him and he had the unreasonable early morning desire to kiss his way down the elegant length. "He won't."

"I'm coming with you," he declared. "Wait here. I need a shot of coffee and a bite of bread."

"No. I don't want you."

That set him back on his heels to chortle. "Now, that, my dear, is a lie."

She shot him a glance that could kill at four yards.

"If you leave without me, I will come find you," he threatened.

She shook her head and tapped her toes on the cobbles. "Oh, well, all right then. Hurry. I have appointments today."

"Have we more cycles or do I have a horse saddled?"

"Three more bikes. Ask Joseph. The groom," she added in exasperated explanation.

He put out a hand. "Do not leave."

"No, no. I won't. Get on with you!" She shooed him toward the kitchen door.

When he emerged a few minutes later, he had a piece of brown bread in one hand and a bit of it in his mouth. She stood, arms crossed, casually talking with a man he presumed to be Joseph the groom, and she was laughing. Her head thrown back, she thoroughly enjoyed whatever they spoke of. And Pierce paused to imprint the picture of her, kissed by gentle rays of morning sun, her hair a thousand shades of red and bronze and gold, the green and purples of her tweed summoning a hearty pink blush to her skin.

Someday soon, he vowed, he'd make her laugh like that. And have another picture of her in her natural beauty to carry with him until he died.

"Here you are," she said when she spied him. "Joseph got a bicycle out for you. Good enough?"

"Perfect." He examined the tall steel contraption. He could do many things. Build steel plants. Negotiate laborers' wages. Invest in the finest shipping. But this?

"Have you ridden one before?"

He shook his head once.

She grinned.

"Mischievous chit," he muttered and Joseph widened his eyes, affronted for his mistress.

"Not to worry, Pierce. You'll learn quickly. Won't he, Joseph?"

"Aye, miss." But he sounded skeptical.

They were off down the alley toward the entrance to Hyde Park, and as he struggled to find his balance, he debated why she was angry with him. He might know...but then again, he might not. Since he couldn't read her mind, unlike other women with whom he was acquainted. Once he maintained a modicum of stability on the wobbly thing, he hailed her.

"You don't have to run off, do you?"

"Want me to appear to be with you, do you?"

"That would help," he said, when he came abreast of her and they reached the pair of broad gates to the Park near old Wellington's house.

"I want to be out this morning." She regarded him and her eyes were dark with a sad determination. "For your information, no. I'm not concerned about appearances. I will be out and about. I will not hide. If that makes me brazen, then..." She shrugged a shoulder. "What I can do is use it to my advantage. A girl gets an idea she can stand up for herself if she sees other women do it. And I won't hide. Not from Connor. Not from the world. Not from you. We can have that talk you want here in the park. A good idea, don't you think? To be among hundreds of people where I can't possibly react except as a lady should. Come along now. Keep up. I know you're eager to tell me to stay away from you."

Then she peddled away.

He caught up to her, but it was no easy task.

She cast a glance at his feet on the pedals.

He chuckled. "You're enjoying this."

"True." She tossed her curls that escaped her tam and threw him a short but apologetic smile.

They ate up a mile or more before she spoke. "I had no idea Connor had that in him."

"I may have."

She tipped her head. "What do you mean?"

"I saw him in the Lanes that day he showed up at your autographing party. He had an altercation with a woman who was very upset with him."

She caught his gaze. "Did he know you'd seen him?"

"I doubt it. When he appeared in the book shop and you introduced us, he gave no indications of having seen me witness it."

She slowed, came to a stop and walked the bicycle.

He was happy to do the same.

A frown marred her brow. "That means his anger last night was a result of what he saw at the theatre."

"He witnessed a lot."

She pressed her lips together. "He did."

"Whisky did not help. But the greater matter, Camille, is that he is not for you. The woman he argued with in the Lanes was no lady."

She faced him then, and she was angry. "Many men have relationships which are not—shall we say—sanctioned by

God. And many women who cannot earn a living wage any other way cater to their appetites. Is it not true that men learn how to behave in the bedroom with women who are in need of their coin?"

He simply nodded and walked his bicycle toward the park bench nestled in a maze of white late blooming field lilies. Resting the contraption against the back of the bench, he said, "You're right. Can I blame him for society's dictums? No. But I can blame him for losing his temper, insulting you and hurting you. But I also know that he may want you for your dowry and your connections."

As he sat, she stared at him with no small bit of fury. "You investigated him?"

"No." He brushed a hand down the crease of his trousers and crossed one leg over the other. He hoped it helped conceal his physical need of her. But attempting to appear nonchalant for the onlooking public was trying his soul. "I asked Victor if he knew him. He does. Well."

She huffed and swung around to stare at the early morning riders, all of them mounted on fine greys or chestnuts. All of them, too, getting a good gander at the two of them. Most of them—men— discreetly shaking their heads or commenting to their companions. News of last night's events, Pierce assumed, occupied their minds.

He patted the wooden seat. "Come sit down."

She shook her head.

He inhaled. "Very well. I shall tell you where you stand. I want you. It's what Connor saw last night. It's what prompted him. It's what I admit. I want you. I want everything about you."

If he had his pocket watch, he might have timed the eternity it took her to turn. But as it was, she froze at his first words and inch by inch turned to face him. A minute? Five?

What did it matter? At last, she stared at him, her lips parted, her mysterious dark eyes flashing in wonder.

He found himself attempting to comfort her with a smile. "I saw you first, as a girl. Impulsive and rambunctious. Quick witted and droll. A new member of the family. You were amusing and my friend. But still too young for me to consider you attractive. For years, I had business on my mind. I didn't search for a wife. I had too much of the world to see. Too much to conquer. Too much to learn about what I was best suited for...and who I was best suited for. As I learned more about what I desired in a lover or a wife, you were never among the candidates."

She surveyed the trees above and the lilies at her feet. "Well, that's not very complimentary."

"I have more that is."

She swallowed and pressed her lips together. "Tell me."

"No."

She blinked, her dark lashes fluttering in confusion.

"Not now. Not here." He wanted to say these things as he'd rehearsed them all through the night. Alone in his cold bed, he'd planned this. Now he was foiled by the hour and the place even if they provided the perfect setting for logic and bargains. Meant for the privacy of a room and his ability to embrace her, his admission and his proposition were such intimate declarations that he feared he'd stumble through this. "But it is best we are here in public."

She took affront. But it covered a fathomless well of sorrow. "I see. You will now tell me we are done? Fine! Save your breath!"

She took a step away.

"No! Stop." He killed the urge to stand and take her in his arms. That would make matters worse. For now...and later. "Look at me."

She clenched her fists.

"Camille. You and I must settle this between us. I see now the best way is for us to match our actions to the moment."

"Oh, really!" She yanked off her tam with one hand and ran the other through her hair, sending it over her shoulders. "What is the moment?"

He blew out a gust of air. "I am trying to be logical."

"You do that little thing!" She arched her back, tears swimming in her eyes, and examined him as if he were the dearest man in the world. "I ache to have you. I've wanted you my entire life. That girl you saw, she idolized you. That girl became a young woman and she spent her days and her years comparing you to every man she met. Was this one as handsome? That one as bold? As funny? As successful in business or law or politics or...or...the art of being you! She found each wanting. Oh. In every way. She found each to be self-centered or unimaginative. Stupid. Or careless with money. Indifferent to family. Insensitive. Or just dull."

His heart swelled with joy and pride at her admissions. "Camille, listen to me."

She whirled her bike around. "I'm going home."

"Camille, you and I will not have an affair in this house or in Rue Haussmann."

"Right you are." She took a step.

And he shot from the bench and caught her wrist. "After Marianne's and Remy's ball, you and I will go away together."

Slowly, she lifted her gaze to his. Disbelief mingled there with fierce desire. "You'd do that?"

He had the insane urge to cup her cheek and kiss her until she sighed in his arms. "We must. Don't you think?"

"I do," she whispered. "I'd say for four days."

He could have shouted in success. "Five."

"Where?"

"I haven't a clue. Yet."

The smile that graced her lips set her whole lovely face

aglow with delight. Alarm replaced it. "You won't change your mind?"

"Never."

"And at the end, if you decide you don't...love me, I promise never to reveal it. Not to anyone."

"Nor will I."

"My mother and your father will never know."

He nodded. "Never."

She regarded him with a winsome glint in her dark eyes. "How good an actor are you?"

"For you? For this? For our family?" He would promise this so easily. "Very good."

"We begin that now, don't we?" Sorrow swamped her features.

"It's wise." He squeezed her hand. "Though I'd much rather kiss you until you cannot breathe."

She swayed against him for one blithe moment. "And go home to retire to your bedroom."

He clamped shut his eyes. "Camille. Don't."

She gulped. "No. I'll be good. I promise. I—I must go to see Mama's manager once more and later to my publisher. He has a new idea for me and I must think of that. And send a telegram to Paris to make an appointment at Worth's and Madame Villette's."

"Ah, a fine idea." He turned to retrieve his bicycle and walk away from the temptation to pull her down into the lush green grass. "A new gown."

"And new lingerie." Her large dark eyes danced in utter devilry.

He set his teeth. "You try me, Miss Bereston."

"Oh, Mister Hanniford, you cannot imagine how I want to."

"Home!" he cried. "Now!"

And off she pedaled, laughing.

~

At peace, he worked the rest of the day on finishing the proposal for the Chinese railroad. He had to calculate the tons needed because something about his first estimate was wrong. He had promised to send the costs via cable to the Shanghai office and his preoccupation with Camille had him day-dreaming.

But he also outlined another project that he wanted to present to a group of French steel manufacturers. He'd invested in the French syndicate years ago and with their contract to supply the French navy, the company's repute was now worldwide. But he abhorred using his product for an item of war. He wished to sell his shares in this company and had to find a way to break the news to many who relied on his strong American dollars.

But his outline for the syndicate and his calculations for the railroad suffered from a more compelling distraction. Camille's smiling face appeared in his mind's eye, and his proposals remained half formed. Luckily when Lee Macfarlane arrived to discuss their project, Lee was preoccupied with his own problems and did not press him on the finances of the railroad.

As she had pedaled off from Hyde Park, Camille had stepped into her role as his friend. An hour later, she'd gone off to dress for her appointments for her mother and at her publishers. She'd returned only at four. At seven, she joined him in the drawing room for sherry. Attired in a low cut dinner dress of pink organza, she was a delicious treat for his covetous eyes. But he was acting friendly. Wasn't he?

Dinner was full of the news of the day.

"My publisher," she said over the fish, "told me today that I have an offer of French editions of my older novels. I'm to call on him in Paris." Camille sat at the other end of the long

157

mahogany table in the formal dining room. Far away from any temptation to brush his fingers over her arms or her throat or…

He raised his glass in a toast. "Always a good idea to operate in more than one country. Congratulations." He'd almost called her 'my darling', but that would wait a week. Then he could call her that and more.

"Thank you, I like the idea myself. More income is always a good concept." She lifted her own goblet and drank.

Pierce approached the more delicate topic with trepidation. "Lee MacFarlane called on me briefly at two. He and I discussed our proposal for a new railroad in China. He leaves for Paris day after tomorrow."

"Then we will see him there. And have him to supper. Where does he stay?"

"The Meurice."

"Not far from Rue Haussmann. Perfect," she said, her attention on her plate, more than him. All of which was wise of her because, in the velvet glow of the flickering candles, her lovely eyes beguiled him.

He cleared his throat. "I thought he'd also enjoy coming to Monet's and Remy's joint exhibition."

Camille met his gaze, her own denoting only friendship. Damn, she was good at this acting. But he preferred her enchanted with him, wanting him. "And the ball."

"Right you are," he said and went back to his dinner. "There's more you should know."

"Oh? What?"

Pierce put down his fork and knife. "He will have company in Paris."

Camille cocked her head in question, but as he took his time to answer, she went quite still. "Who?"

"Lady Brianna joins him. At his hotel. And in a few weeks, they travel together to Berlin."

Her mouth dropped open. "How...how can that be? I mean she—"

"He knows she acts against the rules. But they are quite taken with each other. Lee predicts he may face censure for it, but frankly, he does not care. He wants her."

Camille fell back to her chair. "And she knows what will happen to her for this. She'll be disgraced. No one will receive her."

Pierce felt compelled to explain more about his friend. Such developments, so very unusual, would stun many here, in Paris and even in Shanghai. "Lee does not act out of impulse. He is the soul of restraint and consideration."

"And does he...? I have no right to ask, but I will. Does he have liaisons with other women?"

"To my knowledge he has had a few, yes. And he knows this will shock a few of his European business partners. But he told me he cares more for Brianna than success with them. You see, the man is a millionaire so many times over that he can value love more than money."

Camille stared at him. "A maxim I've heard my mother, Lily and Julian repeat time and again."

"Each of the three faced the same choice."

"And chose love," she said. "Oh, Pierce. I am shocked. I don't know Lee, but I do understand Brianna very well. She does not succumb to infatuations. She does not delude herself about men. She has never done anything like this and may not care about the consequences now. But later..."

He had to ask the ultimate question that had elements of his and Camille's challenge in their own affair. "What of her family?"

Camille put her napkin to the table. "They are not on the best terms. Their opinion, I am certain, would not weigh greatly in her decision to go with Lee. But I do know that once she is committed to something, that is her final word. No matter what her family or society decrees."

He drummed his fingers on the table. If things did not go well between them, life would be difficult to manage. Especially being with the family. He must offer Camille a way out. "If you have any doubts about our decision, you must tell me."

She met his gaze, frank and bold. "I won't change my mind, Pierce."

He narrowed his eyes on her. How far would she go to make love to him, regardless of anyone or anything else in the world? "If you do, I will know anyway."

She tipped up her chin, courage incarnate. "I realize."

I won't allow you to be ruined. "And I won't proceed."

She took a minute to consider that. "I understand."

He made a move to leave the table. "Will you join me for brandy?"

"Forgive me, but no. I'll retire. See you in the morning."

The French ormolu clock atop her sitting room mantel struck one and Camille still walked the floor.

A jumble of excitement and trepidation at her affair with Pierce, she could not sleep. Joy for Brianna mixed with the distress about her friend's decision to conduct an open affair with a man she barely knew also troubled her. Lee was a man from another culture. Another type of family. Another occupation and with very different expectations. Of himself. Of a mistress.

Would Brianna survive such a challenge? Her friend was strong, but this was no problem she'd ever faced. Willingly or not.

Camille sank to her chaise longue and pondered the

empty fireplace. She had accepted her own set of challenges today. While at first, she'd been surprised at Pierce's statements. Excited and gratified. Now she was terrified. And the fright of it had her pulling on her green silk dressing gown and padding across her floor to the hall and his door. And knocking once, twice.

And turning the knob.

She stopped on the threshold. The hot August night air wafted in his open casements, the rustle of the trees a soft accompaniment to the song in her heart for this handsome creature she'd yearned for most of her life.

He sat in dark trousers, his chest bare in his own silken robe, the one he'd had her wear last night, the one he'd wrapped her in. In the moonlight—faint rays through his far bedroom window—he lounged in one overstuffed chair. He looked at once at ease and yet tormented, with one leg up on a hassock, his legs splayed. From one hand, he dangled an empty snifter.

She shut the door behind her.

His large silver eyes skimmed her body with a swift caress and returned to meet her own gaze. "Darling, you should not be here."

"Don't run me out. I cannot sleep and I hoped you'd hold me. Just hold me."

CHAPTER 15

*L*ight-hearted for the first time in weeks, Pierce jogged down the stairs to the breakfast room. He was proud of himself for keeping his hands to himself for hours in bed last night. Being celibate was not a condition he could master for the long term. But he'd been good about simply embracing her last night.

Camille had kept her word, too. Before dawn, she'd stirred and with a soft inhalation of breath she'd laid a hand to his heart and left him.

When she met him in the upstairs sitting room after seven, attired in the white linen shirt and pants he'd given her for meditation, she was well into the role of pretending to be his friend. Their meditation had seemed refreshing for her. Far from it, for him.

"Good morning, Brisbane." He strode to the sidebar to lift the cover of a silver salver, but a glance at the table told him Camille's place was clear. Had she eaten already? "Cook has outdone herself again. My thanks to her."

"She'll happily receive them, sir."

"Has Miss Bereston come and gone?"

"She has. She took her maid and has gone for a walk in the park. She left a note for you. And there is more, sir."

Alarm ran through him. Now that she had agreed to a rendezvous—*ah, be frank, old man*—an *affair*, he banked on it. The fear of losing her had lodged itself like a little ghoul somewhere in the wealth of delight that her agreement had brought him. Silly of him to think she'd back out, but why would a vibrant young woman want him? Why not want a younger man who was not part of her extended family?

He stared at the butler. If Camille had decided not to go to Paris or meet him afterward, certainly, she'd say nothing of that to staff. He was quite foolish over this new enchantment with her, wasn't he?

"What is it?" he asked the man.

Brisbane had detected his anxiety and threw him a pleasant look. "We received a telegram this morning. The courier brought it from the office. It's from Brighton, sir. There." He indicated the yellow envelope beside his place setting.

"Thank you."

He opened it immediately. "Ah. Mister and Mrs. Hanniford arrive on the two-clock train tomorrow afternoon. The two boys come with them. The Duke and Duchess of Seton and their three children are on the same train. They all remain until after Mrs. Hanniford's showcase in the City. The day afterward, we all leave for Paris."

"Very good, sir."

Pierce took up the other note, a simple sheet of vellum folded in half. He read Camille's large elegant handwriting with a mixture of relief and disappointment. Her words were brief, impersonal and she signed at the end with only a capital 'C'. "Miss Bereston says she is off to dine with a friend this evening, and tomorrow morning, she leaves for Paris at nine o'clock."

"Very good, sir. Will you be dining in this evening, sir?"

He thought on that for a minute. It was best that Camille left. There was only so much temptation a man—or woman —could stand.

"I will. Tell Cook not to fuss. Eight o'clock, if that's all right. I'd like an early night."

He predicted it would be a lonely one, too.

The scenery flying past Camille's window going down to the coast and boat train set her mind at ease. She'd done all she could for her mother and her exhibit. The fabrics had come on time and the hall was ready to receive her instructions in the morning.

But Camille had to get away. Take time for herself, for the gigantic job of pretending to be nothing more to Pierce than his step-sister. How she would get through the days ahead she had no idea. Acting took a huge toll on her. It had never been her forte. She was, always, who she was, declaring what she wanted and how. Deceit, lying—anything of the sort— had always been unnecessary to her. She rather expected that many in the family knew of her attraction to Pierce and that they'd accepted it, even as neither she nor Pierce had.

She hoped she might find comfort in the solitude of the train. The constant chug of the engine and the grinding rolling wheels would give her peace in their rhythm. The hum and beat of it would set her imagination spinning. The Channel's churning waters and the site of the cliffs of Dover as they turned east toward Calais and south toward Paris had always filled her with awe. She was a glutton for dazzling scenery.

Just as I am for family and friends. And lovers, too. One, especially.

She crossed her arms and snuggled once more into the serviceable leather squabs. Her rush to arrive to her train on time had been stymied by an overturned carriage, horses and passengers tumbled, blocking the lanes of the Strand. She'd been thrilled to board it on time.

But by teatime, her nine-and-half hour train ride wearied her. With her toe tapping the floor, she endured the train chugging through the northern villages of Paris at a slower pace than in the countryside.

She was hungry, too. Breakfast in her rooms had been toast and tea. She'd dressed serviceably in a simple light grey wool walking suit and lace trimmed cotton blouse. Trains could be cold or hot and one had to be prepared.

Intending to take her mind off Pierce, she'd brought her notebooks to work on her newest novel. She'd given Ivy three weeks of leave to go south to Brighton to visit her mother. In Paris, the staff at Rue Haussmann was sufficient for Camille. Besides, she did not want to have to make excuses in a week when she told her family she was off to the countryside for a bit of seclusion. She needed to meet Pierce for their rendezvous alone.

She forced herself to the examination of the Parisian outskirts. She'd use them, somehow, in a novel, but she knew not how or when. The flat plains of the north that led from the ocean south toward the Seine were a picturesque blend of sparkling meandering rivers, bright green foliage and lush forests of ancient oaks in moist thick black loam. Dotted by white-washed farmhouses with red-clay mansard roofs and chateaus of limestone and pale pink brick, the French meadows of pale grasses danced in the late summer winds. The last petals of wild summer roses dripped like blanched diamonds from thorny stems. But dahlias and asters in a hundred shades of pink blossomed, setting the land to blush like a maiden on her wedding night.

Happy to pull into the large hall of the Gare du Nord, she dug from her valise her receipt for her trunk in the baggage car. She was ready to hop off at first chance. The train huffed to a stop with a last puff and she gathered her purse, her reticule and her writing case. She had no idea if Marianne would meet her personally. She'd sent a cable this morning to her in the house in Rue de Rivoli, hoping Marianne would take her in for the night. But Marianne was nine full months pregnant with her third child, so if she could not come, she most likely would have sent her coachman to fetch her.

Camille took the two steps down to the cement quay and inhaled the unique aromas of Paris. A combination of floral scents, garlic and yeasty pastry, the city was a treasure. So too the Gare du Nord. A tall, spare structure, the iron rafters rose like grotesque skeletons, dark with the smoke from the engines. But it was open to the air and she walked along the quays aside the idling trains and welcomed the exercise after sitting for so many hours. Hucksters in the pavilion cried out their offerings of a thousand delicacies of coffee, croissants, macarons or sandwiches of *jambon et fromage.* Her stomach growled.

And there ambling toward her was the Duchesse de Remy et Princesse d'Aumale, Marianne Marceau, née Duquesne et Roland, the niece of Killian and the wife of an artist as famous as she. Marianne looked nothing like her uncle or her cousins, Lily, Ada and Pierce. Gloriously blonde with golden streaks through her wealth of platinum hair, she was petite, even dainty. Pregnant with her third child, she was twice her normal size. Her complexion was a flawless ivory with cheeks of bright pink highlighting her forest green eyes. A painter who'd begun sketching the Yankees and Confederates who tramped over her first husband's Virginia farmland, she chose now to portray women and often children, particularly her own. By this she was known, along with the Philadelphian Mary Cassatt, for her portrayal of family love.

"*Bonjour!*" she called to Camille and waved a white lace handkerchief. Dressed in a pale lavender muslin trimmed in summer pink soutache, Marianne absolutely exuded good health.

Camille flagged a porter and gave him her receipt for her trunk, then hurried over to Marianne.

"Oh, *ma cherie*! Come, come!" She sounded more French every year.

They caught each other in a fond embrace. Like all Hannifords, Marianne clasped Camille as if she were indeed a blood relative. From the first moment her mother had introduced her to Killian and Pierce, Camille had never doubted her acceptance among them. Now she couldn't help but wonder what Marianne would say if she knew she had agreed to go away with Pierce for five days and become his lover.

Marianne cupped her cheek. "You are hot! Your cheeks are bright pink! Or is this a bruise? What happened?"

"I promise to tell you later. I am so thrilled to be here."

"*Oui,* you must." Marianne ran her hand over Camille's. "You *are* hot. Oh, those trains are little stew pots. We must have Uncle Killian and Pierce talk with their friends who design them and change them up for us, eh?"

"No matter! I'm here. I enjoyed my trip—and you look marvelous. Being *enciente* is so good for you."

She scoffed. "Wait and see how good it is for you!"

Shocked, she found a response. "Marriage first."

Marianne hooked her arm through hers. "A love affair first, why not?"

"Oh, I—I'm not sure." Had she been found out?

"I am teasing you. I thought you said the last time you

were here in March that you were considering one man in particular? No? What happened to him?"

They strode past a flower girl and Camille stopped to buy an armful of pink peonies. She handed over her French francs and tossed Marianne a wicked grin. "He failed my test."

"*Mon Dieu!* Like all the others! You must stop charming all the men in the world and settle on one good one, *ma cherie.* Your mother is always amazed at your collection of odd men. As are all of us!"

Oh, if you ever learn who I've chosen, you will be apoplectic! "I may surprise you one day," she said and handed over her bouquet.

"I hope so!" Marianne lifted the flowers to her nose and inhaled. "Marvelous. *Merci.* Remy will love them. They are his favorites."

"Be serious. Every flower is his favorite." The man—the most renowned sculptor in Europe—loved everything that drew sun and water and air. Peonies, roses or weeds, robins, swans or grubs, his children—Bertrand and Corinne—and especially, his wife.

"At the moment, only one man is Remy's ideal. A famous man and dead, too. Remy works on restoring him to his glory. A new commission, you know. For the City of Rouen —and Remy is obsessed."

"I want to see it. Where does he work on this one? In Montmartre or the estate?" Remy owned a large home and garden up on the Butte of Montmartre. There, beneath the clouds and rising white pillars of the new church of *Sacre Coeur*, he sculpted many of his famous works. His estates, a combination of his family's acquisitions from both Bourbons and Bonapartes, lay to the south of Paris. There, he and Marianne lived most of the year in a rambling chateau that

Louis the Fourteenth had coveted for its pristine architecture.

"Montmartre. He decided to do it there as it will be easier when it's finished to transport it north to Rouen."

They emerged from the wide glass front doors to the boulevard where hundreds of carriages and omnibuses of every size and caliber circled, gaining and discharging passengers in a cacophonous melee. Marianne craned her neck to find her coach. "George must have gone round in the traffic. That's fine. It will give the porter a chance to catch us. We have wine and water in the cab for you."

"I will have both. What does Remy sculpt?" She had to keep herself thinking and in the moment, her mind off any sudden anxiety.

"The famous Norman king Rollo." Her green eyes danced.

"Rollo! The Viking king of Normandy!" Camille opened her large black and white checkered parasol to shield them both from the harsh August sunlight. "Remy must be pleased."

Marianne chuckled. "To fashion his ancestor? Yes and no!"

"Why not? He can call on his instinct to recreate the man."

"Or his guts. Remy says he read an old French *chanson* that says the marauder was as vicious as they come. Remy declared he was inclined to fashion him with a murderous dirk in one hand and a spear in the other. Alas, not so now."

"No? Why not?"

"When Remy showed the town fathers his first sketches, they went away and returned to politely ask for something a little more...shall we say...beneficent? Remy did not like their advice and threatened to return their advance. He believes art must tell the true story. But the powers that be are more interested in inspiring people to honor the past."

"So did they compromise?"

"Of course. The townfolk would rise in revolt if their leaders fired the illustrious Remy. So, now Rollo holds his spear *and* wears a scowl. But in his left hand is a plough."

Camille grinned. "Peaceful. Inspiring cultivation of the fields."

"And of the admiration of schoolchildren." Marianne snorted. "But Rollo stands on a pile of broken shields. Remy's idea, not theirs. They agreed. They have not seen that Remy marks the final form with shields marred by blood and supported by broken bones. He says the town commissioners will not refuse it when it's done."

"The piece is a statement against war."

"Indeed. But as a balance of the vicious Norseman's character, Remy will put a tattoo of the wild poppy on Rollo's right arm in the sign of his love for his wife."

"What a smart man your husband is."

Marianne rolled her eyes. "Never tell an artist what he must create. He'll find a way to foil you."

A little mustachioed man in a blue serge uniform and cap emerged from the station, wheeling Camille's trunk on his dolly. "Here comes the porter."

"Just in time. There is George rounding the far corner now!"

"We're glad you decided to come a few days earlier, aren't we?" Remy looked down the family dining table at his two children, Rand who was eight and Corinne, age five.

"*Oui*, Papa," the children, who sat opposite Camille around the circle of the small dinner table, echoed each other.

"Papa says," Rand added with a boy's mischief in his sky-blue eyes, "that you will read us more scary stories as you did a few months ago. Will you?"

She glanced at Remy for signs his son spoke the truth. Remy, a huge man who'd worked for decades whittling Carrara marble and granite, might look like Goliath to the world. But the tall handsome fellow who sat here was the kind and indulgent father of these two and the husband and lover of his beautiful wife. No sign of the grueling work he did with hammer, pick and axe each day suffused his congenial smile. Here was the man who worked with the themes that drove the human animal to love and cherish the others.

"Well, Rand," Camille said and chewed her *steak frites* and feigned considering Rand's task, "the last time we did that, you had nightmares."

"Not me, *Tante* Camille." Corinne piped up. "But he did."

"I didn't complain," the boy put in, hitching up one corner of his mouth as he scowled at his young sister. "Only you."

Corinne, who was the tiny blonde image of her mother, squinted her large grass green eyes at her brother. "*Non, non, non, Rand.* I am grown up, *Tante.* You see that?" She stretched herself taller in her chair, her brows shooting high to help her grow taller.

"I do, indeed, Corinne. Then we will try those stories after dinner, eh?"

The two clapped.

"A ghost!" Rand demanded.

"A dragon!" Corinne put up her hand and curled her fingers like a claw.

"Both," Camille confirmed. "I think we shall have both."

Marianne sat to Camille's left. "I wonder, Camille, if you might stay here, instead of going to Rue Haussmann? What with Lily and Julian coming along, as well as Pierce, that house will be full. Remy and I hoped you might stay with us."

"I would be happy to stay here." Away from the constant presence of Pierce. Away from the possibility she might slip her role as his friend.

171

"*Oui!!*" Corinne rejoiced. "We could have dragons every night!"

"Ghosts," Rand corrected his sister with a frown.

"Both!" Staying in the Rue de Rivoli would keep her from Pierce and it would be practical since Marianne's baby was due within weeks. "I think it sounds like a very good idea."

The children giggled at her agreement.

"Day after tomorrow, we can take a picnic basket to the Tuileries," she said.

"And go on the carousel," added Corinne with a clap of her hands.

"Oh, that's for babies," Rand grumbled. "Why not go tomorrow, though?"

"I must go see my publisher. After that, I am yours!" she told them.

"Good," Rand said. "I'd like to go to the battlements of Parc de Chaumont!"

Corinne slumped in a heap of dramatic childish despair. "I don't like it. Cannons. That's what he wants."

Rand sighed. "And you want the fish at the exhibit in the Bois de Boulogne! Fish, ugh!"

Camille brightened and took up her wine glass. "I wonder…" She tapped a fingertip on her chin. "Might you like to go see skulls. What do you think?"

"Real ones?" Corinne was a quivering ball of joy.

"Yes." Camille killed the urge to chuckle at Corinne's macabre delights. "Thousands of them."

"Where?" Rand was skeptical.

"The left bank," Marianne said and smiled at Camille. They'd both discussed this on the way from the station as a possible amusement for the children.

"It's true?" Rand was still not believing his good fortune.

His father gave him a grave look of approval. "Indeed. They are victims of the plague from hundreds of years ago."

"And—" said his mother, "from the Revolution."

Rand looked horrified. "So our Bourbon cousins could be in there!"

Corinne looked as if she saw angels. "Real ghosts! For you, Rand!"

"Guillotined!" he declared with resounding approval in his tone. "Oh, *oui!*"

Camille considered the idea sold. "I think we take a picnic each day and after our explorations, we'll look for the best shop for orange ices."

"I agree," Remy said with pursed lips. "Everything is better with orange ice."

"And *tarte au chocolat!*" said Corinne with a firm nod.

"We can invite Garrett and Artie and Beth!" Rand cited his cousins, the children of Julian and Lily, who were much the same ages as Corinne and Rand.

"Liam and Dylan, too!" Corinne chimed in with Killian and Olivia's two.

"A good idea," Remy said but his gaze landed on Camille, full of concern. "But that's a lot of children. We don't want to run you over!"

"Perhaps you'll give me a nanny and a maid?"

"Done," Remy agreed.

"And the big traveling coach, Papa," Rand added.

"Perhaps we give their parents a holiday and have all of them stay here." Camille offered.

Marianne sat forward. "That's such a passel of children. Camille can you handle all of them?"

"Well, I—"

"We'll invite Pierce," Remy said. "He should come here to stay, and we'll give all the adults a respite from orange ices and tarts!" He rolled his eyes.

"A good idea!" Marianne said with a note of finality. "I'd like it too."

"Of course!" Camille agreed. Pierce each day. With seven children. She could do that. Why not? She'd not have a second to consider the lure of his eyes or the charm of his laughter. She shivered and shook her head. "We'll have a marvelous time."

"And be on your best behavior," said Marianne. "Now. No more of this. I see you are both finished. It is time for you to change for bed."

Both children slid from their tall chairs and curtsied to their parents, each one in turn, then to Camille.

"You will come upstairs for stories?" Corinne turned on Camille the raptured look of expectation only a child can produce.

"Within the half hour! I promise!" As they scampered from the room in a hail of 'yay and 'huzzah', she grinned and said, "They are wonderful."

"You see them at their most amused and with their best manners," Marianne said.

"It is the end of summer and we have worn them through working at the chateau with the crops. They are active. Very much so." Remy put his serviette aside his plate, pride in his children mixed with concern. "Rand refuses to return to his school in Reims. They bore him, he tells us. I agree. I see the signs. He needs more than the average boy his age. And as for our *Mademoiselle* Corinne, she will have a new governess in two weeks. She wore out the first one." He chuckled.

"What do you think would bring out Rand's interests?" Camille wanted to know.

"Your stories, he likes," Marianne added. "I think he writes his own, though he will not share them with us."

"He has an eye for color and movement, too," Remy said. "He comes to my shop and will sit for hours drawing my models, but in different poses. He is beginning to understand the body. How it moves."

"And if he does not return to school," Camille asked, "he will not miss his friends?"

"It seems not. He is sociable enough, I think," Marianne told her. "He has two friends who live in the Place des Vosges. Neither of them will return to boarding school either but are precocious and need tutors. Both are a year older than Rand."

"Let us not forget his two other older friends," added Remy with a hint of sarcasm. "The barman and the garçon at the *Purple Cow* at the top of the Butte!"

"Older friends," Camille mused. "Always the way to learn about life quickly."

"Or too quickly!" Marianne shook her head.

Remy scoffed. "Rand knows how to draw a proper beer from a keg."

Camille burst out laughing.

"You will be good for them." Remy said.

"Safe, family fun, eh?"

"You bring them a *joie de vivre* they both love." Marianne smiled at her husband. "We're glad you agree to stay here. We won't leave you with them all to yourself. We have a few things in mind for the entire family. Parc Monceau has a new carousel. But also we thought we'd hire a well-outfitted barge for the fifteen of us and sail down the Seine to Mont-Valérien. It is a famous fort and not only Rand will like it, but we'll enjoy the views down into the city. And I'll love the breezes."

Remy eyed his wife as she took up her fan. "*If* you can climb the steps to the fort, and *if* that baby will wait a bit, you can enjoy your breezes."

Marianne put a hand to the large mound of her belly and gazed at her husband with the look of a woman in love. "She is not as active as Corinne."

"Ha! This time we may have a child who is serene?" Remy

mashed his lips together and frowned, playful as his children. "I don't believe it."

Marianne turned her face to one side and fanned herself like a coquette. "Just you wait and see, *monsieur le duc.*"

"Well, as we wait," Camille said, as they all chuckled and rose to adjourn to the salon, "I'm ready for fun. Forts and bones and catacombs!" The prospect of entertaining seven rambunctious children might defeat another, but she welcomed the numbers and the chaos.

Poor Pierce had no idea what awaited him!

.

CHAPTER 16

The next afternoon, she gazed out the window from Remys' sumptuous town coach and pondered the noisy traffic circling the Opera Garnier. The bejeweled women in the swan-like corsets and enormously brimmed hats contrasted with the popinjay French men in slim tailored day suits and top hats. The extravagant joys of people-watching in Paris gave her little tingles of joy. London was...well, docile compared to the jolly *hauteur* of Parisians in their capital city.

Now, if she accepted the offer of her new French publisher, she had the opportunity not only to see her works published in French but also to join the French on a more permanent basis. To open the conversation, he had offered a chateau, available at her call, rent free for a year, two staff to run it plus a generous annual stipend of two thousand Francs.

On that, she might be able to afford to buy the gown she'd ordered from Worth this morning. And perhaps the négligée from Madame Villette, too.

She grinned at the fact that the man had done more. He

increased her royalties. On each copy sold, she could live in the country quite well. Support herself. Over time she might be financially secure and be able to afford to live in Paris. Rent a small apartment, perhaps near here. Or up in Montmartre, she could afford a house. Live near many of Marianne and Remy's invigorating, accomplished friends. Writers, like Alexandre Dumas. Artists. Renoir. Mary Cassatt. Berthe Morisot.

She had no illusions of her own abilities or accomplishments as an author. She wrote stories of amusement. Not literary works of any elaborate worth. She had aspirations, but they were financial. She did not seek awards or acclaim, but readers. Thousands, millions if she could get them. The French were ravenous readers. Acquiring them and others around the world who spoke the language, she could sell more novels than she'd ever dreamed. Then she could live quite well in France.

But. What then of her other more immediate aspirations and desires?

With Pierce so near and now so very dear, more than he had ever been, she was alive with sexual desire she had so long denied. Mulling over this new opportunity gave her a different thrill, certainly. Just as she had jumped at the possibility of an affair with him, she relished this offer, too. She would not—would not—turn it down out of hand.

It was the kind of offer few authors received.

Few *female* authors received.

So the fact that she was not the finest of literary writers did not mean that she could not value this excellent chance to become something more than she'd anticipated.

To value it was one thing. To take it, another.

And the truth was that she wanted to accept. The very fine compensation was four times the amount she had earned from four novels for her London publisher. Plus, the world-wide benefits of the French copyright laws were grand, allowing her to keep her rights —fifty years beyond her lifetime—and grant them to any children she might have.

That socked the air out of her.

Children.

She ran a hand over her brow and squeezed shut her eyes.

Always, children belonged to others. Never had children been a feature in the future she saw for herself. A man, one man always came to her mind first.

And she had never had any reason to hope of having him. This, she'd pushed off that thought.

But if or when she married, she would welcome children.

And now…she allowed herself to jump ahead for a glimpse of a future with Pierce and a baby or two.

Then she caught her rampaging mind back.

She would not throw over the chance to write the types of novels *Monsieur* Daumier requested. She had no idea how that might work if Pierce and she found they wished to go on together as more than lovers. But certainly she could not write the kinds of novels *Monsieur* wished of her if she had not the opportunity to absorb the *milieu* he wished.

The carriage idled, and the groom pulled open the door.

"*Merci beaucoup,*" she said to him and walked up into the grand marble foyer of *Palais de Remy*. Two footmen were carrying up the grand staircase a large *bombe* trunk and another footman held a man's black leather valise.

"*Bonjour, Mademoiselle.*" The majordomo of the house took her gloves and parasol.

"Is *Madame* available?"

"She awaits you in the grand salon," he said in French. "*Monsieur* Hanniford has arrived."

~

Why was it that each time he gazed at Camille now, she appeared even more luscious than the last?

She lit up Marianne's finely appointed gilded grand salon with a verve that took his breath. He had missed her. And damn his soul, he had to appear not to, didn't he?

He stood to greet her and it took all his discipline not to grab her, but to hug her in a brotherly embrace. "Good afternoon, Camille. You left London unexpectedly. Out to your publisher, Marianne tells me."

Of course, he knew she was going to see the man, but he had not expected she'd leave London so soon.

"I was." She smiled, all too briefly at him, and tore her gaze toward Marianne, then took a seat in the lemon and lime Chinoiserie wing chair. "I thought it best to see him right away."

The contrast of the cheerful appointments with her eye-popping fuchsia afternoon gown made her resemble a fondant he should eat. He sat down himself, happy to cover his erotic physical reaction to her in front of Marianne.

"And you?" Camille inquired, all business, the tease.

He'd act as cool, one leg over the other. "I've come early, yes."

Marianne looked to each in turn. He'd arrived as she was in her studio so she was dressed in her painter's smock, daubed and smeared with paints of all colors of the rainbow. A spot of vermeil dotted her cheek. A bit of lapis lazuli decorated the back of her hand. "He telegraphed this morning that he wished to arrive in Paris early. So I invited him here straight away. It's what we hoped you'd agree to do, Pierce."

"Is that so?" he asked. "Why is that?"

"Rand and Corinne have wrestled Camille into doing their bidding at entertainments. We thought we'd put all the children together here and give your mother and father and Lily and Julian a holiday. It would be great fun for the children, plus I hoped you might give me a chance to go help Remy with the placing of the sculptures."

"Happy to," he said and caught Camille's eye. "You're good with children."

"Hmmm," she said and smoothed her skirts. "As you always said."

He gave a laugh. "Did I?"

She locked her gorgeous chocolate eyes on his. "Because —you said—I was one."

"Ah. Well. That was long ago!"

"Two years ago," she corrected him.

"You two," Marianne said as a footman entered with a tea tray, "must stop your rivalry."

He raised his brows at that. "Is that what it is?"

Marianne paused, thought a moment and blinked. "Isn't it?"

"His eternal teasing," Camille put in, the glint in her eyes part challenge, part denial. "We'll stop. Won't we, Pierce?"

Indeed we will. This relationship is changing, by God. And soon.

That night after dinner, Camille excused herself. She hoisted her skirts and took the grand staircase at a run.

Soon, quite soon, she would scream if she didn't get away from Pierce. He'd driven her to flights of fantasy all through the meal. Discussions of his clients, his new projects and his life in Shanghai fascinated Remy and Marianne. Meanwhile, Camille had amused herself with imaginary conversations with him about how she'd like to have him first. In a bed? On a chaise? In a garden, roses in her hair and thorns pricking her thighs!

She gulped back laughter. Fought back her visions of him

naked, his arms around her, him inside her. Oh, hell. She ran more quickly.

"Stop!"

At the sound of his voice, she grabbed the rail and spun. He was running up the stairs two at a time.

"What are you doing?" she hissed. "You can't leave right after me."

He wrapped one arm around her waist and urged her up toward the landing. "I had to. I couldn't watch you any longer and not touch you."

He backed her up to the wall and one of the frames of a portrait of Remy's ancestor nudged her scalp.

"Let me go, you idiot. This painting is coming down on my head and you can't—"

But he did. He kissed her. Her arms went around his shoulders and her heart hammered. She hauled him closer. He spoke on her lips and whatever he said tasted of raw desire.

"We can't do this." Was she pleading or ordering him? No matter. She grabbed his hand. "Come upstairs."

They both ran along the hall and she led him to her own rooms. But reason raced in her head. It won the night when she flattened herself to her outer door and spread her arms against it like an altar sacrifice. "You can't come in."

He nudged his knee between her legs and pressed his very aroused body to her compliant one. His lips were on the bare skin of her collarbone and his breath, hot and heavy, warmed her even as his hands, sure and seductive, slid along her ribs and cupped her derriere. He crushed her to him, his impressive erection calling forth her loud moan.

But with a ferocious curse, he was gone.

She opened her mouth wide to let out a silent scream.

Then beat the door with the back of her fists and went to bed!

He went down early to breakfast, Very early. Six-thirty. And he lingered. For more than two hours. The butler and footmen surely thought him daft or very ill-informed. He'd read every word of four morning newspapers.

She finally appeared. Nonchalant and breezy, she flounced into her chair with a little wiggle of her elegant brows.

He swallowed the urge to scoop her up and take her down to the table for morning kisses.

When the footman left to the kitchens to fetch her a fresh pot of tea, Pierce picked up his own much-used coffee cup and saucer, moved next to her at the intimate circular table and sat down.

"You are very late," he accused.

"So are you." She batted her long brown lashes at him like an artless child.

"I waited."

She picked up her napkin, put it in her lap and asked, "Are you ready to go to see the giraffe?"

"Is that what we're doing today?"

"And an octopus."

"Lots of legs." He mused about what he'd like to do with hers.

She snorted. "I thought you said you were going to meet your partners. A business meeting, hmm?"

"I put it off."

"A problem?" she asked, seduction in every syllable.

"Yes. But I can deal with them. It's us I am concerned with."

She glanced about as if she'd spy the problem out there in the world. "Nothing wrong there."

He examined her with narrowed lids. "But there is."

"What?"

"I want you without all your pretty finery." He reached out to flick the butterfly sleeve of her morning dress. "I envision you only in your skin."

She shivered, the smile on her face one Salome must have used. "I do hope I'm flawless."

His guts churned with his need of her. "You are."

"I want to equal you," she whispered.

He couldn't help himself. He caught her chin to brush his mouth on hers. "I'm busy searching for a good place for us to go."

Her pink lips parted. Her eyes met his in erotic longing. "Do hurry."

"I'm trying."

"Good," she said, licked her lower lip and ground her pretty bottom into her chair. "Because you are a terrible actor."

He ground his teeth. "I'm going to pay you back for this."

"You'd better!"

The next day, the two of them took the family's large landau and escorted Rand and Corinne to the Left Bank and the Catacombs.

The skulls were piled floor to ceiling. The explanation by the docent at the entrance was that this was the burial ground for plague victims of centuries gone by. But Rand was quick to grieve over the many who had died in the Terror.

"Our aunts and uncles," he said with wild eyes and the ghoulish delights that only an eight-year-old boy can find in gruesome bits of lore.

The dampness and gloom was not improved by the odd

breezes that wafted through the tunnels and blew out the lamp that Pierce held.

But Pierce's arm around her waist did inspire a laugh.

His lips on the back of her neck had her nipples hardening.

But when she sneezed, he grew alarmed.

"Take this," he told her as the flames inside her flickered. "Let me give you my coat."

"No, no. Let's just collect them and leave."

He was ready with an offer they could not refuse. "Hot chocolate and cakes!"

And the two children headed for the exit.

The following morning, Camille returned to *Monsieur* Daumier's office to ask more questions about his offer. Might she start at any time? What if she didn't want to remain in France a full year? Might she still take advantage of his generosity for less than a year?

That afternoon, Pierce and she escorted the two children to the Parc de Chaumont. One cannon, well rusted, amused Rand. A military band arrived, marched in order to a stand, played a few ditties and left. Rand grumbled. He was cheated! Sweets from a patisserie helped assuage his loss.

At tea time, they arrived home at Rue de Rivoli to learn from Remy's butler that Marianne had received a telegram from Killian in London. He announced the family would arrive at rue Haussmann tomorrow afternoon and all, children included, were invited there to an early dinner tomorrow night at eight.

The butler passed over to her the telegram. "*Madame* says you or *Monsieur* Hanniford know how to communicate this dinner invitation to your friends."

The invitation her stepfather extended was to Mister Lee Macfarlane and Lady Brianna.

But Killian also wanted them to know that he'd invited another couple and their daughter. Camille had met the young woman years ago at a house party. She was good company and accomplished at the piano. An American heiress of a reputed one-hundred thousand dollars or more, she was also outspoken. It was the reason she'd not yet landed a proposal from the gentleman titled enough to impress her parents. The home of the Randolphs was Hampton Roads Virginia, distant relatives of the famous American Randolphs. They'd lived in London for three years now. Looking for Eleanor's prospective husband. Making new contacts for her papa who had made his fortune building merchant marine ships of huge proportions. They rivaled Killian's transports in size, sales and quality.

So the night would be partly about business. Killian's. Pierce's. And perhaps even Lee Macfarlane's.

Camille had a good idea that the evening would also be about Eleanor's search for a match. And the lady was not shy about letting her preferences be known. Pierce would be her quarry. After all, he might not have a title or English blue blood, but he had looks and millions in his bank account.

The evening promised to be lively—and irritating.

CHAPTER 17

The dinner was the usual deluge of laughter and conversation. The room was chock full of children and adults. Remy and Marianne had come only to greet everyone briefly beforehand, then left to supervise the last-minute details of his exhibit tomorrow. The addition of the Randolphs, jovial folks, added to the joy of it. Then too because Eleanor was so far down the table from Pierce, her presence and her interest in him, the only single man at table, was negligible. Camille breathed more easily.

"How did your own show go, Mama?" Camille was able to get her mother alone to ask after dinner.

"Quite well. And I am grateful to you for finishing the acquisitions in London. I could not have done it without you." She cupped Camille's cheek—and Camille was thrilled that her bruise had largely disappeared. "I say. Are you well? You seem tired. Are you certain you want all the children? Neither you nor Pierce is used to that commotion!"

"It's only for two days. They are yours again the morning after the ball. I am off to visit a friend in Tours that morning." That was a lie, but her mother accepted it only with a question.

"Very nice. Do I know this person?"

Quite well. "A school friend. Dorothy Scarborough."

Liv thought on that a moment. "The American girl from…Ohio, was it?"

"Exactly."

"Hmm. Didn't she marry an Irishman from Tipperary?"

Dear God, had she? Camille should have investigated who to fib about.

"Yes," her mother said. "And he has some connection to the pretenders to the French throne."

"He does? I didn't know. How wonderful. Or is it, eh?" She had to get away. "Excuse me, please, Mama. I must have a word with Lady Brianna."

Her escape to Brianna brought her relief of a sort. Her mother, however, had frowned over the fate of Dorothy from Ohio. If Doro had in fact married some chap from Tipperary, Camille was now officially stupid for having forgotten. Not the way she wished to leave Paris. Well, what could she do now but try to cover her tracks?

"You do not look well, Camille." That from Brianna was no help at all!

"I'm not ill. Or perhaps I will be. Can you tell me if you remember Doro Scarborough from finishing school?"

Brianna stared off into space, collecting her thoughts. "Blonde. Pretty. But her teeth were…"

"Yes. Protruded."

"Poor thing. She had trouble speaking. Her s-s were caught in her tongue."

"Did she…" Lord, she hated to know. "Did she marry a man from Tipperary?"

"He loved horses? Yes. Yes, she did marry him. Sweet fellow."

Camille ran a hand over her brow.

"I say, you are not yourself. What's the matter? Headache? Chills?"

"No. No. I am fine. Really. I just had forgotten that Doro had married."

"Lucky girl. He loves her madly. Quite rich, I understand. Breeds racing stock and has notable French relatives in the bargain."

"He does?" Camille grabbed Brianna's hand. "Fabulous. Where? Do they visit?"

Brianna was alternately amused and confused by her words. "Yes. She and Lord...what was his name? A second son who inherited. Papa knew the first son, hated him. But Doro's man is a swell fellow. His family have French relatives in the Loire Valley somewhere. Why? What is the matter with you?"

"The Loire. Oh, thank heavens. Tours is in the Loire." Her mother couldn't be too upset with her.

"It is indeed. Why are you concerned about Tours?"

"Oh. Well. Because I...I am...going there myself."

"Is that so?" Brianna pulled back, skeptical. "When?"

"Soon."

"I see." Brianna arched a brow. "Why?"

"I.... It's a secret."

"Good to know. Why?"

Camille struggled with an answer. "Because it is."

"My goodness. Is it really so? You do! Ha! You have a gentleman."

Camille sank into the settee. "Am I so transparent?"

"You? Yes!" She chuckled. "A man for Camille."

Camille widened her eyes. "Please don't."

"An affair will be good for you. Who is he?"

Camille shook her head. "I can't tell you."

Brianna pressed a hand to her heart. "I am almost insulted."

"Don't be."

"No, I won't. I won't because I know." She paused to scan the room and lit upon the tall, dark elegance of Pierce in his swallowtail evening suit. "It is he."

Camille could've turned to stone.

"It is then! Congratulations, darling. He is superb."

"You don't understand."

"I do, sweet girl." She patted her hand. "I definitely do. Enjoy him, whatever you do. Enjoy him and take him forever if you wish him. It's what I would do. Will do."

"Really? What are you going to do? I am concerned about you. Pierce has told me you'll travel with Lee."

"I will. I am. We go to Berlin Monday."

"Is that wise? Have you thought it through?" She took Brianna's hands in her own.

"I have. Most thoroughly. In fact, I've news for you. On Monday morning in the Paris City Hall, I will marry Mister Lee Warren Macfarlane of Shanghai."

"Marry!" Camille squeezed her hand, delighted and full of fear for her friend. "Oh, that's wonderful. Wonderful. I am so very happy for you."

Brianna's eyes rested on the man who would become her husband. "I love him. He is everything I need. Adventurous. Kind. Ethical. And totally mine."

"Oh, Brianna. And have you told your family?"

"I wrote just this morning. My father will read my letter first thing tomorrow. Thereafter, you will hear this ghastly explosion from across the Channel."

"He'll not approve, will he?" Camille knew the answer to this, having heard Brianna speak of her narrow-minded family for many years.

"Of course not. He's interested only in his own self-defined sterling connections. At the news, my father—God deliver me from him—will suffer a stroke. My mother will put a finger in the air and forbid the match. A Chinaman as her son-in-law. Disgusting! And as for my brother, he will embrace any creature who has deeper pockets than he has. Insurance, you see, against his debts, his spendthrift wife and his own failures to make the estate earn profit."

Brianna inhaled and caught the gaze of her intended across the crowded room. What passed between them was love and comfort for she reflected that to him in her own smile. "Lee has come to me at a perfect time. A moment when I am my whole self, assured of that, and old enough that they cannot destroy the marriage nor take my inheritance from me. Not that I need the money. It is, quite pitiful compared to the sums that Lee has earned. No. I do not need my family's approval. Nor their money. In fact, the day may come when they need mine. I love Lee Macfarlane and he loves me. We will be wed Monday morning. Then I am his, and he is mine for every day thereafter."

"I applaud your courage."

Brianna gazed at her squarely. "You can claim your own."

"I feel like a school mistress herding all these children into the carriages." Camille plunked her hands on her hips as Liam boarded and took a seat beside Rand in the black lacquered coach.

Pierce shot her a look that told of his own frustration. Whose idea was this that we take them all?"

"Mine? Marianne's? I forget," she said with a wince, fanning herself with her straw hat.

"Their parents will owe us for decades to come. Ah! Ah!!"

He spun to catch Dylan by the collar and turn him back toward one of the two landaus.

"I cried off for any expeditions tomorrow. We won't go anywhere," she said as she handed Lily's youngest, Beth, the doll that Liam had taken from her.

"Good. Because I have to go talk with my French staff again tomorrow."

"You can't help me with this menagerie?"

"For an hour or so. But I'll return afterward."

"I might not be alive," she said, closing one eye and glaring at him.

"I promise to bring macarons."

"If you bring two dozen from Ladurée, I will forgive you your absence!"

He grinned and flourished a hand. "Your favorite flavor, *Mademoiselle?*"

"Strawberry. With French vanilla cream."

The journey from Rue de Rivoli to the Champs de Mars along the Seine took only ten minutes. Traffic was sparse mid-day as most Parisians chose the shade of linden trees or the comfort of cafes for luncheon.

As the two carriages—one with Camille in charge, the other with Pierce—pulled to the grassy expanse where the iron tower by Eiffel rose, the children went silent. Their mouths open, each boy and girl gazed upward to the bulging iron girders that had reached now the height equal to a building of two or three stories.

"We'll climb down now," Pierce announced to those in her carriage after his own had dismounted. "You must stay together. No running off. The workmen have their orders and their timetable. You must not interfere. And you will all line up here, single file and quietly observe."

Horses drew long carts with lattices of all widths and lengths. Men positioned huge swathes of iron to the foot of the cranes. Derricks stood at the four corners of the tower, sentinels to what it would eventually become.

"They began," Pierce said, "by drilling the foundation into the water-bed of the Seine."

"How can they do that, Uncle Pierce?" Garrett asked. "They'll be drowned."

"The tubes were air-tight, Garrett. They forced them into the river with steel drivers."

"When did they start to build this?" Dylan wanted to know.

"Last June," he told them all.

"More than a year and they're not finished," Camille said in awe, gazing up at the black iron beams that arched and bent and stretched at odd angles to the sky. "And yet it is lovely."

"I read the newspaper reports that it stands one hundred and fifteen feet high as of August fifteenth."

That was days ago. "Astonishing," she said "And they predict they will finish it in time for the May Exhibition."

"*Monsieur* Eiffel demands they embrace the schedule. During the winter, they worked nine hours each day. Now that it is warmer, they work twelve."

"That's exhausting."

"It is," he said, his gaze never leaving the cranes that rose inside the structure. "They are demanding higher wages."

"I would think they deserve it."

"I would agree. However, we do not know what the original contracts stated."

"Will Eiffel hold them to that?"

"I've no idea. But I will say that many laborers are coming

to the conclusion that they undervalue their own work at the beginning of a project."

"Human nature, I would say."

He stopped to consider her with a look of wonder on his face. "What do you mean?"

"We don't know what we're worth until we try it and excel at it. This," she said with her hands up, "will be a wonder of the world. More will attempt such lovely structures. And many will build them. Don't you think?"

He nodded, his expression stark.

"So then," she said. "The more skillful workmen become, the better compensation they demand."

"May I quote you?" He chuckled.

"Of course. To whom?"

"My partners?"

"You meet again. That must be an intricate proposal you have."

His silver eyes seemed to melt into hers. "I have quite a few I'm making."

"Do you?" she asked, breathless at his implications.

He inched closer. "I have a house for us."

Her whole body tingled at the idea. "Where?"

"A chateau in Amboise."

Amboise. Delightful little place. "A small town."

"Have you been there?" Dylan piped up.

She had to laugh and hope she did not blush. The boy had been listening! "Once I was there, yes. Years ago. A friend of mine had a little house near the one that was owned by Leonardo da Vinci."

Dylan frowned. "Who's he?"

"A famous artist. A painter."

"Like Aunt Marianne." The boy nodded, unimpressed.

When Dylan returned his attention to the workmen who were hoisting a huge iron girder up to the second story of the tower, Pierce leaned closer to her. "I will have a coachman call for you."

"At Gare de l'Est," she told him in a rush. "I know it should be Gare Montparnasse but that's what I told Marianne. I am sorry. I am nervous and not a good liar!"

Dylan spun to her. "Are we all going to Amboise?"

She swallowed laughter. "No. Just me."

"Why?"

This young boy was more inquisitive than was healthy for her! "I will visit a friend."

"Oh. Okay." He was back to his absorption with the tower.

Pierce cleared his throat and mouthed, "We'll talk more later."

That evening, with all the children at their suppers, Marianne, Remy, Pierce and she climbed into Remy's town coach for the short ride to the Rue Saint-Georges, the Galerie George Petit, and the joint exhibition of Remy's sculpture with the impressionist painter, Claude Monet.

Remy, usually so ebullient, was for such a large and assertive man, silent.

Marianne threaded her fingers through his own and touched her cheek to his shoulder. "A remarkable evening," she breathed and caught his smile.

He touched the end of her nose and winked at her. "There is a new piece for you, my love."

She was surprised but by her look, honored too. "Really?"

He gave one nod. "Truly."

She shivered in expectation, but put on a silly face. "Tell me. What am I? A barge upon the Seine?" She swept a hand over her stomach. "A Viking matron with shield and babies all around?"

He laughed, a booming sound that filled the carriage. But he directed his blue gaze to Pierce. "You see how I am plagued by disrespect?"

Pierce smothered a grin. "The best kind of disease."

Remy leaned over and kissed his wife on her cheek. "I will never be cured of her!"

Marianne took it with good cheer. "He is oppressive, this man I married. But you and I, Camille, will see what he has done and declare him an observant creature."

"Observant? Piffle!" Remy snorted as the carriage idled to a stop before the old Rococo building. "I had better be or I'd best retire to the south and devote my days to growing my children and crops!"

Marianne patted his hand. "And we know, my love, how well you would do that too. Come now. I want to greet *Monsieur* Monet. I understand he has done a new landscape and I wish to admire the brushstrokes. That way, I can regain my own humility. We need some, you see, Camille, in this family."

"Ba!" remarked Remy. "Humility! Out! Out now!"

Inside, the arrangement of Remy's life-size marbles and enormous bronzes juxtaposed with Monet's prodigious colorful paintings had Camille standing before so many, lost in the wonder of their creators' imaginations.

She walked about, happy to go alone to absorb the wealth of emotion in the works. She'd always admired and been enchanted by the scope and depth of Remy's creations. She'd seen so many. His Samson, blind and tormented by his failure to see the duplicity of the woman he loved. An Artemis, lovelier than any painting of her, rendered faceless but nonetheless seduction incarnate with her aggressive stance and a mark of a huntress. An agonized Job, sitting upon his pile of ashes, face raised to the heavens to ask God why he was punished so brutally when he'd been good, very good.

The complement of Monet's work, the gardens, the women, the people enjoying themselves, lifted up her spirits. She watched the man as he stood across the room, accepting the accolades of those in attendance.

She would never be this talented. This insightful. But she didn't mind. She didn't yearn for talent like this. She had her own and she was happy with it. She had her forte and her purpose. She had a greater landscape of her own to claim.

"You look pensive." Pierce came to her side and placed a flute of champagne in her hand. In his glistening gaze, she detected the edge of fear. "Are you reconsidering coming away with me?"

"Oh, no."

"Yet you seem far from me."

"I'm not. Not at all. Oh, don't you see? This acting is making me miserable. And I'm bad at it too."

"I thought you much too good!"

She laughed. "I will never agree to lie again."

"Thank God."

"Oh, Pierce." She admired him, his sleek tamed hair, his large iridescent eyes, the shape of his nose and the lush curve of his bottom lip. "I have to stay far away from you. I cannot be close for long or I will do shameless things. Put my hands on you. My lips. I want to be in your arms, your bed. I want all of you around me, inside me. So never say I do not want you. I cry without you near."

His expression was one she'd never seen. He turned toward the wall. "I'm afraid you have just undone me, my sweet. Stand here a bit, will you, and pretend we're speaking of the weather?"

She threw back her head to laugh, then sobered. "Ahem. Of course! What was I thinking when you approached me?"

"That's good. Yes."

"I'm appreciative of their work. All of them. I've always liked what Remy created. Marianne too. They are true artists. Like *Monsieur*."

"Do I detect there is a comparison in that statement somewhere?"

She took a sip of the very fine sparkling wine. "Yes. There is. A good one."

"Will you explain it to me?"

She tipped her head and hesitated.

"Now. Tell me now. Each second I have with you brings a new discovery. I fear I have not enough minutes left in my lifetime to learn every aspect of you."

She widened her eyes. His sentiments ran through her like strong red wine and she gathered her impressions. "I looked at Eiffel's creation today and thought how audacious of him to design such an unusual object to no purpose but its aspiration and its beauty. Though he says they will tear it down after the exhibition, I doubt it. So dramatic a structure will draw admiration from those not yet born."

She took a step toward Remy's newest sculpture, the homage to his beloved wife Marianne and what he spoke of during the carriage ride. Unmistakably she, the bronze was a replica of her, her head thrown back, her thick hair blown about by some unseen breeze, the smile on her face one of love and her hand caressing her pregnant belly. "I look at what Remy creates and Marianne paints and I value the emotions they draw from the beholder. Love, pride, pity are all there for the absorption and edification. These works are art for the ages."

He narrowed his gaze on her. "And your view of your own work?"

She demurred and considered the champagne in her

glass. "An amusement. Enjoyable. But not durable. Not..." She swept a hand toward the Monet on the wall. "Not this."

"I've read the novels I bought in the Lanes. I plan to read all you've written. But I think—"

She put up a hand. "Do not praise me out of hand."

"I've no intention to," he shot back. "I would not lie to you."

She inhaled and fortified herself for his assessment. "Very well. Tell me then."

"You write well. And your readers have proven that. Your income grows. And this French publisher? You've not told me about your meetings."

"No."

"Whatever he said, you need not tell me now. But one thing I glean from his invitation is that he would not have asked to meet you if your work had not impressed him."

"That's true," she admitted.

"Then you think your writing is not worthy of...what? The Champs de Mars?"

She grinned and shook her head.

"Not worthy of an exhibit with Marianne's and Remy's and Monet's?"

"I do not lie to myself, Pierce!"

"Well, then, do not denigrate what you do either."

"I do not pretend that what I create will inspire others for centuries. Nor do I imagine that many sit for hours to marvel at what I've imagined. I write romances about women who search for another to love and to struggle and to conquer the challenges they face. I do not change my readers' lives."

She paused as he gave her an arched look. "And?"

"I change their opinions of how to choose a partner. I encourage them to seize the power in that. I change at the least, the pleasure in their evenings." She turned to gaze at the bronze figure of Marianne. "And at the most, I change their attitudes toward themselves."

"And is that not what you have done for yourself?"

She studied him for a long silent time. "It is."

"And why you would really like to change women's lives more than their evenings? Run for Parliament? Change the world?"

She glanced away, honored by his insights and his attentions to her aspirations. "First I must be able to vote."

"You will."

She eyed him. "You have such faith."

"I know you, Camille Bereston. I have the privilege of observing your drive."

"I love that you don't object."

"Why would I? I have my own."

"That you do, sir!" She chuckled and drained her glass.

"I admire you, my darling. Never doubt it." He took a drink and purposely scanned the room for a very long look. "I think if I cannot demonstrate how well and soon, I will wither away."

"Do not think of it."

He gave an outraged laugh. "it's that or throw you over my shoulder and stride away like a caveman with my prize."

"How exciting!"

"What a scandal, eh?"

The courage that Brianna Price had claimed blossomed in her own heart. "We won't make one."

"No, my darling. We won't." And then he told her that he'd hired a carriage to meet her at the main entrance to the Gare de l'Est day after next at ten in the morning.

She gave a little shake of her head, barely able to look at him without walking into his arms. "Will you be in the coach?"

"I would not waste a moment without you."

By the time he assembled in the foyer of Marianne's and Remy's palace the next evening to enter the ballroom, Pierce was alive with nerves. He'd endured much too long knowing he was soon to enjoy Camille and watching her laugh with children and smile at others and tempt him. Tempt him with every glance. Every sigh.

Tonight, she strolled down the curving marble stairs in a gown that buckled his knees.

"Ravishing," he said as he lifted her hand to his lips. "The blue-green lights up your eyes."

"Monsieur Worth calls the color Adriatic. I call it expensive, but justifiable to see you approve."

As Marianne and Remy made their way down the hall toward their ballroom, he leaned closer to catch the fragrance of jasmine and honeysuckle. "When did you have time to visit him?"

She tugged on her elbow length gloves and teased him with a smile. "The first day I arrived. Afterward I had an appointment with Madame Villette, too."

The famous designer of lingerie. "I hope that visit was satisfactory."

"Hmm," she crooned as she looped her arm through his. "You must tell me."

"Tomorrow." He patted her hand. "Tomorrow."

CHAPTER 18

Camille stepped down from Remy's town coach at the
grand entrance of the Gare de l'Est and thanked the
groom for his kindness.

"Shall I hail a porter for you, *Mademoiselle?*"

"No, *merci,* Andre." The graying man, concerned, had long
been employed by the family. He was a jolly fellow whom she
had always liked. She hated to fib to him. "If you will put my
trunk and valise beside me, that will be good. I expect a
friend."

"I will wait with you then."

"That is not necessary, Andre. Most kind of you. But no
one will accost me here." She tipped her head toward the
chattering crowd gathering on the cobbles, many emerging
from cabs with their own luggage and boxes and bags.

"*Mademoiselle,* you have no maid. I fear for you."

"Andre, if someone wishes to attack me, a maid would be
no use. Besides," she offered and brandished her parasol. "I
have this!"

He grimaced and muttered a French curse.

Around the corner, a large black cab fit for country travel

202

rounded a lorry and another town hack. The window was open and inside, she was most certain, sat Pierce. She hoped he could see that Andre lingered. If Pierce had his coachman stop for her, Andre would know he and she departed together.

Every muscle in her body was alive with fear of discovery. "Honestly, Andre. You may leave me."

The man shook his head, climbed up into his box and flicked the reins at the two matching Percherons. Off he went with a doff of his hat.

The large cab that had idled at the corner approached behind an omnibus and stopped by her side. The cabbie climbed down, opened the door and lowered the step, then faced her with his hand out.

"My ride?" She peered inside at the man who welcomed her with a grin.

"I am indeed. Climb in, my lady."

And up she went straight into his embrace.

"Oh," she sighed against him, her head tucked under his jaw, his arms hugging her close. "I never thought to be here."

He put a finger beneath her chin and examined her eyes. "Nor I. It's been a devilish long time, but we'll make up for it."

Her gaze dropped to his lips. "Soon."

He pressed the flat of one finger to her lips. "I daren't touch you that way yet. Not yet. We've a train ride to endure."

Three hours later, they climbed down to the quay inside the tiny Tours railway station. Their trip to Amboise by horse-drawn coach took another hour.

She'd slept on the train trip, leaning against Pierce in their first-class compartment. She felt at peace with him on the train journey, having escaped the tensions of keeping this affair from their family. At his nudge and urging that they had arrived in Tours, she awoke refreshed. But at once wary of the moments to come, she could not look him in the eye. Dreaming of this for so long, the first thing she had always thought she'd do would be to make love to him. And now... now that the time was nigh, she worried that she would not know what to do or how or when to invite him to her bed.

As they approached on the north side of the river, the town spread across the wide Loire and the red brick curtain wall of the fortress of the medieval French kings, the Palace of Amboise spread along the banks.

"Oh," she said and squeezed his hand. "That is stunning. May we go inside?"

"I've no idea. I'm sorry. I did not think to ask my friend. I'll ask about in the town."

"Thank you." If he became bored with her, they could divert themselves with contemplating historical treasure. Or go back to Paris.

The coach crossed the little bridge and passed through the cobbled streets. A small patisserie sat on one corner, a cafe on another. A little girl sold flowers on the green. Then the village fell away and a long limestone wall curved into a circular drive to the front of a small chateau with the charm of the French Rococo and the colors of rose and white.

"It's lovely," she told him.

And he answered with a tight smile. "We have two servants at our disposal. A major domo and his wife who live in a small house to one side of the vegetable garden. The man is our butler and his wife, our cook. They are discreet and not in attendance in the chateau except for the mornings."

"*Monsieur Barrère*," Pierce greeted the young man when they stepped from the coach. "I am your guest, Mister Hanniford."

"My wife," the caretaker said in English, then with a nod at both Pierce and Camille, he turned toward his wife. "We are happy to receive you, sir. *Monsieur* De La Croix wrote to tell us you will stay for five days. Is this correct?"

"Indeed. My friend, *Mademoiselle* Bereston, and I are not demanding. A good breakfast, Coffee, bread and jams. An early evening dinner."

"My wife is an excellent cook, *Monsieur, Mademoiselle*. If there is anything you would like, we are at your service. And if you need anything at all that we have not provided, do come to us in our little house. We will happily provide."

At that he helped the coachman down with their two trunks and left the two of them to enter the chateau together.

The house was an elegant but cavernous creature. With two salons, one pale blue the other peach, one as grand as the other, the house trailed onward to a huge dining room fit to seat twenty at the long table. A smaller dining room stood at the back of the house and led onto a glassed-in orangerie whose doors opened to a veranda. The kitchen led off that small dining room. From the sunny orangerie, one could see the small house where the Barrères lived.

"Shall we tour the upstairs?" Pierce asked her as if to examine the house were the most normal thing to do.

At her agreement, they took the curving staircase up. The carving on the marble pillars denoted that once the house was owned by families who spent much time hunting and fishing. Animals of every size and sort and fish of every type stood in carved relief in the white marble that led up up up to the second floor. And there, to each side, west and east were two bedrooms separated by the central corridor. Both were of the same size. Each consisted of a dressing room, a smaller linen-hung toilette for bathing, plus the main suite, the bed huge, well hung with formal drapes reminiscent of the Empire style. As in the decor below, one bedroom was pale blue, the other peach.

"Which do you prefer?" he asked her when they stood beside the huge bed in the blue room.

That took her aback and at the same time told her he would not presume anything about this liaison. "The peach. I think whoever built the house intended the separation of the sexes that way."

"I would agree. Very well. I will inform the Barrères of that." He strolled about, commenting on the drawers and shelvings in the blue dressing room and admiring the porcelain fittings in the toilette. He turned the handles on the side of the giant porcelain tub. "I am impressed. They have installed new plumbing for running water." He looked up, following the line of a pipe. "Fed by a cistern to collect rain."

"That is surprising. I hope they have it in the other room, too." She hadn't had presence of mind to notice.

"If they don't, use this one."

"I will," she said with a grateful smile and felt the heat of a blush that crept up her cheeks.

"Why don't you go settle in to your suite and come join me in the orangerie when you wish."

He couldn't believe she was suddenly shy of him. Yet her body told him it was so. And he would not force her to any act she did not wish. He'd told her and in effect, promised. That still held.

Patience was his best solution. He went about his business of settling in, taking the opportunity to test the efficiency of the running water in the basin of his shaving sink which was fed by another cistern. He smiled and changed his clothes.

Refreshed, he went downstairs to see what Madame Barrère had put out for them.

He had visited the Loire River area only a few times. Never had he been to Amboise, but he liked the looks of the little town. Quiet, compact, it sat to one side of the ancient fortress of the palace where so many French kings had ruled. Even the two Napoleons had lived there for a spell. The lure of yesteryear drew him and he'd taken little time over the years to learn more about the past. The future had always consumed him.

Now the present did.

He prayed he had not misjudged the value of what he did here. For his own life, he had few questions. To Camille's best interests, he was devoted.

When she appeared in a flowing summer cotton gown of grass green printed with a thousand yellow butterflies, her hair loosely pinned and barefoot, he questioned if she was presenting him with the virtual innocent she was or the lover she wished to be.

Her large dark eyes took in the al fresco offerings upon the tiny round table. Cheeses of every color and shape, sausages, fresh strawberries, cucumbers, and pickled squash piled high and offered up with fresh baguettes. "I am hungry. Are you?"

"I am." *And while what I crave is not spread upon this table, I must discover if what I want is still on offer.*

He pulled out her chair and she sat, sending the fragrance of her jasmine to mix with his raging need to taste the skin beneath her earlobe or the pulse beat at her throat.

"I know what you think," she said, not looking at him but focusing out the window toward the veranda and the sunshine.

He dare not answer. Instead, he served himself from the array before them. His plate full, he waited.

"I'm here but hesitant. Not..." She swallowed and occupied herself with choosing cheeses and sausage tidbits for her plate. "Not because I've change my mind."

He contained the urge to groan his approval of that.

"I have not..." She faced him, her gaze locking on him for the first time in days. "I have not changed my mind." Her lashes fluttered. "How could I? I have never wanted any man as much as I want you."

A bit of bread stuck in his throat. He had to wash it down with a good swallow of fine white wine.

"I simply don't know how this is done, you see. I've never gone away with a man. I even debated after my bath, if I should put on my corset again."

He choked on his bite of bread then. And reached for his napkin. When he recovered, he stared at her.

And she giggled. "I didn't."

He nodded. His brows wrinkled in feigned horror. "I'm very glad."

"Oh good. I must say, I hate corsets."

It was his turn to chuckle. "Wise."

She rearranged her napkin in her lap. "I wish to never wear them again."

"Wiser still," he said seeking another good draught of wine.

"Tell me what you think of the house, really."

So they were making conversation, were they? What to say? "It's lovely."

"It's perfect," she said wistful. "The Barrères are, too. And far away."

"Unobtrusive," he agreed, his aspirations for their solitude this afternoon taking flights of fancy and encouraging his cock to stand tall and hard and beg for her.

Suddenly, she dropped a morsel of cheese to her plate. "Pierce?"

He tipped his head, the look in her eyes that of a cat in heat.

"Can we do this now?"

Now?

If he hesitated, he would vow afterward that he did not remember.

What he did recall was that she reached over to him, put her hand to his jaw and kissed him. Her lips were warm and tender, appealing to him with short sensual blessings to his mouth. He'd been approached by women before, but none with the bright allure of Camille Bereston's soft, warm lips to his own.

He wrapped his fingers around the bare skin of her upper arms and drew her flush to him. She made a little noise of delight and insinuated herself to sit on his lap. Her arms wended around his shoulders and her heavy pointed breasts with hard little nipples drilled into his chest. Her kisses grew longer, hotter as she settled against him and he cradled her near him.

She put her fingers to his shirt, dislodging buttons and her lips followed upon his bare skin.

God. He moved in his chair. He had to get up and out of here. But she was devoted, hunger in her lips now and he was gone to the desire she inspired.

He met her with his own madness, tongue in her mouth, the caress of her intimate flesh there what he wanted. Until he had to have more. And he caught her face in his hands. "My darling, you must stop."

"No," she whimpered and dropped her face to his shoulder.

"I mean to say, come upstairs."

"No." She pulled back, defiance hard on her face.

He would have objected.

But she shot to her feet and grabbed his hand. He

followed. Of course, he did. Where else would he go but with her, always.

She led him, a man enthralled, blind to whatever she wanted. She took paces and there before him, she unbuttoned the little hooks down the bodice of her charming gown, pushed the short sleeves from her shoulders and revealed to him the essence of Camille Bereston, naked, stunningly beautiful like a Venus from the sea. Her skin was cream. Perfection. Her arms, long, her fingers, too. Her breasts were full, her nipples large, larger than he had imagined, a pale rose satin he longed to lick and lave. Her waist was trim. Her belly slightly rounded. Her hips wide. Her thighs inviting. Her blonde hair over her mons a sweet v he promised he would honor with his fingers and his tongue.

"You are exquisite, my darling."

She shivered, her breasts quivering and her huge nipples beckoning him to still her desires with his lips to her there and everywhere.

Her offering deserved his own. He blinked, forcing himself to stop staring at her and do her the service of showing her all of him. He took down his braces, undid the rest of his buttons, tore off his shirt and dropped it to the carpet. His trousers came next and with an assist from her deft fingers, the garment drifted to the floor. But his damn shoes obstructed and for those he had to waddle to the nearest chair. Free, he stood and discarded his underclothes. His garters and socks, too.

But she waited, her arms crossed beneath the lovely wealth of her breasts with those nipples he intended to enjoy for the rest of his life.

He stood and pressed against her. The warm length of her aroused him to painful degrees. His hands cupping her breasts, he bent and took one large pink nipple in his mouth. His tongue ran over the chiffon of her skin and his knees grew weak. He lifted his face to peer into her eyes and unable to move on without a sample of her other breast, he lifted that one for the homage of his tongue and his teeth.

She arched against him, and the brush of her nether hair against his thigh was enough to make him wish he could take her on the floor.

He broke away. "Come upstairs."

"No," she said, her expression one of dire need. "Here," she pointed to the chaise longue by their side.

She'd found it. She'd seen it.

He'd not. He'd been so fearful she was leaving him. Instead, she was looking for locations to seduce him! Oh, what he needed to learn about her could fill libraries!

She twirled around and sat, then arranged herself like an odalisque. Her arms wide, Her shapely thighs open, he was going to die here a happy man.

One knee to the longue, he loomed over her. "You are the most unusual woman."

She gave a laugh. Her fingers traced up his ear and into the wealth of his hair. "I hope that's good."

"That's perfect," he whispered. Then he kissed her, his mouth taking all of her supple one. He nestled between her thighs, wishing he could wait longer to savor each inch of her with his tongue, but fearing his own release would come too soon to honor that. "I'm not able to wait."

"Ohhh," she crooned, "Please don't." She rubbed her breasts against his chest and arched up to press her mons against his groin. "We have days to go slowly. Days and days," she said and her words were lost in the kisses she bestowed.

He gave her kiss for kiss, but where was his reason? He'd brought letters. French Letters. But they were upstairs and this was now. Now. He hated the damn things anyway. "But I won't let you get pregnant."

She smiled, the smile of a naif. "Good, but do hurry,

darling. I am so very needy." And at that she wrapped her hand around his cock and the heat of her made him groan.

She drew him near and he found her core. She was wet and warm and when he entered just a bit, she arched into him. He sank further inside. And oh. She was succulent, silken.

He sank further and she was his. His.

She found his mouth and kissed him with a fervor that tore into his brain. God, he had never had the pleasure of making love. Not like this. Never like this.

The urge to move was primal. He kissed her and the madness of what they were together burned through him like a fire. He sank inside her once and then again, each time deeper, dearer. She urged him on, her nails scoring his skin.

She moved with him, her lithe body his solace and storm. She cried out and he knew he had to give her more. He fingered her slick little folds and found the nub that would give her the heights she sought. She bucked and moaned. His. She was totally his.

He told himself to stop. Stop.

And he pulled away.

Later—much later—he grabbed his shirt from the floor, then went to find a pitcher, water, cloths to clean her skin and his own.

She cupped his cheek and searched his gaze for the answer to some question that clouded her eyes.

"What is it?" he asked, dropping a kiss to her palm.

"That was…" She rolled a shoulder, confused. "I have no words."

"Nor I, my darling." He let the playful side of him emerge,

the one few saw, the one he had so little call for...until now. "We will call it indescribable."

"And worthy of repetition?"

He burst out laughing. "Indescribable and worthy of repetition! Of course. I will go to my grave repeatedly enjoying such indescribable pleasure."

~

To live with him night and day set her aflame. She could think of nothing else but the delight of his hands, the joy of his mouth, the ecstasy of his body on hers, in hers. He was everything and more she had never hoped to claim. The idea of him as hers was such a fantasy that this idyll with him approached a heaven she had questioned but now believed existed here on earth only with him.

He was a careful lover, tender and considerate. He was an ardent one, demanding and after that first comparatively short coupling, became a man of many ingenious means to bring her to fulfillment. Indeed, she had not imagined the variety and versatility of how men and women could pleasure each other.

But he was skillful, good natured, and she allowed and welcomed from him every exciting moment. His hands on her hips, his lips on her breasts, his mouth on her most intimate places, his cock inside her for long luscious minutes, as he feasted on her skin and told her tales of how next they'd enjoy each other. Sitting cross-legged on the carpet, spread across his huge bed in the blue room or on the chaise longue in the flower garden, the sun bright on their faces, he buried deeply inside her...and only to the point where he would not bring her consequences they did not intend.

The day before they were to leave, she ignored her dread of their parting. She rolled into his embrace as they lay upon the bed and traced with one finger the perfection of his bones. He caught her finger and bit her. She kissed him—and he reached for her and rolled her beneath him. Once more, they'd have each other.

She loved him. Simple and forthright, she could tell anyone. Though she had not yet told him, she would save it. Decide if she should employ it. But only if she thought it beneficial. And she would not use it to persuade him to any action. No, she would not. Nor would she bargain with herself about any ending. If he loved her, he would say. If not, then not. She would accept it. Had vowed it.

But today, she wanted something different. Other memories to mark the ending, a set of images that told her of the normality of life.

They had awakened late, the sun rising to midpoint and bathing the world in the glory that was in the lush valley of the Loire. They strolled to the village, hand in hand, and paused to marvel at the white limestone and pink brick chateau along the lane that once had belonged to the artist Leonarado da Vinci. He'd agreed to come to France to the Court to work for Francis the First and it was here after two years, Da Vinci had died. The house, given to him by Francis, remained the property of the French monarchs until the Revolution. Pierce had no knowledge of who owned the lovely little house.

There as they considered the career of that famous artist, Camille told him the details of the offer of her French publisher Daumier. "The chateau is in a town west of here. Blois. It's another town like Amboise, small, old, once a center of the French monarchy. But the house comes with two servants, so that would be helpful."

"Have you accepted?"

"I told him I would consider it."

"It is a fine offer. I don't know how many such offers an

author receives. Is it not practice to simply pay on acceptance of a manuscript for publication?"

"It is. Plus the offer of a house and an annuity is unusual."

"What holds you back?" he asked, turning toward her, his black hair glistening in the summer sunshine.

I want to live with you. Go to Shanghai. Live anywhere you are. And yet, I also want to have my own ambitions, not live through yours. And since she had no resolution yet for her own personal desires, she had to approach discussing those elements with him with care. "I am not certain I want to live in France and I don't know this town of Blois," she said, and that was part of the truth. "I love London, family. My readers. My work with women's rights. How can I live here apart?"

He frowned at that. "I understand. And I commend you for admitting to wanting all of that. What makes you whole is the sum of all your talents and ambitions. I know that well."

"I think you do."

"I have my own desires. Had, perhaps, indulged in too many of them. Now I must trim them. Make my days more..." He waved a hand and sighed. "Manageable."

Too late she realized she might have given him the wrong impression. That she would not go anywhere. That she would not have him, not consider living with him. "Much to ponder."

"For us both." He pushed a lock of her hair from her cheek. "Let's go to the curtain wall, shall we? I want to climb up and see the line of the river flowing past."

When they returned to the chateau, aperitifs had been laid out for them. Cheeses and breads and wine. But Camille was hungry for him. Only him.

She excused herself when they arrived and ran upstairs.

Quickly, she drew a bath and afterward, donned her dressing gown and nothing else. Then she went downstairs.

He was standing on the patio, quite still, gazing at the garden and drinking wine.

When she drew his attention, she smiled. "Come inside. I need you," she whispered.

And he followed.

She led him toward the chaise longue where first they had made love.

A quizzical look on his face, he sat down and she crawled up over him, her legs spanning his. She was brazen, outrageous to do this, but she wanted to lead today. Needed to lead. She bent and kissed him.

He caught his breath. "When we go home, I want to change so much, Camille. I've too much to order. So much to correct. I've lived trying to control too much. I fear I've made mistakes."

Alarm ran through her like ice. He couldn't mean this was a mistake, could he? Did not these days together convince him of the rightness of what they were together? She put two fingers to his lips. "No words of parting, please."

He kissed her fingertips. "None. Ever."

Whatever he decided, whatever she decided she wanted for a full life, even if they broke apart now, to one extent or another, they'd always be a part of each other's lives. The family would meet and strive and celebrate together for decades to come. It was what they were together, what they valued when apart. Pierce and she were as much participants in that family as any of the others. "I want to remember you as you are now."

"Do you? As do I." His silver eyes burned with fond desire. "I will remember each sigh, each laugh, each exquisite arch. The geography of you." He put the flat of his palm to her breastbone and slid it down to her waist. "I love the valleys of you as much as the heights."

She grinned, wiggled at his touch and arched her neck.

"You are fine and lovely country, my darling. This valley here." He slid his palm up between her breasts to her throat and on to the hollow behind her ears. "The delicate one here…and here." His hand lifted one aching breast. "And this." He dipped his finger in her belly button. "Here is a lovely valley." The crook of her knee he caressed and she sighed. "And this." He smoothed his hand to her core, fingered one frilly fold and made her grab breath. "And this one." He slid his fingertip along the length of another. "But this one…" He sank two fingers inside her and she heard the succulent parting of one fold from another as he slid up and circled the button that brought her so much delight. "This one is my favorite valley."

A second later he brought her the release she sought and minutes later, she fell against him. He turned her, taking her beneath him and opening the placket of his trousers. "But I love the peaks of your lovely landscape too, my girl. And how you climb them with me." At that he sank his penis inside her and she undulated beneath him. "I want you, sweetheart. All the time. Each day. Each night."

He proved it to her then. A glorious culmination of all he'd shown her was hers in that one moment of love.

Minutes later, he brushed her hair from her cheeks and peered at her. "I want more than this, Camille. I want more than five days with you."

Her heart beating like a drum, she caught her reason. Was this what she'd waited for from him?

He threaded his fingers through her hair. "I hate that I have things I must settle. With my French colleagues. With Victor. With my father."

"I don't understand what you're saying."

"Give me some time. I cannot properly do right by you until I can take good care of my businesses. Give me time."

Her disappointment was tempered by his bargain. She could not wait for months or years. She'd already waited much of her lifetime for him. "How much? How long?"

He shook his head. "A week. Two. Three, most likely. I must talk with Victor."

"You'll go to Brighton?"

"I must."

She looked away but tears stung her eyelids.

"Don't cry, my darling. I never want you to cry."

"Can you…will you tell me what you discuss?"

"I can." He got up, offered her his hand and pulled her to her feet. "I think we need our clothes for it, though."

She snorted and reached for her robe and his shirt.

Minutes later, he told her of his worries that he had made mistakes to negotiate a deal with the French steel makers for Lee Macfarlane and him. "I've priced the steel too low. To make it affordable for the Chinese, I priced it too low. I'm not sure Lee or Victor will approve. And Lee has gone to Berlin so when he returns to Paris, I must meet with him to remedy that."

"And how is Papa involved in this?"

"He isn't. That is a different problem. I promised him when I first returned home that I would help him with a laborers' dispute in Liverpool. I am to be the negotiator. Those meetings are to be in two weeks."

"I see."

"I don't want to leave you like this. And I feel as though I cannot offer for you in limbo as I am."

She didn't understand why he couldn't make a decision about their future without settling his business issues. Would his business matters always come before his personal ones? Before her? Could she live like that?

He pressed his lips together, his expression stark. "And you have decisions to make, too. Will you accept Daumier's offer? Do you want to stay here in France to live for a year? Or more? And what of your other ambitions to be influential in politics? Does one limit the other?"

"I haven't made any decisions on those. I wanted only to be with you."

"Then we are the same."

She saw his point. But she didn't have to be happy about it. The fact that they had no resolution at the end of their affair, tortured her. "We are."

The next morning, his departure hung over her like a shroud. Still she would not utter the fears that consumed her. Instead, she threw herself into absorbing her last minutes with him.

As it was, they had to rush to the train station in Tours. They'd lingered much too long at breakfast and dressing and kissing goodbye at the house. Monsieur Barrère had obtained a carriage from the village that took them the twenty-odd miles to the small station. They arrived just as the train going south from Paris arrived.

They got to the quay and conscious of the crowds around them, they stood apart and waited for the southbound Paris passengers to disembark. But as it became clear that their minutes dwindled to nothing, Pierce looked into her eyes and snaked an arm around her waist to press her near. He was all warmth, all passion, all the love she'd ever wanted for herself alone. They shared one glorious last kiss, his lips tender and yet possessive.

"That will keep us both, I hope, until you arrive back in

Paris," he said, more jovial than his sad gaze told her. "Two days."

"Not long at all," she lied because she missed him already and he was but inches from her. She put a brave face on it just as from the corner of her eye, she glimpsed a finely dressed woman gaping at them.

Camille pulled away from him, her heart in her throat.

"Oh my! Lady Barnet!" Camille tried for light-heartedness.

"How good to see you," the woman remarked. But the lift of her brows and the tip of her head declared she knew that the scene she'd just witnessed was not that of affection between step-siblings.

Pierce acted as polite and politic as ever. "Lovely to see you, my lady. And you sir," he said to her husband.

The man grumbled the usual nonsense when one does not recall the other's name.

Pierce turned to Camille and with tight lips said, "Smile at her with friendship in your eyes."

She did as best she could but feared she failed.

The porter blew the whistle. Pierce turned for the steps up into his compartment, gave her one last loving look and was gone.

Others drifted to and fro around her.

She stayed only a moment. After all, one didn't linger after saying goodbye to one's brother.

But Lord and Lady Barnet had seen more in that half minute than mere affection.

Camille knew it and now far more than she had feared in London when Aldridge Connor had been so uncouth, she was shaken that here her actions had given far more proof to Connor's accusations.

How could she live this down?

She strode away, angry at herself. Climbing up into the

rented carriage to take her back to Amboise, she threw herself into the squabs and clenched her teeth. She cared not about critics of her novels. People loved them or they didn't. Her moral reputation she did care about. Immensely. Used to holding her head up in social circles, used to pride in her mother, pride in the Hanniford clan, pride in her own simple accomplishments, she had known she could never wear well the mark of a fallen woman. Nor would she bear up well under scrutiny of one who had seduced her step-brother. For that blame, like so much else in this world, would go to the woman, not the man. Men were entitled to tarry and roam. Encouraged to it, for their own education, poor excuse that it was. Women could not afford the chance they would pay dire consequences for their indulgences. Pregnancy was a hard load to bear without a concerned partner, a husband, a father. Raising a child was doubly as difficult.

The driver flicked the reins and the horses left the station.

There in the seclusion of that carriage, she was aware that the sun had hidden behind a few clouds, that the day grew darker. But as she looked out upon the passing trees and saw the rushing Loire drift past, she decided that she would never give up her support for women's equality. She might love a man to fierce distraction but she would never allow that to deter her from the effort she'd always believed was her higher calling. She could love Pierce, could support him in all his endeavors, negotiations, building projects, here or to the ends of the earth, but so too she deserved the same from him.

And if he truly loved her, then he would acknowledge her right to pursue those goals.

Her challenge would be to find a way to do that, wherever they lived.

And only as his wife.

CHAPTER 19

*A*s his train headed north toward Paris, Pierce sat alone in his first-class compartment. The verdant French forests whizzing past his windows in a spectrum of greens and browns inspired contemplation of a thriving future with a woman he enjoyed and admired. This was the quietude he always sought to sort his life.

Devoted to ordering his options, listing positive and negative probabilities, he had promised himself this time. He'd concentrate on the same reasoning about his personal life that he'd given every business he'd ever made. His days and nights with Camille had not been conducive to that. He'd been too randy, too taken with her, too enthralled to demand reason of himself. Charmed by her and his irrepressible drive to make love to her, he now needed to be alone. Alone with his mind on logic, his body cool and composed.

He always thought he'd make a terrible husband. Too obsessed with work. Too devoted to every small detail to make a business blossom. What woman wanted a man who was never there? His father served as the fine example. From his childhood, he recalled that his father would order his days so that he was home for breakfast and home for supper. Then after Pierce's mother died, his father hired a manager for the shipyards and for the factories in the port of Baltimore and made the same commitments to his three small children and his niece. Pierce as an adult with his own commitments had never perceived how his father had regimented himself to order that. But Pierce grasped its importance now. After days with Camille, he understood love as he had not before. Proper nurturing required time and attention, nothing taken for granted. His gratitude to his father grew even as his love for Camille did.

The rendezvous with Camille in one way had not been his finest hour. He winced at the admission. But it was true and he never shrank from truth. Guilt however was not an emotion with which he had much acquaintance. His affairs, few as they had been, had been nigh unto business agreements themselves. Grounded in sex, they were strictly regulated, formally agreed to and then officially dissolved when the attractions withered. His fixation on Elanna, the ill-fated Countess of Carbury, had been his irrational obsession with a woman who knew no order or discipline. How a woman lived like that— how anyone could—bewildered and appalled him. He fixated on her, he had concluded lately, more to learn how to avoid that than to think he could ever survive loving her.

Finally, there was May Macfarlane. His love for May had been more admiration than desire. He smiled to himself, remembering her selflessness, her quiet dignity in life and death. Perhaps May's fortuneteller had been right. He would go on to become more whole with another woman. For surely, what he felt now when he looked into Camille Bereston's eyes resembled nothing he'd ever experienced before.

Oh, yes, he'd noticed a different Camille the minute he walked down the gangplank of the *Manchu Empress* weeks ago. He'd met her when she was a girl. Coltish and buoyant, she'd been irreverent and a challenge, even an irritant. As she'd grown, she'd matured into the stunning creature she was today. All ebullience and dedication, yet careful of her reputation and devoted to her family. His family. Her family. No shallow girl bent on capturing some lust-dazed fellow and hying off to the countryside for the rest of her days, Camille had built a career for herself. Done well at it. If indeed she wished for more, even a career in politics, he applauded that.

What he had done all his life was strive for more, better, finer. What he could do, so could a woman. May had wanted that for herself in her own culture, in her own way. Now before him was Camille who climbed different barriers, fought other restrictions.

He could help her. If she wished it. He could ease her way. If she let him.

But if she didn't, if she barred him, that was fine with him too.

Because he loved her.

He would treasure her. Admire her. Encourage her.

Marry her.

And adore her.

For the rest of his life.

But now in Paris, he'd settle his own affairs. He would write to Victor and describe the change of administration he had decided was imperative for them both for their Shanghai company. He would argue for his own assessment and hope Victor could agree and soon. Much had to do with Lee Macfarlane. To that end, Pierce would also wire Lee Macfarlane to alert him to the necessity of a meeting in Paris before he and his new wife boarded a steamer for New York. If Pierce's plans for the future of his Shanghai business were to succeed, he'd need Lee's agreement and insights.

First in Paris however, Pierce had to visit with his father. Mark the changes there that meant a different dynamic in the family when his father's step-daughter also became his daughter in-law. And Pierce's own step-mother, became his mother-in-law. Both would welcome the news of his marriage to Camille. Of that he was certain. For both of them had big hearts and open minds.

He caught his reflection in the window glass and frowned.

Camille would have him, wouldn't she?

He hadn't asked. Hadn't declared himself. He needed to be grounded in his own matters first. Or he had thought it to be so. What if he'd been wrong?

A stabbing pain shot through him. To have had Camille as he did for days in lavish rapture and then to think she might not want him, might refuse him, eviscerated him.

She hadn't said she loved him.

But she did.

He loved her.

And in a few days, he would prove it to her.

The following morning, Pierce appeared at Rue Haussmann and requested to see his father. Arriving late yesterday afternoon at Gare Montparnasse and not wishing to return to Marianne and Remy's house, he had hired a carriage, crossed the Seine and taken rooms at the Hotel Meurice in the Rue de Rivoli last night.

The butler showed him upstairs without delay.

"Thank you for seeing me, Papa."

"Of course. Why not?" He greeted him with open arms and extended a hand toward the visitor's chair. "Did you return yesterday? Come in. Come in!"

"I did. I am not with Remy and Marianne. I chose not to disturb them at the odd hour of my arrival. But I would like to talk with you at length this morning, if you have no other appointments."

Killian met his gaze with a measure of curiosity. "I have no other commitments. You haven't said how your trip was."

"Enjoyable." Pierce sat, facing the man he'd admired since a child. A man he tried to emulate, even in business. Now even in his private life. He'd told him little detail about his trip, whom he was to meet or where or why. Even now, Pierce wished to keep the experience of his time away to himself. He doubted his father would press him for descriptions. Because his father was not intrusive, did not however mean he was blind. Pierce had predicted that his father and Liv would realize that he and Camille had left town together. Perhaps even that they had planned it a while ago. He had gone away without his valet and she had sent her maid Ivy away for a vacation.

Pierce cleared his throat, ready for the discussion that he hoped would go without contretemps. "I've come to a few crossroads, Da. My thinking about much has changed in the past year."

"I gathered. Otherwise, you would not have returned to us, would you?"

"No, sir. I like Shanghai." He gave a small laugh. "Hell, I like Tokyo, Aden. Joppa! Venice! If I did not have this other drive to develop new products, new industries, for the adventure I'd stay in China or choose another city for another few years. But I won't."

His father settled back in his leather chair and folded his hands. "And instead? What will it be?"

"Paris, perhaps." A flicker of his days in Amboise danced over him and mingled with the memory that Camille's publisher had offered to give her a chateau in Blois for a year. He'd never been to Blois but the prospect of living with Camille tucked away for weeks and months spoke to his burgeoning need for quiet and reflection. "Somewhere in France. But trips to London and Brighton to visit you. All of you."

His father's broad Irish face lit with pride as he clamped a hand to his chest. "I'm devastated to hear it."

Pierce chuckled. "I can see that!"

"But honestly," his father said, "Liv will be thrilled to hear this. So too Lily and her brood. Ada. Victor. All of us."

"Before I make any decision, I must talk with quite a few people. My own man in London and definitely Victor. I owe him much to allow me to partner with him and I have learned much about dealing with men from other cultures. Living abroad brings a perspective that aids working with others long term. But now, if I stay here, I question much. I question if he and I can or even should make a profit from the Chinese as they modernize their country. They are very reluctant to adopt new machinery or even roads, let alone trains. Our iron and steel can help them modernize only if they embrace the opportunities. But they've kept their peasants in such poverty and ignorance that I fear it will take centuries to bring them forward. And before they accept advanced education or intricate machines, they will endure more rebellions like the murderous Tai-Ping that killed millions. They'll kill each other and take many of us with them. I doubt I am a person to witness that and not become jaded or strike out irrationally."

"I doubt that last, Pierce. You are not such a man. Responsiveness to opportunity is your forte. More than mine."

"You are complimentary, sir. I take the praise and say that once I was that man. But now? I doubt it."

"Why do you say that? What you've done in Shanghai is triple the value of Victor's company and your's."

"True." But money alone did not make the man. Killian knew it, had lived by it, and Pierce would not utter it to proclaim the obvious."I've made mistakes, I fear. The latest is with pricing a new project. In sympathy for the Chinese, I priced the steel too low. So low it would go at less than manufactured price. I cabled that pricing to our office in Shanghai over a week ago. I should have waited to examine it once more. And while I can say I was not thinking correctly because I was distracted, I cannot make mistakes like that. I need partners. I need another person with whom to sift and winnow ideas. I cannot give away thousands of francs of product out of sympathy for the customer.

"And so, having told you that," he said as he crossed one leg over the other and locked his gaze on his father's, "I wonder if you might consider having me around more so that I might learn from you."

"You would do me an honor, Pierce, if you wished to work with me more closely again. I valued it years ago. I would do so now." His father glanced away and knit his brows. "I am not doddering, but I grow older. I see trends and opportunities but I don't keep up with the inventors who will make those new industries run more efficiently. Plus, I wish to take more time to enjoy what I've built. More time to enjoy Liv. Lily and Ada and their families. More time to educate Laim and Dylan." He turned his silver gaze on Pierce. "And I would like to rely on you to help me with them both. My business is half yours when I am gone, but they should have a working knowledge of it.

You would be a great value to me in educating them in that."

Relief swept over him at his father's largesse. "I'd be honored to teach them. But I'd also insist that if they find a product or industry they wish to learn, then they must have a piece of the business. Even if they aren't attuned to management, they are your sons and they are entitled not only to learn the businesses but to share in the rewards of them. And there is more. I want your advice on a merger."

Killian opened his hand. "I'd love to hear your ideas."

"What is your assessment of Lee Macfarlane?"

"I liked him. He seemed measured, wise. You liked him, valued him. That is what I know most of all."

"I know your time to get acquainted with him was short but what do your instincts say?"

"You trust my instincts. All well and good but I must say I do not have much experience to read Macfarlane. I know he married Lady Brianna Price quickly. That, I must say, belies my impression of prudence. She is a lovely young woman, but they've known each other only days."

The issues of time were irrelevant to many. "Didn't you fall in love with Liv quickly?"

His father inhaled and threw him a crooked smile. "You have me."

"I'm eager to meet with Lee again when he comes through Paris. I must talk with him about the pricing on that steel which I so miscalculated. But also, I'd like to talk over another plan I have. And it involves Victor. I consider discussing with Lee buying sixty percent of my shares in Victor's and my company. That would give him local control. Too because he is part Chinese, he understands the people."

"A significant proposal. Do you think he would consider it if Victor approves?"

"I think so. Victor is more interested in politics. His business is merely his income to him. He does not care much how he achieves it as long as it is honorable."

His father nodded. "On that, I do agree. So then what of Lee? What is your assessment of his thinking on the matter?"

"Lee is aggressive but careful. Devoted to details. Usually never impulsive." Pierce smiled. "His love for Brianna Price aside."

Killian laughed. "I say then if your instinct says approaching him is the right thing to do, then do it."

He took a calming breath. "I have more to discuss and for this, I hope you will give me your blessing."

That last word changed the tone and Killian tipped his head. "What is this?"

"I'm going to get married."

His father was not so much surprised as concerned. He set his jaw and narrowed his gaze. "Do I know this lady?"

"Camille." Pierce licked his lips. "If she'll have me."

His father frowned, his anxiety aging him. "I dare say there is no question of that. Camille has worn her heart on her sleeve for you for many years. I want to congratulate you, son. I want to say the same to her. But I am troubled. Liv and I have known, seen how Camille cares for you. But we thought you did not look upon her in the same light. Camille knew it, too. As a result, she's fought hard to look elsewhere."

"I'm aware of that. In fact, I knew she cared for me but I pushed the idea aside thinking she'd grow out of the attachment. I always thought she'd find another man. She's no longer a child, but a woman with fine attributes and ambitions. In the ensuing years, I've come to know her, full grown. In the past weeks, I've grown to love her. Now I want to marry her."

His father looked away.

Pierce worried he couldn't convince his father of the

rightness of his regard for Camille. He knew not what else to say. "I hope you and Liv will approve."

The worry that had creased his father's brow melted away like sun over snow. His grin brought brilliance to Pierce's day. "My dear son, why would we not?"

Relief swept over him. "I have much to do before I ask her. I've a few men to see, a house to rent. And I assure you I've not forgotten my promise to you to negotiate the Liverpool laborers' issues."

"Mid-month. You'll still want to do that amid wedding preparations?"

"If the lady accepts me, I hope we can set a date for later in September."

"Thank you. As long as your bride agrees. I would not wish to stand in the way of anything Miss Bereston wants when it comes to you."

Pierce laughed but his heart hammered at the bigger question of whether she would want him. "Nor I, sir."

His father came around his desk and opened his arms to him. "Congratulations. I am delighted for you. I know you'll be happy. We must tell Liv."

"Yes. Now would be best."

At the news, Camille's mother found a chair in which to sink. In her own office with samples of Lyon chiffon in a rainbow of colors spread across her work table, she stared at Pierce and could not for the longest time find her voice. When she did, tears muffled her words. "Camille loved you from the first moment she met you. She loves you as a woman now."

"She does."

"Never has she regarded you as her brother."

"Nor should she." By affection they'd always been bound.

"A happy marriage," she said in a wistful note. "Helps a person become his or her best self."

Pierce nodded. "I make arrangements to begin that. Now. Here. Before I see her."

"So then. She is not in Tours with a friend." Liv's statement reflected her understanding of how they'd gone away together.

"No." He wouldn't offer explanations.

Liv chuckled. "I wondered why Marianne said Camille had asked to go to Gare de l'Est when all trains from that station go east, not south to the Loire."

Pierce tipped his head in apology. "A slip. She's not used to fibbing."

"Commendable," Liv acknowledged.

"Camille returns to Paris tomorrow."

"And you propose then?" Liv asked with a twinkle in her eyes.

"I do," he said with a grin at the spark of delight at Liv's acceptance.

"I hope you have something wonderful in hand to make that a reality," she said with a wiggle of her brows.

He laughed at the ceiling. "I make my first stop to a jeweler."

"Smart man." Liv pointed a finger at him. "Pearls are my first purchase."

As Pierce shrugged into his dinner coat, he dismissed for the evening the hotel valet whom he'd allowed the hotel to provide for him. A knock came at his sitting-room door.

"Shall I answer for you, *Monsieur?*"

"Please do, Albert." He was about to take his dinner in the restaurant below with his manager of business here in Paris. Exploring new ways of working was his agenda and Pierce wished to honor the man who had worked for him for six years with a preview of his thinking on restructuring. This would be one of the last items on his agenda for business. Today, he'd visited the British and American embassies and the rector of the American Church in Paris. His last stop had been to a very fine jeweler on the Champs-Élysées. Tomorrow he'd have a long talk with the owner of a chateau near Chantilly about renting it for a year and then much of his work for his wedding and honeymoon would be done. He grinned at himself in the mirror.

Murmurs of an argument reached his ears.

A woman at his door demanded to see him.

Albert was fuming at her. "*Madame! Monsieur*, the lady was—"

"Pierce!" Marianne strode into his bedroom. Her face red with exertion, she was breathless.

"Marianne! What's wrong? Albert, you may leave us. The lady is my aunt. Come sit down," he said as he rushed forward to take her hands and lead her toward a chair. Earlier, he'd sent a message to her home that he would remain at the Meurice for a few days as he would be in an out of meetings and did not wish to disturb her household. Or her. She was far into her pregnancy and from the looks of her she was overwrought. "What's the matter?"

"Is Camille here?"

He startled. "No." Fear gripped him. "Why?"

Marianne sat, checking his expression. "Camille did not arrive at Gare de l'est this afternoon. I sent our coachman to fetch her at four but he never saw her."

Pierce sat down with a thud. To keep up the ruse of visiting a friend, Camille was to have disembarked from the train from Tours at Montparnasse and taken a hack to Gare de l'est to meet Marianne's coachman. "Perhaps she's gone to Rue Haussmann instead of your house."

"No. She did not go home. I've just come from there. Liv

and Uncle Killian have had no word from her. Your father told me the two of you were together these past few days. Honestly, I'm not surprised. How could one look at the two of you and not guess? Where is she Pierce?"

"I don't know." It killed him to confess it. "But I—. She didn't say a word to me about not returning today."

"Where else might she have gone?"

And why?

CHAPTER 20

The next afternoon, Pierce jumped down in the drive from the rickety open landau he'd hired at the train station in Tours. The quaint Amboise chateau sat nestled in its charming gardens. But it looked deserted, its windows closed, the drapes pulled across the glass. The flower pots full of reds and pinks and lush yellows that had welcomed him and Camille drooped, wilting in the late afternoon September sun.

Anger that Camille had not come home drained away as he looked at the chateau where once he'd found happiness in every minute. Fear clawed away the remnants of his rage.

He mounted the broad steps and knocked upon the old blue varnished door. No one answered. He motioned to his driver to wait for him. Then he was off to tramp around to the side of the house. He tried the gate. It did not give. But he peered through the spokes of the large wrought iron fence into the vegetable garden. At the little house beyond, neither Monsieur Barrère nor his wife appeared.

And neither did Camille.

He traipsed round the other side of the house and jogged

up to the back kitchen door. He banged on the door. Got no answer. Then tried the latch but it was locked.

He took the path to the stables, fighting alarm that Camille had not simply fled him but all the family. And why. Because they'd been seen in the station kissing?

No.

He scoffed at that. There was more. More. Love, career, travel, Shanghai. He should have broached more before he left. Settled a few things.

But he understood one fact well. That she would flee and not return home because she wanted solitude to think. It was not like her to allow her family to worry about her, but even that was a measure of her discontent. Still, he understood the need for a solemn communion with one's self.

Hands on his hips, he stood in the stables in an open stall and hung his head. He prayed he'd find her, assuage her concerns that…what? What?

No answer came to him. And the only sound was that of the mice skittering about in the rafters. Outside, farther along the lane, the chickens clucked and pecked. The wind from the river blew soft and warm and swirled around him in the stables. Its caress drained him.

He strode back to the front of the house and stood back to view it one final time. An old stillness settled about the place. He ran a hand through his hair. In town, he'd search for the Barrères and ask after Camille.

He jumped up into the landau. The coachman winced as the old thing creaked and groaned.

"*Bonjour, Monsieur Hanniford!*"

Monsieur Barrère bustled around the far side of the chateau. The smile wreathing his face dropped at the sight of Pierce's frown.

"*Monsieur?*" He met him in the grass. "You return. May I help you?"

"I'm here to see *Mademoiselle*." He examined the chateau once more, its closed sad state so reflective of his own.

"She is not here, *Monsieur*. She left the day after you did."

When she had not come home, he'd feared the worst. "Where did she go?"

"I am not certain, sir."

"What, exactly, did she say?"

The little man shuffled his feet. His wife ducked her head around the foliage of a huge rhododendron. She curtsied and kneaded her fingers in the white cotton of her little apron.

Barrère bit his lip. "She asked for a carriage to take her to Tours. I presumed she was returning to Paris."

"Did the coachman perhaps see her buy a ticket for Paris?"

"No, *Monsieur*."

"No?"

"He thought it odd what she did do."

Pierce had agonized over her fate for interminable hours. Odd was not the word he'd use to describe the fright Camille's disappearance had cost them. Especially him. "What did she do?"

"Once the carriage arrived, she asked him to take her to Blois."

North east to Blois? The opposite direction from Tours? Blois! Of course! She'd gone to Monsieur Daumier's chateau. Where she could contemplate her future...alone. Pierce panicked. "You saw him afterward?"

"*Oui, Monsieur*. Later in the town."

"And you asked him where she'd gone?"

"*Oui, Monsieur*. He knows."

"He can tell me the address?"

Barrère acknowledged that with a grunt. "I can take you to him, if you like."

"I like. Very much. Might we go now, Barrère?"

CHAPTER 21

*C*amille had always prided herself on making good choices.

Looking around the salon of the chateau she'd been given by Monsieur Daumier, she questioned if coming here was one of them. The fourteen-room house sat on a moat connected to its gardens by a land bridge. To marvel at the house from the side surrounded by water, she could see that it appeared to float in the mist of the mornings and evenings. She took long walks the past two days and admiring the house gave her a distance from much that occupied her.

The chateau itself also fascinated her. So too the stories of the estate agent, Monsieur Cartot. He spoke excellent English and she was certain Daumier had told him to be on his toes to speak the new tenent's language with her. The frail little man had been kind to welcome her, indeed to let her in when she arrived unexpected, trunk in tow and valise in hand, frustration knitting her brow.

Cartot's stories had consumed her. And she absorbed them because they were vital to feeding her imagination— and essential to keep her mind from her worries.

The chateau was a treasure. Built, Cartot told her, by a cousin of Louis the Thirteenth, the ducal abode was constructed of sturdy, creamy Loire limestone. Camille could examine the high vaulted ceilings for hours and with each new look find another animal amid the acanthus leaves, his demeanor always feral. The five boudoir apartments on the third story were expansive rooms of such gold paneling that when the sun shone upon the veneer, her eyes hurt. The marble sculptures of Venus and Eros, Alphios and Arethusa standing in the halls stole her breath with their artistry. But their poses and expressions were angry, inspiring a distaste in her. The paintings on the walls were no better. They could take her to Renaissance Florence or hunting with Louis the Fourteenth, but they showed mobs or bloody hunting scenes. The tapestries, some threadbare, others vibrant as the day they were woven, lined many walls, ten or fifteen or twenty feet tall and twice as long. They were of battles won, the enemy broken and bleeding on the ground. Every piece of art was surely priceless. Rare. She asked Cartot how he managed to keep thieves away, but he lifted a set of old iron keys and shook his head. Robbers could not get in or carry away the glories easily. Camille pondered who would come to steal away such horrid scenes. Few would find delight in them.

And the owners of the chateau? Where were they? Ah, Monsieur Cartot pressed a hand to his heart and said he was sad. The government, he told her, had passed a law two years ago expelling former reigning families from France. The owner, a Bourbon descended of Louis-Phillippe, the last king, had given the house to the State. A young rich man purchased it, and it was often used by many businessmen as a temporary residence.

She felt at ease in the cavernous house, though it had not the touch of home which she'd loved in the chateau in Amboise. This one was a hulk, a relic, remnants of people and events gone by. A revolution. A terror. A restoration. A house of old memories, cold and unloved.

Though she'd been here two days, she'd spent at least half of them in the mind-numbing work of rearranging furniture and putting one large table and old Louis Quatorze chair in the sun of the southwest window. It fronted on a small balcony and there she discovered the perfect vista from the hill down over the rooftops of the town to gaze upon the medieval royal castle. It was a mélange of grey stone, red brick and dirty limestone. There, one French king had solidified his rule over this portion of the Loire and the belligerent knights who abused the people and commerce of the longest river in France. The only sign of any more tender emotions were the *bas reliefs* sculpted into the rafters of animals in various poses, ferociously mating.

Her man of all work, Monsieur Cartot was polite. In that, he resembled Barrère. He had no wife. But a cook, he claimed, could be had from the town, if she wished. *No, merci,* she had begged off. She rather liked to cook for herself. And the local greengrocer's stall stood not far away down the lane. So too the patisserie.

But as her history lessons ended all too soon, she told herself she should write. Never a job to her, writing came easily.

But not now.

The sun blazed in a long red line to the horizon on the west as she rose from her small repast of fried squashes and onions, bread, and razor clams from the *poissonnier.*

She picked up her plates, headed for the kitchen and a quick clean up from her meal. But the sun dropped like a stone over the landscape. She lit a candelabra and puttered about the old kitchen. But her longing for Pierce suffused her.

She sat again in her kitchen chair, pausing, breathless with concern for Pierce and their future.

She closed her eyes. Consoling herself that she'd been right to write to her mother yesterday to tell her where she was, she pushed away the knowledge that she'd hurt Pierce by not writing to him as well.

"What would I say to you?" she asked the sultry night breezes. "I'm sorry?" *I'm not.* "I don't know why I'm alone here." *But I do.*

I do know. I came to see if I want this.

And I don't.

Not without you.

Without you, I want a few bright pennies to mark my life. My family. My writing. A few good friends. Adventures in a few new places. But not many. For I am first and foremost an adventurer of the mind.

The longer she sat with these affirmations, the better and happier she was.

By the time she climbed the grand staircase to make her way to up to her boudoir, the huge French Rococo clock with the funny porcelain face of plum peonies and ivory roses chimed the ninth hour.

Tomorrow she would return to Paris and declare what she wanted in life.

She had just put her feet up under the downy coverlet when she heard horses pounding the stones along the front drive. No one came up that lane at this hour of the night.

But then there was a banging at the main doors. A loud banging.

She pushed up on her elbows and listened to Cartot yell his response as he went to answer the summons. He conversed in abrasive tones with another who demanded entrance.

Urgent, irritated, their caller was determined to have answers that it seemed Cartot could not give.

She had barely donned her robe when she heard footsteps run up the stairs and her name called. Over and over.

The bass voice she knew. And treasured.

Barefoot, she padded toward her sitting room when her door flew wide.

"There you are!" Pierce stood on the threshold of her apartment, panting but triumphant. In the shadows of the night his devastating silhouette filled her doorway. He also filled her heart with gratitude that he'd not only come for her, but that he had found her. That was truly romantic. Worthy of a plot, too, though she'd never share this with her readers. This love affair was hers alone to treasure. But that sentiment must come later, eh?

"What are you doing here?!" She very well knew. Of course she did. She was not daft. But her letter to her mother would not have arrived until this afternoon at earliest. He could not know from that she was here. So he had searched for her. She liked that.

He whirled his hat to the floor and stalked her.

His determination was a new aspect she'd never witnessed. Not in regard to her, at least.

She stepped backward.

"Why did you leave?" He stepped into a ray of light and the kiss of reflected moon brightened his midnight hair to silver. His luminous eyes, alive with fear and relief, danced over her and she shivered that here was the creature she adored.

"*Why?*" She folded her arms. Well, she had no coherent answer prepared for that yet. So she lifted her chin and shook her head.

"Because we were insane when you didn't arrive!"

That she understood.

"Why not come to Paris as you promised?" He kept coming for her.

She mashed her lips together and held her ground. "I didn't mean to worry you. I will apologize to everyone."

"You certainly will! Why not to me? Now?" He stood before her and the overwhelming masculine hurt he showed her warmed her very cold toes.

"I do. I am sorry, Pierce."

"That's good. Is there more?"

"No." She showed him the full force of her integrity. "I will not grovel. I wanted time. Time to myself. I am allowed to take that. Have it. Use it."

That seemed to wash over him and drain away a bit of his ferocity. "Yes, you are. What did you decide?"

She ran her gaze over the marvelously carved rafters. Shimmering in that same moonlight the cream limestone was alive with the animals and foliage of the lush French forests. "It was a mistake to come here."

He blinked. "What?"

Oh, she did so like confusing him. A smile of triumph curved her lips. She couldn't help it. "It was a mistake to come here."

"Why?" He glanced around. "It appears to be...beautiful."

"It is. Full of the art of men and women who have lived and loved, full of the memories of men dead and alive, departed but near. The walls burst with the passions and the troubles they'd beheld. I love it. But I hated it..." She took a step toward him and put a palm to his heart. "I hated being here without you."

He gripped her upper arms. "I was wrong to leave you as I did."

Progress! "You were."

"I should have told you more about what I wanted to do and why."

She arched her brows, in total agreement. "Indeed."

"I wanted to settle all my issues and come to you a whole man."

She liked his sentiment. "You were always a whole man to me."

He gave a harsh laugh and threw his head back to consider the ceiling. "I can be too organized."

"A good foil for me."

"Oh, yes. You, my darling, are too impetuous. You need me."

She nodded. "I always have. But only now may I have you as I should."

"I hope you will. Have me that is."

She frowned. He needed to ask her. Ask her! "Why should I? How can I?"

He came so close she could inhale the application of his cologne and revel in the obvious attraction his body exhibited. "I sent cables to Victor and to Lee Macfarlane. Victor wants me to come to Brighton next week. Ada has false contractions and he dare not leave her. Lee Macfarlane confirms he and Brianna return to Paris on the tenth. I go to Liverpool for my father's negotiations on the thirteenth. I've rented a house in Rue du Faubourg Saint-Honoré. But if you want to live here, I will do it."

This was why she and he were a proper match. He, the planner. She, the spontaneous one. "My. You have been busy."

"Very. I've spoken with the American ambassador and the British, too."

She didn't understand that. "Was that necessary?"

"Indeed. Neither you nor I can marry in France without certificates from them both."

"I see." She bit her lower lip and fiddled with the button

of his frock coat. "And that marriage?" He had to ask, and if not, she had other options.

He stilled her hands. "Look at me. I am a good man. Too used to taking care of details, all my business before I enjoy myself. I am not impulsive. But measured. Too measured. Too contemplative. I want to change. Will change."

"And how has this to do with marriage?"

He raised her hands and kissed her fingertips. "May I now proclaim what I should have days ago?"

"That would be wise."

"I love you." He strode right up to her. The light in his eyes was electric and she'd remember him thus until the end of time. "I love you."

She liked those words. Raising her chin, she curled her shoulders like an ingenue infatuated with a new beau. "You do."

He snorted. "You knew?"

She rolled a shoulder. "How could I not?"

"So then why are you mad at me?"

She really was angry now. "Continue as you were, sir. Or we will stand here all night!"

"Can I kiss you first?"

"No."

He sighed and looked at the ceiling again.

She had a good idea what he was taken with up there, but this was no time to discuss *bas relief* sculpture. "You were telling me why you are here."

He shook off the vision of the sculpted ceiling and grinned down at her. "I was. Am. I love you. I will for eternities. Only you."

She took back her hands and watched his face fall to despair. Good. She would not save him that small morsel of horror. For she had suffered her own. For so many years, she had lived with the danger that she would settle for less than the charm of living with him. Less than the bliss of loving him day in and out.

She pushed away, determined to have her say. "You cannot imagine what I've lived through, wanting only you. Seeing you in every circumstance. With Lily and Ada. Their children. Your friends, their husbands, with my mother. I've watched you laugh with a million ladies, waltz with a hundred others. Seen you flirt with dozens of girls. Known how you attracted them all, but never chose one.

"I wanted to be the one.

"Always your one and only.

"I couldn't understand what you sought in a woman and I thought, why not me? I wanted you. Had for years and years. Age, be damned. It didn't matter to me. And if it did to you, well…"

She laughed. To her own ears, the sound was almost bitter. "As time went by, age no longer meant a thing. Because every hour, every day, every year, I wanted only you. No other man compared. And god knew, I looked. I sampled. I tried. And each one came short. Because each examination of another man meant only one thing.

"I wanted your hands on me. Your eyes on mine. Your lips on mine. But I was confounded. Stymied.

"I didn't know how to make me less your sister. Make me more your lover. I lived in a fortress built by other people, their mores, unable to declare how I loved you. And this time when you came home, I told myself I would not want you. This time, I vowed I'd show you, force you to see that if I could not have you, I'd have another, the best I could find.

"Because I was tired of trying to break through the barriers of custom and time.

"Because I could not go on without the love I saw all around me. With your sisters and their husbands. With your father and my mother. I deserve to be loved. And if you didn't. I would have a man who did."

The wary expression on his face spoke of his doubts she still cared for him. "You deserve a man who wants only you every hour of his life."

"I'm glad you agree. So then." She spread wide her hands. "Could you live in our little chateau in Amboise for a few months?"

"I could."

"And take me to Shanghai once or twice for visits?"

"I can do that, too."

"And we'll have babies?"

"I think, my darling, we will have many."

"Oh, delightful. And we'll visit London and Brighton and Lily and Julian's brood in Kent?"

"Often."

She stilled. "And you will applaud me if someday I can run for Parliament?"

"And write pamphlets and appear in lecture halls to discuss the rights of women. I certainly will."

She threw her arms around him. "You are the most extraordinary man. I vow to make you happy with every breath I take."

"I'd ask for nothing more in life."

"Nor I," she rubbed her nose on his. "So then, will you marry me?"

He stared and grinned and drew her flush to his warm hard body. "My darling, I could think of nothing and no one in this world I want more."

"I love you, Pierce. I have forever. I will forever. I cannot love another as I do you. Marry me, will you?"

He threw back his head to laugh then. So heartily did he roar, that the old house seemed to vibrate with it. "I love you, my darling. I want your joy and your enthusiasm, your impetuousness and your thoughtfulness. I want to live with you anywhere and everywhere in this world. And perhaps beyond it too. I must learn to live with you, in all your impulses. And I do. I want to. And I will learn that from you, too. But you must forgive me now one thing."

"No. I mean, yes. But what?"

"I had thought I would do the asking to marry you."

She giggled at his feigned hurt and toyed with a button on his shirt. "You may still."

He cupped her cheeks., the look of adoration in his eyes a joy she would recall until she died. "Ravishing Camille, will you marry me?"

"How could you ever doubt it?"

"Never." He swept her up in his arms, took her to her bedroom and down to her broad bed. Securely pinned beneath his weight, she wiggled to become more comfortable. His kisses ensured more excitement than she planned. And her robe and negligee came off so easily. Naked, she let him have his fill of her skin as she tugged at his shirt and his trousers.

"We'll not get anywhere quickly if you don't help me dispense with your clothes and your shoes, sir!"

As if she'd set fire to him, he shot from the bed and disrobed with charming alacrity. She had only a second to admire his figure and his very virile desire for her when he climbed back beside her and cupped her chin.

He was well into a thorough laving of her breast when she curled her fist around his manhood. "May we dispense with those hideous French letters?"

He raised up on one arm, focusing on her question with a satyr's leer. "We may." Then he drifted lower and savored as he went.

She hated to intrude on his journey, but she had to know.

"Do you think the end of September a fine date for the wedding?"

He seemed to hum his answer and she really did not mind that he had a tendency to focus on one thing at a time. She told herself to ask him that question again after…well after he finished bringing her to a delicious pulsing climax.

But then he added another delight of sinking inside her and this time, finishing his journey there. That done, she was quite lost to memory or logic.

He curled her beside him and made a practice of tracing a lock of her hair around her areola so that she squirmed, even in her lethargy. And of course, she was soon ready for another round.

But he sank his fingers into her hair and said, "Monday, October first at ten in the morning at Rue Haussmann, the minister of the American Church will preside over our wedding."

Overjoyed, she gave a shaky laugh. "Have you chosen my gown as well?"

He pulled back, considering. "I can if you wish."

She ground her teeth and rolled over him. Twining her legs with his, she grinned. "Should it be silks from Shanghai?"

"It can be burlap for all I care. I have one stipulation only."

She sighed, feigning forbearance. "Which is what?"

He got up from the bed and cast about for his frock coat. When he found it, he dug around inside a pocket and returned to her to hand over a red satin pouch. "It must look good with these."

She sat up, reached inside and extracted the longest strand of pearls she'd ever seen in her life. She checked his happy expression and, naked, scrambled from their bed. Standing she let drop the strand. The thing was as long as she was tall.

"I see by this," she said as she put the strand around her throat and wound and wound and wound it up into layers of pearls, "that you expected to propose to me in grand style. I like all your organization, Mister Hanniford. Continue, do, with it."

"Some other time," he said and beckoned her waggling his fingers. "Come here. Show me how you like them."

She took a good long time at that. Most of the night, in fact.

The sun climbed high in the sky when they awoke, laughing at the day before them.

"Tell me one thing," he said as he pointed to the carved vault above their heads. "Is that a male lion on the ceiling?"

"It is." She wiggled her brows and ran her palm over his honed muscles which were more enticing than that of the creature above them.

"And his lioness?"

"Indeed."

"Mating?" He chuckled.

"They are." She kissed his ribs and pecked her way down his torso to his other intriguing accoutrements.

"How kind of them," he said as he sank his fingers into her hair and gave himself up to her and more of what they both wanted.

EPILOGUE

May 5, 1889
122 Rue du Faubourg Saint-Honoré
Paris

*C*amille stretched and yawned. Rays of spring sunshine radiated through the lacy curtains of the bedroom, foretelling lovely weather for the opening of the Grand Exposition and the Eiffel Tower. Every one in the family, except for the babies, were to attend the events which so many had anticipated for months. Exhibitions from thirty-five countries promised to be an eye-opening experience for anyone who went, adults and children alike. The Hanniford children had chatted for days of nothing but where they wished to go or what they wished to eat.

All in the family would arrive at the main gate at exactly ten-thirty. They would assemble as a group and walk in together. After that, the adults agreed they would be hard put to keep the family together. Everyone had different desires.

Even Camille and Pierce had lists that did not match, but given her condition, Pierce had decided it was best to take Camille everywhere she wished to go first.

"I am forever at your service, Mrs. Hanniford," he had declared more than once.

She ran a hand over the mound of her belly and smiled at the grand designs she had for their future. This child, conceived in the chateau in the village of Amboise last September, would enjoy new machines and inventions all her life. Some of them would be on display at the Champs de Mars. Many would come later.

This baby's father would help to bring them to the people of the world. And Camille would be so proud to declare that the man who accomplished such things was her husband and her only love.

She stretched both arms out across the bed and inhaled the fresh air wafting in through the open casement.

She was so fortunate. She had the luxuries many wished for. A caring and talented mother. A step-father who was attentive and wise, famous for his business acumen and known for his ethics.

An ardent husband who set her heart a quiver with his charm and his devotion. And soon, they would add to their joy with the birth of their first child.

Pierce had always been the man she adored. And rightly so. For his skills at negotiating conflicts between workers and owners, for his kindness and understanding of the reasons people wanted and needed a fair income from their labors, Pierce Hanniford had turned his talents at diplomacy to the art of creating plans for four towns in the United States. The small towns had seen exponential growth in the past decade and their city councils had voted to plan not only the streets but also the water lines, sewers and electrical grids. Pierce had a team of engineers who were specialists in that detailed planning. He was attending the Exposition at the Champs de Mars not only as a visitor but as a consultant to the City of Paris on the construction of the exhibits.

The hall door swung wide and Pierce appeared, smiling and carrying a breakfast tray.

"Still waking up?" He shook his head and smiled. "If you don't get up soon, we'll miss the ten-thirty meeting."

She pretended to frown at him. "I don't take that long to get dressed."

He cast her a wary eye. "I don't know by what clock you judge your habits, Madam, but I'd say you need to sit up and eat this now or we won't be at the gate until noon!"

He had donned his summer robe of navy blue and the color contrasted with his impressive black Irish good looks. He stood, gazing at her with those twinkling silver eyes of his, waiting for her to prop herself against the head board.

"You are a pest, Pierce Hanniford. If I could go without a corset and petticoats, I'd get dressed much faster." And at that, she put her hands to the bed and pushed up.

Her grin vanished as a stabbing pain raced up her spine.

"No dawdling, my darling. This tray is heavy."

"I...Yes. Of course." She sat up and sighed against the pillows. False labor. She'd felt the pangs for the past week. Happy to have her coffee and croissants, she arranged the covers around her tummy. Her lap had disappeared long about January and she had marveled at just how much her figure could expand for one baby.

Pierce settled the tray over her. "Sit a bit higher, sweetheart."

She pushed up and another pain cut through her good humor. "Oh! I...there."

"Hmm." He gazed down at how her stomach lifted the tray off the flat of the bed. "I will have to buy a tray with taller legs."

"Unnecessary, sir! Just let me levitate this one." She rubbed the sides of her stomach where now a muscle cramped and took her breath.

"More false labor?" Pierce bent and lifted her chin. He took in her expression and knit his dark brows.

She nodded. "A pang or two."

"Good. Well! I have to tell you we have the morning mail and a note from New York."

She lifted her cup and drank. "From the Macfarlanes?"

"Lee writes that they've decided to return to England in September. They think that traveling will be easier for Brianna and the baby by then. They plan to return to Shanghai three weeks later. They'll leave from Southampton."

Lee and Brianna had discovered she was pregnant last November while they were in the United States. Brianna had had a difficult first three months and so they decided to remain in New York until she had her baby. The child, a boy and the heir to the Macfarlanes' vast fortune and international company, was born two weeks ago.

"Finally," Camille said, "they're going home. Will they come to Paris?"

"I doubt it. Lee divested himself of all involvement with the French and Germans. He prefers to deal only with the British and the Hannifords, I'm proud to say."

"That means that we should go to London when they arrive. We need to coo to all the new babies." She longed to see Brianna and her child. Ada had given birth to twin daughters last September. Marianne had had another girl that same month. The next baby to arrive in the Hanniford clan was to be her own and Pierce's.

"I'll go to London but if you're not fond of traveling, you need not go, sweetheart."

"I want to," she said when another pain shot through her and she doubled over the tray.

Pierce was there beside her. One hand to her back, one to her wrist, he bent down and captured her gaze. "This is stronger than the ones you've had previously."

She licked her bottom lip. "They are."

"They?" His voice rose. "How long have you had them?"

"Just as you came in the room."

He scowled at her. "Not before? You're sure?"

"I am."

"I'll send a messenger to the doctor."

She grabbed his hand. "No, don't. Monsieur Lavare and his wife are looking forward to seeing the Eiffel Tower."

He clamped his hand over hers and squeezed. "Monsieur Lavare will not be seeing the tower today, my love."

"He said not to send for him until the pains are one minute apart." She smiled just as a red hot spiral of pain shot through her hips. She gasped. "Oh, my."

"That's enough for me." He strode to the bell pull and yanked at it.

When a footman appeared, Pierce gave instructions for one messenger to go to Rue Haussmann to fetch Camille's mother and another to go to the offices of her physician, Monsieur Lavare.

"What can I get you?" Pierce returned to her side, took the tray away and urged her to recline.

"Nothing. Nothing. I'm to sit up. It is better, I was told, for the pain."

"Do you want to eat?"

"No."

"Tea, perhaps?" He looked as if someone strangled him, his complexion gone white.

She laughed and clutched her stomach in another pain. "Ice. Just some ice."

He lifted her hand and kissed her there. "I'll be right back. Don't go away."

"Oh, to be sure, I think I'll stay." She laughed but the next pain shocked her with its force. She gulped, happy and breathing again when it ended and she felt at peace. "Ohhhh, that was...strong."

Then she looked up at him. He hadn't moved but stood nailed to the spot, luminous eyes wide in shock.

"You'd better send a message to your staff whom you're to meet later this afternoon that you won't be available today because..."

She fell backward to the pillows. Eyes shut, she threw off the covers and lifted her knees, feet flat to the sheets.

As a crippling pain tore through her, she heard him curse beneath his breath and dash away.

As it was, Lavare was quick to arrive, medical bag in hand, full of concern for his illustrious patient, the author Camille Bereston-Hanniford. But his services needed were few. Indeed, he cut the umbilical cord. Then he turned and declared to his patient's husband and mother, both of whom had assisted at the very quick birth, that the placenta was intact. Assured that his patient was hale and hearty, he checked the breathing of the baby boy and promised to record in the city hall the birth of Brendan Patrick Hanniford.

The baby's mother was happy to see the doctor, but hurried him on his way. After all, she'd been in labor for only one hour and ten minutes and she wished to celebrate quietly with her husband, who marveled at her strength and resilience.

. . .

On the fourteenth of April, 1900, the Hanniford clan were to once more assemble at the gate to the Champs de Mars for the opening of the Inauguration of the Exposition of 1900. Everyone had great expectations for the show of the world's achievements during the past eleven years.

The Hannifords themselves had much to celebrate. Killian, the patriarch was sixty-eight years old and still in good health though he had retired to Brighton and left much of his enterprises to Pierce. Training Liam and Dylan during their holidays from their American colleges, Pierce also kept to his word to pay just honor to his private life as the husband of the noted author and women's rights activist, Camille Bereston-Hanniford, and their two children. Brendan would be eleven years old next month and his sister, Justine would turn eight next week.

It occured, too, that they were about to add another child into the fold. So it happened that on the morning of April fourteenth as Camille awoke, nine months pregnant as she was once more in the spring, she pushed up from her bed at nine-fifteen, smiled at the man who always lit up her world and who brought her tea and croissants each morning, and she said, "I regret, my darling, that I will not be attending the family gathering at the gate this morning."

This time, Pierce did not ask what to do next, he simply went to the pull, summoning help, and returned to her side to take her hand in his.

"How strong are the pains?" he asked as he pushed her hair from her cheeks.

She pressed her lips together, but tried to smile at him, ever patient and dear Pierce. He was quite charming with his good looks and his excellent care of her. At forty-seven, he retained an athletic physique crowned by a full head of silver hair. He'd become an even more striking creature whom she adored more each day. "Very."

Lavare arrived within the hour. He stayed to do as he always did, proclaim the newest member of the family a healthy babe, and declare the child's mother a strong creature who birthed her children in record time.

"Now only fifty minutes of labor," said Pierce with glee lighting his magnetic gaze. The baby, Ruark Damon Hanniford, had nursed and was at peace in his bassinette. "He's beautiful, my love. I like his red hair."

She sank further into the comfort of her pillows. "The next child I have will be born as I ask for my morning tea!"

He dropped a kiss to her forehead. "You are a marvel, my darling."

They spoke of the family and how they would laugh at her speedy delivery. Again.

Camille chuckled. "I have to ask. Are there suggestions that there will be another exhibit in nineteen-ten?"

He paused to consider. "Plan on going to the opening, do you?"

"Of course! But we do need another child to even the numbers. Don't you agree?"

He kissed her then. "I love you. If you want more, we shall have them. And I will celebrate each day the delight you bring to every moment of my life."

I hope you loved this story of the Hanniford family. Read on to the Earl of Carbury, Nate Langston's romance which starts in a ballroom in London in 1906 when he meets a young lady who changes his life.

IF YOU WERE THE ONLY GIRL IN THE WORLD begins the second generation of the family so many of you adore!

IF YOU WERE THE ONLY GIRL IN THE WORLD, BOOK 6, THOSE NOTORIOUS AMERICANS, STEAMY FAMILY SAGA

October 1906
London

*N*athaniel Langston, the Earl of Carbury, had attended so many similar balls that he was inured to all the attending social rigors but the the charm of the music. He liked to waltz. Odd, perhaps. Most men his age thought it an obligation to be quickly embraced and discarded. But he, along with his innumerable Hanniford cousins, had been taught to waltz by his Aunt Lily in her grand ballroom and anything she did had always been a boon to his life.

But tonight, he left the floor and his fiancée and his favorite Viennese waltzes to wend toward the terrace. A few would notice his departure, but for that he was old enough not to care. Plus he was wise enough not to dwell on the reason. His fiancée was behaving badly. And prudence said he should overlook it.

One did not marry easily in this new century in Britain. Did one ever? But that was irrelevant, wasn't it?

His problem that made him cringe was the very essence of which he thought her incapable. True, Felicity Northcote liked dancing as much as he. Liked it more so, it appeared, with other men. Tonight more than ever. And her favored partner seemed to be James Erlander, Lord Carterham, a baron of some landed wealth and little more to his credit except bad debts.

One cannot account for poor taste, eh?

Nate strode out the garden doors and headed for the wrought iron bench among the roses. He sat, swirling the glass of whisky he'd taken from the footman's station and inhaling the crisp night air. The night was still young and no one else had sought the solemnity of the gardens. Solitude afforded him the chance to ponder what his options were. Ignore Felicity's penchant for dancing. Speak to her about it. End the negotiations for the marriage, her dowry and all the heinous money-changing that denoted the merger of an earl and the daughter of viscount. Then call off the wedding.

He took another swallow of his host's excellent Scotch.

The far door opened and the woman who emerged fled to the railing.

Fled seemed like an odd term. But then, he'd witnessed many young women seek peace amid the garden maze at grand events.

This girl—one hand to the balustrade and one to her ribs —gasped.

He sat forward.

Was she hurt? Crying?

"No," she said as if it were a vow. "I won't."

In the silver rays of moonlight, her fair hair shone pale gold. Her dark eyes stared straight out upon the parterre and in her expression lived despair. She was lithe, petite, and in the extravagant white lace and peach silk gown she shimmered like a fairy of the night.

Did he know her?

No matter. He stood, better to announce himself than scare her half to death later. "Pardon me."

"Oh!" She whirled toward him and clapped a hand to her generous décolleté. "Who...? Oh, Lord Carbury!"

He put a hand out. "Forgive me, I did not wish to frighten you."

"You...you didn't." She tried to smile but couldn't quite bring herself to the fullness of it.

"Miss Schubert, is it?" He strolled forward, his gait casual so as not to alarm her further. Indeed, he was surer of her identity as he approached her. She was the American heiress from Chicago, her father the owner of department stores. Lovely as the ripe summer peach of her gown, she was a bright young thing whom many an impoverished young swain had taken to enchanting this season.

"Yes, pardon me." She turned for the doors.

"Don't go." He stretched out a hand. "I came out here for some silence. I wouldn't want to rob you of the pleasure of it."

She straightened her spine. In the effort, she stretched to perhaps another one quarter of an inch taller so that the tip of her towering coiffed hair, white gardenias included, reached his jaw line.

"Thank you. I do like the night. Oddly, I feel safe at night. I know most don't."

Such revelations were rare to hear, especially at grand balls in London in the midst of the fall season. So close, he could appreciate the length of her lashes and the almond shape of her large dark eyes. Were they brown? Green? "Safety among the stars. I understand."

"It feels safe to confess to them."

He raised his glass in a toast. "The moon never tells, either."

Her gaze centered on his hand and his drink. "May I?"

"Of course."

She took the crystal with eagerness and pressed it to her lips. Her full pink lips. She drank deeply. "Sorry," she said, when she'd had her fill and pressed a fingertip to each corner of her mouth. "I've made you seek another."

When she handed it back to him, he tipped the nearly empty thing and drained the rest. "I like a woman with enthusiasm for her choice of liquors."

She snorted in laughter and it brought delight to her lovely face. "But not too much enthusiasm."

"Never. That way…" He pursed his lips. "Disaster."

"Do you escape disaster in there?" She tipped her head toward the throng that chatted and whirled about inside the gilt-edged ballroom of the Duke and Duchess of Edington.

"I question if it is disaster. Yet. And you?"

"Mine may be already calling at my door."

"A man you don't wish to call?" He'd met so many rich American girls and understood their plight to be dangled before the likes of eligible British males with titles. Two of his aunts had once been women who'd faced similar challenges. One of his cousins, too. All had survived the rigors of the chase and married men they adored.

"A man I don't wish to wed."

"Ah. Tell him no."

"That's not easy to do," she tossed back, anger in the set of her mouth.

"I know. But it's best. You should not marry without full confidence in the prospect." He should listen to his own advice.

"My father wants it."

Nate gave a rueful chuckle. "But he doesn't have to live with the chap."

She frowned and turned to grip the railing. "That's what I've said."

"Does your father gain something from the marriage?"

On that she stilled. "What do you mean?"

"Why this man? Why not another? One you like? Love."

"I don't like or love anyone. I don't want to do that."

"You don't want to marry or there is someone back home who—"

"No. None of that. I want to go to college."

"Good of you." He applauded women with ambition. "What will you study?"

"I want to become a doctor. And he won't let me."

"Your father doesn't approve of education for women?"

"He wants the notoriety of my marriage."

"I see." His Aunt Lily had taken nursing courses when she was in her forties. As Duchess of Seton, she shocked society but she cared not. Nor did her husband, his uncle, the eighth Duke. She still nursed the sick and dying in her husband's estates. His Aunt Ada, the wife of a noted Member of Parliament, was an active campaigner for women's right to vote. His distant cousin, Marianne, the duchess de Remy et princess d'Aumale, was a famous painter of women and children. And his other aunt, Camille Hanniford, worked with Ada and Lily to lobby Parliament to increase women's rights and their health care and lying-in hospitals. "What does your beau say about your desire?"

"Lord Carterham?"

That pronouncement soured him and he turned toward the view inside. He leaned backward upon the railing. As if pre-ordained, the crowd parted to reveal a picture of Felicity, her palm on Carterham's spiffy white cravat, laughing up into his eyes.

Miss Schubert followed his gaze. "You know him?"

"A little."

"Is he...? Is he trustworthy?"

"With what?" he said far too promptly.

She exhaled. "Well. That tells me much."

Nate frowned at her. He'd spoken on impulse. "Forgive me. Don't take that as proof."

She pushed away from the railing. "No? Why not? Yours was the most honest reaction I've heard since I stepped foot on English soil."

"That's my fiancée you see there with him. They are old friends. I responded quickly."

"As well you should," she said with a nod. "And so will I. I am indebted to you, sir. Good evening."

She marched away, her shoulders squared, her hands fisted, her flowing peach silk swaying around her legs. Skirting the crowd, she disappeared from Nate's sight.

He did not see her again that night nor any other. Nor did he expect to.

But five days after the Edington's ball, he read in *Lloyd's List* of her departure from England on Cunard's most recent steamship out of Southampton, headed for New York.

That same day he called off his engagement to Felicity Northcote.

WHO IS CERISE DELAND?

Cerise DeLand

Cerise DeLand loves to write about dashing heroes and the sassy women they adore. Whether she's penning historical romances or contemporaries, she has received praise for her poetic elegance and accuracy of detail.

An award-winning author of more than 50 novels, she's been published since 1991 by Pocket Books, St. Martin's Press, Kensington and independent presses. Her books have been monthly selections of the Doubleday Book Club and the Mystery Guild. Plus she's won nominations and awards for Best Historical of the Year, Best Regency and scores of rave reviews from *Romantic Times, Affair de Coeur, Publisher's Weekly* and more.

To research, she's dived into the oldest texts and dustiest

library shelves. She's also traveled abroad, trusty notebook and pen in hand, to visit the chateaux and country homes she loves to people with her own imaginary characters.

And at home every day? She loves to cook, hates to dust, goes swimming at least once a week and tries (desperately) to grow vegetables in her arid backyard in south Texas!

Lady Fiona's Tall, Dark Folly, #1

Lady Mary's May Day Mischief, #2

Miss Harvey's Horribly Lovable Fiancé, #3

Lady Willa's Divinely Wicked Vicar, #4

Miss Weaver's Last Handsome Frolic, #5

Box sets, Historical romances:

When You're Mine, A Medieval, Regency & Victorian Romance Collection,
4 complete novels of 4 different series

Victorian Romances

Those Notorious Americans, Steamy Family Saga series:

Wild Lily, #1

Daring Widow, #2

Sweet Siren, #3

Scandalous Heiress, #4

Ravishing Camille, #5

If You Were the Only Girl in the World, *#6, January 2022*

Let Me Call You Sweetheart, #7, *Spring 2022*

Medieval erotic romances:

Knights of Passion Series: Re-releasing soon!

At Her Service, #1, *in* **When You're Mine**, *box set*

For Her Honor, #2

With Her Kiss, #3

Military Romances

You Were Always Mine, #1, 7 Brides for 7 SEALs

No Getting Over You, #2, 7 Brides for 7 SEALs

SEALs Going Hot, box set

Burning for Nero

Conquering Zeus

A Long Time Comin' (erotic romance)

Contemporaries

Is That a Gun in Your Pocket? (erotic comedic suspense)

Tall, Hard and Trouble, box set, romantic suspense

Santa, Cutie, Holiday Box set, December *2021!*

Always, A Collection of Romances, *Coming Soon!*

Sign up for Cerise's newsletter: Cerise's Bon Bons

And if you would like to read more by Cerise, she writes under her own name, Jo-Ann Power! Do sign up for her newsletter for tales of historical fiction and great mysteries!

www.ingramcontent.com/pod-product-compliance
Lightning Source LLC
Chambersburg PA
CBHW060904250626
47159CB00008B/2866